D0820254

THE CROCKFORD'S FILE

OTHER BOOKS BY WILLIAM ODDIE

Dickens and Carlyle: The Question of Influence (1972)

What Will Happen to God? Feminism and the Reconstruction of Christian Belief (1984)

After the Deluge: Essays Towards the Desecularisation of the Church (ed.) (1986)

THE
CROCKFORD'S FILE

GARETH BENNETT AND
THE DEATH OF THE ANGLICAN MIND

WILLIAM ODDIE

Hamish Hamilton · London

HAMISH HAMILTON LTD
Published by the Penguin Group
27 Wrights Lane, London w8 5tz, England
Viking Penguin Inc, 40 West 23rd Street, New York, New York 10010, USA
Penguin Books Australia Ltd, Ringwood, Victoria, Australia
Penguin Books Canada Ltd, 2801 John Street, Markham, Ontario, Canada l3r 1b4
Penguin Books (NZ) Ltd, 182–190 Wairau Road, Auckland 10, New Zealand

Penguin Books Ltd, Registered Offices: Harmondsworth, Middlesex, England

First published in Great Britain 1989 by
Hamish Hamilton Ltd

British Library Cataloguing in Publication Data
CIP data for this book is available from the British Library

ISBN 0-241-12613-4

Printed in Great Britain by
Richard Clay Ltd, Bungay, Suffolk

IN MEMORIAM

Gareth Vaughan Bennett, Priest

1929 – 1987

Contents

Introduction

On Saturday, 5 December 1987, Gareth Vaughan Bennett, priest of the Church of England, took his own life. His personal tragedy reached its lonely consummation as two mutually uncomprehending worlds were locked (not for the first time) in a kind of ritual conflict, a conflict which had now become deadly: the worlds of Fleet Street and what Bennett himself had described as 'the liberal ascendancy' of the Church of England.

It is true that the victim himself succumbed to what still seems remarkably like an unholy alliance of the two worlds, in which for a time each supported and pursued the other's short-term aim. 'Already the vultures are circling around this man', one diocesan bishop was reported in *The Times* as saying, two days before Bennett died; but it seemed, from the way he was talking, that it was the Church as much as the press, who would supply the vultures with their prey. The two worlds, for a moment, had the same objective: to find the culprit. And the press manhunt was given its journalistic piquancy by the cries of bitter and affronted rage emanating from deaneries and episcopal palaces. If everyone had adopted a mantle of dignified silence, as did the Archbishop of Canterbury, there would have been no manhunt. A manhunt was what both worlds instinctively wanted: the press because of what it was, the Church of England because of what, by the end of the 1980s, its ruling caste had become. But the underlying conflict between them was never truly resolved, then or later.

In particular, the antagonism felt by some elements of the Church's leadership towards the information media, even before the *Crockford's* affair, had reached a condition very near paranoia; to find a parallel for it, we have to go to the world of secular politics, to such embattled figures as Harold Wilson, Spiro T. Agnew and Richard Milhouse Nixon. Hostility to the press is not necessarily a sign of righteousness and inner tranquillity, or that there is nothing to hide. Certainly, this intense hostility in some Church circles was by no means wholly inexplicable, as we shall see; but neither was it the sign of a mature and confident leadership, and it showed itself afterwards in a shower of recriminations against 'press harassment' from some who had done little to discourage it at the time, and who would have done well to look to the beam in their own eyes.

The Underlying Cause

The Archbishop of York's famous attack on the unknown author, which did more to intensify the atmosphere of crisis than any other single contribution, was not wrung from him by media pressure; it was issued on his own initiative as a statement to the Press Association who, as he intended, transmitted it to every newsroom and radio and television station in the country. He used the information media to make his views known; they did not use him.

The press were not the prime movers in the *Crockford's* tragedy; Fleet Street was not what the sociologically minded like to call 'the underlying cause' of it. It may have been a catalyst; but the explosive chemical reaction which shattered the unquiet calm of the Church of England on that dark December day was already under way. All the gentlemen of the press did was to shake up the test tube and retire to a safe distance; the ingredients inside it had already begun to splutter ominously.

Nor, ultimately, were these traumatic events caused by those involved in the writing and publication of the preface itself. The death of Gareth Bennett, if we trace back the line of causality to its source, was not the consequence of his writing, or the General Secretary's commissioning. Nor is it adequate to relegate the affair by talk of Bennett's 'flawed' personality, or his supposed bad judgement or malice or guilty feelings or partisan bias. It was assumed by many, it is true, that some such rationale had to be found; it was beyond them to entertain the possibility that this dreadful outcome said anything about the Church of England itself. It had to be explained by halting the inquiry at the state of mind of Dr Bennett (there were hints that the inquest would reveal a history of mental instability or depression), or by waxing indignant at the supposedly irresponsible and conspiratorial actions of ill-disposed senior members of the Church's bureaucracy. To suppose that there were lessons for the Church in what had happened, beyond those to do with better public relations skills, was unthinkable.

A week after the publication of the *Crockford's Directory*, the General Synod's policy subcommittee discussed what, for those who decided the meeting's agenda, was the great burning question. Not 'was the preface correct in its general analysis?' Not 'was the reaction of the leaders of the Church to its criticisms, anonymous or otherwise, to their credit or discredit?' The question was this and this alone: 'how could it ever have been commissioned and pub-lished in the first place?' One member of the committee, it is true, asked, in effect, 'why should it *not* have been commissioned and published?' But he was not allowed to discuss the substance of the preface, to ask, quite simply, whether it was *true*; he had to issue his remarks to the press afterwards for want of any other audience to listen to him. But this was the real question, and remains the real question: what is the underlying condition of a Church in which such things take place? It is true to say, certainly, that if Gareth Bennett had not bent his powerful historian's mind to the analysis of what was wrong with the Church he loved, he would be alive today. But the analysis was necessary. It is more fitting to say something else: that if the Church of England were other than it has become, *then* he would be alive today.

If Gareth Bennett had not killed himself, he would have lived on as a man disgraced; not because he had done anything of which to be ashamed, but because he had done that which is unforgivable to the establishment mind: he had rocked the boat. And his disgrace would have been just as much an indication of an underlying disorder in the Church as was his death. He who had been accepted, though with reservations, as an insider had come to see that what he was part of was in some ways, though not in all, corrupt and irreligious. But many others had come to that conclusion and had made their accommodations with the way things were.

The Unforgivable Sin

Many indeed, spoke about the Church's failings, but not so that it would make very much difference. Some of them even, unlike Garry Bennett, shared the underlying assumptions of the establishment of the modern Church: they were the licensed critics, institutionalized and sanitized prophets of the new status quo, court jesters of the 1960s revolution. They were there, many of them, to urge the revolution on, not to undermine it; their pinpricks in the flanks of the stodgy old C of E seemed to show how tolerant the Church was, how lovable and diverse and comprehensive the Anglican tradition had remained despite all the changes in teaching and practice that those in the pews had had to absorb. Dr Runcie might humorously remark that in his retirement Bishop Montefiore had come to Southwark in order to harass him, but he was safe enough from any real awkwardness from that quarter.

Garry Bennett had committed the unforgivable sin. A man of the establishment by instinct, he allowed his religion to take him over, to overrule all the deep caution of his nature and habits, to become more important to him than his longing for high office in the Church, a longing which remained with him until his dying day. And so he spoke; but not as a court jester. He mounted, not a licensed demo, but a devastatingly effective military ambush; his intention was not simply to have his say and feel better for it, but to make a real difference.

He knew what the consequences of discovery would be, and he seems genuinely to have believed that he would not be discovered. Anonymity in such matters was not strange to him; it was, on the contrary, a well established operational tactic in ecclesiastical controversy. He wrote in the opening paragraph of the preface that it was 'a *fortunate circumstance* that there exists a longstanding custom that each edition of *Crockford's Directory* should have an anonymous preface in which Anglican affairs are subjected to the scrutiny of a writer who is given complete independence.' [My italics.]

It was not, for him, a bizarre anomaly; it was 'a fortunate circumstance'; a fragment of the Anglican tradition that had somehow survived from the age of Archbishop Sancroft and of Bishop Atterbury – the subject of his greatest work, and one of the most unbridled exponents of the anonymous pamphlet – into later and more mediocre times when the one thing that had not changed in the Church was the fate of those who kick too far over the traces. He knew what that fate would be; if he had been temperamentally given to rebellion, less instinctively a man of the establishment himself, he would have been better able to survive it.

In a Church boastful of its tradition of comprehensiveness and toleration, he would have become an outsider. Those who before had accepted him would have become cold and distant; one after another, the doors would have closed. A handful would have rallied to his cause; but his fate would have deterred all but a small minority from pursuing their support beyond certain limits. He would have been voted off the Synod by the clerical electors of Oxford University. His seat was already marginal; he was elected in 1985 by a majority of only one vote. The departure from the university of two or three of his supporters, including the author of this book, had already made his continued membership of the Synod doubtful; his disgrace over the preface would have made him unelectable, probably he would not even have stood. He would still have had his New College fellowship, but his life in Oxford had become onerous, even hateful to him; he longed for escape from it. Among friends, he once speculated wistfully about how much capital a man might need to be able to retire into private life and devote himself to writing, once all else had failed.

Even before the storm broke over his head and engulfed him he had come increasingly to realize that his hopes for advancement in the Church were now slim. Not only did he suffer under the handicap of orthodox churchmanship in a Church the ideas of whose ruling caste were formed in the 1950s and 1960s, in the age of 'secular Christianity' and the 'death of God'; by a strange quirk he had become tarred by the same brush as modernist theology's most indiscreet and embarrassing exponent. He was an academic, the Bishop of Durham was an academic; academics, so the thinking apparently now went, were all like that, liable to come out with embarrassing theological speculations the man in the pew was not ready for and which it was unwise to have discussed too much in the newspapers. The Jenkins affair changed the prospects for academics; the Archbishop of Canterbury himself, Garry confided to friends, had told him so. It was a nonsense of course; he was an historian, rooted in traditions of careful, solid scholarship to which the airy and undisciplined flights of the Lord Bishop of Durham

were anathema. His aside in the preface about the Bishop of Durham
– that 'the appointment of a man of such imprecision of mind and
expression under the guise of being a theologian was a minor
Anglican disaster' – was heartfelt. He was no Jenkins; no one could
have been safer. But there it was. 'There's no preferment now from
the universities', he once told me; not bitterly but with some
sadness. He was not a bitter man. Disappointed perhaps; but certainly not sour, still less vindictive.

He longed for high office, not merely for worldly ambition but
also to become more deeply immersed in the real Church of England,
the Church of pastoral care and the worship and love of God. It
might be thought that he could have thrown it all up and gone into
a parish, become a latter-day John Keble; but he knew himself well
enough to understand that this most demanding and particular
vocation was not his. He knew his worth; he felt that he had
qualities of intellect that the Church needed. He was right; but his
views were not those acceptable to the liberal establishment of the
Church, acceptable, that is, in one to be accorded a position of real
influence in the present dispensation. One after another, preferments
which he would have filled worthily came and went. On the
weekend before he died, he had come to accept that the latest of
these, the Deanery of St Paul's, had now eluded him. So many
doors had been closed; and now, even those which had opened
would soon close too.

The Suicide Note

The death of Gareth Bennett, it is not too much to say (overused
though such language has become) was a symbolic moment in the
history of Anglicanism in the late twentieth century. Ecclesiastical
historians are not, normally the stuff of which history is itself
made. As Dr Bennett's literary executor, the theologian Dr Geoffrey
Rowell, put it afterwards, 'the lives of academics are not in general
marked by dramatic incident or stirring events. The patient analysis
required of the historian as he investigates the past may lead, as
Garry Bennett's own work did, to a reinterpretation and new
evaluation of a particular historical character or period; it will rarely
be on a par with the events so studied.' But Gareth Bennett's quiet,

scholarly life became, by the manner and circumstance of its dissolution, eloquent of larger themes. His death was not the private death of someone who had taken his own life for merely private reasons. It was a public death and its reasons were public. Garry left no suicide note on his desk, precisely written out in his small donnish hand. But there was a document attached to this suicide nevertheless, and because of this death it was to have a currency it would not otherwise have attained.

There was, in a sense, a suicide note; it had already been published by the Church Information Office and distributed to the press. Its message was to do, not with the success or failure of any particular prelate, but with the increasing failure of the Church of England itself. The message was that the Emperor no longer had any clothes and that he ought to acquire some or die of pneumonia. It was anonymously written, because the Emperor had shown over the years by his treatment of earlier messengers that it was not always a message it was agreeable to deliver in person.

His death was the ultimate exclusion; self-inflicted at a time of his own choosing, rather than quietly administered, inch by inch. But the process had, in one way, already begun years before; it was not unleashed by the *Crockford's* affair. The moment he began to question, in the Synod itself, the intellectual and spiritual basis of the revolution within the Church that had more or less coincided with the installation of Synodical government, he was absorbed into a process that had affected hundreds, even thousands of other clergy. There was nothing explicit; nothing, necessarily, consciously intended in this process. It was simply that a revolution in the mind-set of the establishment had taken place, and those who were not part of it found that they were less and less likely to be in the places where the decisions were made, or where the mind of the Church was formed.

The revolution was able to take an explicit political form because at exactly the right moment, the right political conditions materialized. In 1970, effective control of the Church's affairs passed into the hands of the General Synod; in 1979, the appointment of bishops passed into the hands of a committee appointed by that Synod. The choice of the Church's leadership was now made by the opaque agency of its own political and bureaucratic structures. It would reflect the ethos of those structures; no longer would prime ministerial patronage (theoretically indefensible, in practice often splendidly effective) maintain a right balance between Catholic, Evangelical and Modernist. Nor was there any longer room for the inspired or the unsafe choice (if it could be identified in time). There would be no more Mervyn Stockwoods, often outrageous and wrongheaded but never dull, whatever else you might say a believer. A more serious consequence by far, there would be no more Michael Ramseys, holy, unworldly, hopeless at political manoeuvrings and committee work and small talk, in every way, you might have said, an appalling choice for the bench of bishops, certainly for the Primacy of All England, in the event the greatest and most beloved primate of the century. Only those who fulfilled certain criteria could be got through the committee; not just this committee, any committee, because committees make different kinds of decision. Committees like mediocrities, men who will not make waves or cause questions about their judgement (Bishop Jenkins was a mistake). Committees are subject to pressures both implicit and explicit. They reflect the balance of political realities around them; and by the late 1970s there had been a major shift in that balance, a real revolution had occurred; that, more than the particular influence of the two archbishops, was the explanation for the Crown Appointments Commission's decisions. But in the end the effect was the same: the bench of bishops was overwhelmingly 'liberal' in its composition; the Evangelicals and Catholics who had slipped through, with few exceptions, were low-key and not given to making trouble.

The Quiet Revolution

The political revolution flowed from a theological and spiritual revolution. In a quite brief period of time, the fundamental doctrines of Christianity had been simply dispossessed of the authority of revelation; the resurrection of Christ, say, or the doctrine of the Trinity, were, in the words of one of the successful revolutionaries, Leslie Houlden, no longer to be seen as objective and unchanging, 'stable rocks in a sea of shifting and developing human beliefs and notions'. They were themselves, he went on, 'despite the continuing names by which they are identified, within the swirling waters, and the names are to a large degree convenient labels whereby a body of related but distinct ideas and institutions may be recognized'. Those who utterly rejected this approach were decreasingly likely to be appointed to academic positions; partly, this was because they would not always find it easy to gain the basic credentials in the first place. Not necessarily because they lacked the intellectual ability: but because in a liberal theology faculty (and in the end that is what they all became) the theologically conservative found it increasingly difficult to gain first-class degrees. It was not necessarily that there was a conspiracy against them: it was just that, in the words of one graduate student – speaking despairingly of a senior theology professor – 'if you really believe in the creeds, if you take them seriously, they think you must have brain damage: they simply think that you're not very bright'.

A story (perhaps apocryphal), is told of the undergraduate days of one young evangelical student at one of the ancient universities. To prove he had understood the theology he had been taught, that he was not brain-damaged, he wrote all the examination papers in his finals from the standpoint of the 'liberal' theology of the 1960s. At the end of each paper, he wrote, in red ink: 'I feel in conscience bound to state that I believe nothing of what I have written.' To the credit of his examiners, he was awarded a first.

The revolution had taken place; but it was for the most part a hidden revolution. Developments were to be natural, or to seem so. Where overt changes were to take place, it was not to be in the name of liberal theology, but of the recovery of the ancient roots of the Christian tradition, the paring away of 'accretions'. The Book of Common Prayer disappeared in church after church; not, it was said, because it stood in the way of progress, but because it represented a deviation from ancient tradition. The new services, so ran the claim, were modelled on the liturgies of the early Church. Hence, the liturgical revolution of the 1960s and 1970s had the support of many whose theology was orthodox. In parish after parish, the Book of Common Prayer was removed, or was retained only for evensong. In many parishes, to be sure, the new services were a success, welcomed by the people, genuinely the basis of 'renewal'. Nobody could legitimately argue that it was wrong to make them available. But the 'Alternative Service Book' soon became, not an alternative, but the only option. The Book of Common Prayer was still officially the Church's liturgy; but it became increasingly difficult to find a church on a Sunday morning where the worship was centred on it.

Many orthodox clergy had supported this change; but the disappearance of the little black books was not without its drawbacks for those who wanted the Church's faith renewed but not replaced. Patristic in its structure the new liturgy might be, but as a safeguard for sound doctrine and as an aid for teaching it was a non-starter. It had no roots in the people's affections, nor did it have any doctrinal status: the old prayer book was still the repository for the official teaching of the Church. But the faithful in the pews were losing touch with it; less and less could a preacher point to the catechism, or to the exhortations to pious observances through which they had so often thumbed their way during dull sermons. The book was no longer within reach; it was collecting dust at the back of the church. The doctrine of the Church of England was no longer guaranteed by any external authority; it was a matter for majority votes in the Synod, taking place at the end of scrappy and perfunctory debates.

In all this upheaval, both liturgical and doctrinal, the role of the theological colleges was crucial. I began training for the priesthood, as a late convert, in 1975. I had been confirmed in 1973. The first Prayer Book service of Holy Communion I attended was one I also celebrated some years after my ordination. It was not a technically competent celebration, I kept losing my way; we had never been taught to use the book. Once, during my training, I had been writing an essay in which I was called on to compare various liturgies. I went to the chapel to find a copy of the 1662 prayer book; they had all been cleared out, not one was left. In the end I found a copy of the Book of Common Prayer in the library, in the 'comparative liturgy' section, but the English 1662 prayer book itself was nowhere to be found; I used the old South African prayer book which was based on it.

Thus do revolutions become entrenched. First capture the education of the next generation; in the Church, of the next generation of clergy. There was no obvious suppression of mainstream biblical and traditional Christianity in most Colleges, some indeed – notably those of the Evangelical and Catholic traditions – were dedicated to its defence. But these establishments came under increasing fire from the centre for a time, on the ground that they were 'divisive'. Most colleges had a tendency (implicit or explicit) to install the doctrines of 1960s radicalism as the only rational option. Some did so with all due deliberation. One true story illustrates the process poignantly. A very eminent theologian, one of the greatest exponents of classical Anglicanism who had left the university and become a bishop, retired to a cottage near a well-known theological college in the province of Canterbury. The principal of the college was also a theologian but of the new school, and by no means as personally persuasive. The retired bishop, a man of great holiness of life, had always loved the young; one of his greatest joys had been the intellectual and spiritual nurture of young men training for the priesthood, over whose priestly formation he often exercised a powerful influence. He had been looking forward to helping at the college; in the past such help had been eagerly sought wherever he had gone. But here it was not only not sought, the principal of the college took every necessary step to ensure that his young men should not come under any such retrograde influence. They were effectively cut off from his company, and he from theirs. The old bishop was treated with such unkindness that he sold his cottage and moved far away.

The New Fundamentalism

There was in the air a new intellectual inflexibility, cold and hard; almost a new fundamentalism. But this was a strange kind of fundamentalism: not the fundamentalism of revelation once for all delivered, recorded in the bible by the hand of God, literally applied, to be clung to without deviation through thick and thin. This was a *liberal* fundamentalism, which often seemed to have more in common with the austere tenets of secular humanism than with mainstream Christian tradition. The intellectual debt indeed was occasionally acknowledged; at a mission to Oxford University one senior bishop of the Church of England told bemused undergraduates that it was the logical positivists who had taught him how to think. It was, some of them felt, a strange kind of thinking to be spoken of so fondly by a Christian prelate.

'Unless a proposition can be verified, it has no meaning.' A mechanistic Victorian scientism, literally applied, to be clung to without deviation through thick and thin, that was the new fundamentalism. Miracles do not occur. Why? Because they cannot be demonstrated to have occurred; if the bible says they do, that part of the text is to be subtracted from the dwindling remnant to which credit may still be provisionally attached. 'However much help we may get from the Bible', wrote Dennis Nineham, then Warden of the formerly Tractarian Keble College, 'we must decide for ourselves, with the help of such light as we can get, what our stance before God, and our attitude to our neighbour, should be.' In the end, human reason is all we can rely on; we are on our own. It was cold, comfortless stuff for a Church through which, already, faith in the nearness and power of God in individual human lives seemed to flow with such agonizing torpor. In the end, the 1960s revolution turned out to be a counter-revolution, a return to man's imprisonment within himself, a refusal of the irruption of God's fire into man's world, a turning back of wine into water.

It all left the faithful with a question, which more and more perplexed and bothered them: is the Church of England as it has become remotely like the Church that God intends? It is a question Anglicans sometimes find themselves asking when they experience the worship of others, especially perhaps at moments of crisis in their own Church. On the day after Garry Bennett's death, but before anyone knew of it, the veteran Church affairs correspondent, Douglas Brown, stood at the back of a Church in Paphos with his wife. At the end of the Orthodox liturgy, as they pondered on the faith of the vast congregation, on its mingling of rich and poor, young and old, they were given the *antidoron*, the blessed bread, from the remains of the loaves from which the bread of the eucharist is cut, invited by this act into the community of faith on the periphery of which they stood. On his return to England, Douglas Brown spent a morning reading through the press cuttings on the *Crockford's* affair, still pondering. His questions and his conclusions were and remain those of many faithful Anglicans:

I have had the good or bad fortune, whichever way you look at it, to be far away when all this happened, and write with hindsight. But, prompted by renewed experience of Orthodoxy in practice, I can't but feel that the Church of England has to some extent lost its way. I am forced to ask whether liturgical revision and other trendiness, preoccupation with ecclesiastical politics, with doctrinal and theological mind-bending, has done anything to refill the pews, to renew the Faith.

I can do no other than turn my mind to the unchanging changelessness of Byzantium: to the packed churches; to the sight of priests, their child on one arm, their shopping basket on the other, lingering among their people in the markets and coffee shops; to the faith-affirming liturgy; to the serenity and spirituality and transcendence expressed in the scores of icons I have seen of late. And it is against such things that I find myself mourning the death of a priest of the Catholic tradition who, shattered by the state of his Church and by the consequences of having been persuaded to expiate it in the manner he did, was apparently hounded to his death.

In a long working life largely given to reporting Church affairs, I have not known anything more harrowing.

This has been a difficult and often intensely harrowing book to write. Every day I have gone to my study, to write about the cold and lonely death of a friend, and the current spiritual condition of my Church, of the Church within which I found faith in my thirties after a lifetime of atheism or agnosticism. When priests tell me, sorrowing, that 'it isn't the Church I was ordained into', I know exactly what they mean. God gives us free will to reject him or accept him. I thank God that I asked my own hard questions about the viability of secularist assumptions before those assumptions had so wholly pervaded the upper reaches of power in the Church.

One day, the meaning of this terrible episode will be assessed by a writer who has the advantage of time, distance, objectivity, documents still secret, the memories of those who have yet to speak. I cannot claim objectivity. I am a priest of the Church of England. Like many others I was concerned about the Church in the same way that Gareth Bennett was, and had often discussed current tendencies with him. I was not one of his intimates, very few were, but he and I thought of each other as friends; some, deceived by his shyness and his controlled manner, thought him cold; but I was fond of him, and knew that he was warmer and deeper both in his personality and his spiritual life than was sometimes assumed. His death was a personal loss, and I still feel it as such. I have another personal interest to declare: The *Crockford's* tragedy and its aftermath unfolded in, and to some extent through, the pages of the newspapers; like the chorus in Greek tragedy, they recounted the events and formed part of the drama itself. In a small way I was part of that story, and contributed to the coverage of the *Daily Telegraph* throughout.

An Unfinished Story

To be so closely part of a story of this kind has its disadvantages but it has its advantages too. I reject any suggestion that I am incapable of putting the events themselves 'into perspective'. If my view is subjective, so is that of everyone else in the Church of England who cares about its future; there is no one who can claim to be objective, and they would be cold indeed if they could.

This is an unfinished story. In a leading article published two weeks after the appearance of the preface itself, and ten days after the suicide, the *Church Times* spoke for many when it said that 'the main good to be prayed for after this tragedy is a greater spirit of reconciliation between all the groups said to be opposed to each other both in the General Synod and in the Church at large'. But that telltale phrase – 'said to be' – itself confirmed what it seemed to question, even in the face of evidence so terrible and so impossible to ignore: the existence of real and potentially disastrous divisions within the Church. One way of seeing the division, indeed, was as a gulf between those who did and those who did not perceive it. Those who generally supported Archbishop Runcie did so because of his supposed success in maintaining unity – or at least accommodation – where division might have been expected. Those who did not accept the dispensation over which he ruled were – it was said – misfits of one kind or another, representing only the extreme fringes of Anglican opinion. One of the discoveries of the months that followed the *Crockford's* tragedy was how numerous the 'misfits' were: in a Gallup poll taken within weeks of the publication of the *Crockford's* preface, of those who expressed an opinion (around three quarters), twice as many clergy supported the analysis of the preface as rejected it.

The *Church Times*'s hopes for reconciliation were not fulfilled. The divisions remained; if anything they grew deeper. The root causes of division grew: 'agreement' – in the house of bishops and later at the Lambeth conference – became a code word, meaning agreement to disagree over issues of fundamental importance. Within the Church of England, feelings within the Church over the circumstances surrounding the *Crockford's* tragedy remained strong beneath the surface, despite the restoration of the bland civilities of Anglican life; reconciliation had been starved by a dearth of two essentials for any Christian community: penitence and forgiveness.

Before there can be either, there must be a recognition of the facts, of what has actually taken place. There was never a real recognition of the significance of these events; only when there has been can healing and new growth once more take place. That is why I have felt impelled to write this book. It has been a grim labour to recall the events surrounding Dr Gareth Bennett's tragic death; it has been scarcely less grim to write about the growth – within the Church of which I am a priest – of an intolerance from which many have suffered, but of which he was the most tragic victim. On hearing of Garry Bennett's suicide, I wrote an article (with which I end chapter three) containing these words:

Garry Bennett is dead. Nothing will bring him back. But it is important that he should not have died for nothing. What needs now to be placed under scrutiny is the context in which his tragedy unfolded. For it has to be understood that this is no isolated act, whose significance is confined within its own boundaries.

That still seems to me to be true over a year later. Garry Bennett's death was emblematic of something that had happened to Anglicanism; and by a great irony, much of what had happened had already been perceptively analysed by him in the preface itself. The immediate circumstances of his death remain relevant, and ought to be branded on the memory of every Anglican. But the roots of the incapacity to cope with dissent, so dramatically illustrated by the 'liberal' ascendancy in the days following the publication of the 1987 *Crockford's* preface, require scrutiny too. Its roots, I believe, are theological and not merely personal, and have to do with the displacement of classical Anglicanism by a school of thought describing itself as 'liberal' but often marked by an apparently paradoxical illiberality in the behaviour of its exponents. The answer to the conundrum of why it should be the case that a school of thought which seeks to dissolve dogma and open up free inquiry should lead in practice to the 'marginalization' of its opponents has, at one level, an obviously political dimension. But there is also, I believe, a theological explanation of which it is my intention to attempt the beginnings in part two of this book.

It may be as well to indicate what it is *not* my intention to attempt. There will inevitably be other books dealing with the life and works of Gareth Bennett and examining in detail the arguments of the preface. Though these themes have inevitably formed a large part of this book's raw materials, it has not been my intention to conduct here a systematic examination of them. Nor is this a treatise of moral theology: I have not taken it upon myself to offer any considered judgement, as others have not hesitated to do, on whether or not it is right to tell lies under certain circumstances, and whether or not such circumstances existed to justify Dr Bennett's denials of authorship. I believe that suicide, as a cool and considered act, is a grave sin; I believe also that there is no sin so grave that God does not remember our circumstances and the balance of our mind at the time. Gareth Bennett is in the hands of a loving and merciful God, to whom I am content to leave the assessment of his guilt: 'judgement is mine, saith the Lord': it is certainly not mine.

If this is not a moral theology, neither is it a biography. Bennett's life cannot in any case be written until his unfinished autobiography and diaries are made available to scholars. Dr Geoffrey Rowell has published an autobiographical sketch which draws on these materials, together with his indispensable collection of Bennett's essays (including the *Crockford's* preface) which appeared in 1988 under the title *To the Church of England*. I am myself not competent to assess his historical scholarship. And the arguments of the preface itself, though I have considered what I take to be the most important of them in this book, and have examined certain key areas in detail, have been examined here in the perspective of the furore they provoked rather than as the subject of an objective and balanced study. The *Crockford's* preface can probably not in any case yet be read wholly objectively at least in this generation; and the way its author died will probably always be in the minds of those who read it. This book deals with the area of overlap between what actually happened and what the preface itself said; the questions it tries to answer have to do with how the two can be seen to illuminate each other.

Most of the topics dealt with in the preface are at least touched on in this process, though not necessarily at the same length. Some mention for instance, at least in passing, of such bureaucratic entities as the General Synod of the Church of England, the Crown

Appointments Commission, and the Anglican Consultative Council can, unfortunately, not be avoided here. Garry Bennett took these bodies more seriously than I have ever been able to do; we did not agree on everything, only on the essentials. But he would certainly have agreed, I think, that the ineffectiveness of these bodies is a symptom, rather than the cause, of the ills of contemporary Anglicanism; the cause, I believe, is to be found in a loss of vision and coherence, the sources of which need to be diagnosed at a level less functional than that of the workings of human institutions. I have looked at two institutions more closely than others (though always inside my general perspective), because they illustrate my argument (and Gareth Bennett's) with particular aptness: The Episcopal Church of the USA, and the Lambeth Conference, as exemplars of the problems of modern Anglicanism.

On This Rock

In publishing this book, I will without doubt be accused of disloyalty to the Church of which I am a priest. But the Church does not consist of bishops and archbishops, still less of boards and synods and committees. Nobody but a confirmed atheist could look down from the press gallery of the General Synod at the proceedings and the personalities to be observed there and imagine for one moment that in any essential way they represent the reality of the Church of God. None of this *is* the Church. But the leaders of the Church of England, the bishops, do have a function in God's providence. They are described in Anglican documents, in the solemn language of the middle ages, as holding their office 'by divine permission'. I hold their office in honour, and believe them to be descendants of the apostles themselves. It has not been pleasant to have to describe the actions of some of them, during the *Crockford's* furore, in the way that I have. I am aware how easy it will be to dismiss this book by describing it, as one prelate described the preface itself, as 'sour and vindictive'. But I do not seek revenge; only the healing of the wounds caused by this terrible affair, a healing which can only come when the truth has been told and acknowledged. I seek something else: an end to the injustice already being done to the memory of Gareth Bennett and what he stood for by a process of what is being called 'setting the record straight', or putting the affair 'into perspective'. This process has so far involved a more or less subtle denigration of the dead man and a rewriting of what actually happened.

I am well aware of what awaits me too when this book is published. I have written seriously and soberly out of concern for my Church, but if I am not now misrepresented in certain quarters, I shall be astonished. It will not, after all, be the first time such a thing has happened. I have already been accused of making capital out of the affair for 'partisan purposes' and of 'doing a disservice to Dr Bennett's memory'. My 'partisan purposes', if that is how they are to be described (certainly, they involve taking one view of the Church rather than another), are precisely the same purposes that animated Gareth Bennett in writing the preface. What is meant by 'doing a disservice to his memory' is actually refusing to acquiesce in the establishment view of how that memory should be cut down to size.

I have subtitled this book *Gareth Bennett and the Death of the Anglican Mind*. This may seem unduly gloomy until we remember that resurrection is the underlying principle of Christianity. But it rarely happens as we expect it to. The works of great Anglican theologians like Michael Ramsey and Eric Mascall may have been driven from our seminaries; but they are read with respect, I understand, in the Gregorian University in Rome and other intellectual centres not easily dismissed. Their Anglicanism is still believed and practised by many faithful people throughout the world. Whatever the fate of the Church of England's currently prevailing institutional manifestations, the faith which has, through the centuries, animated the true *Ecclesia Anglicana* – that is, the faith of mainstream Christendom – will still be breaking down the gates of Hell. The Church is always dying, but it is always rising again, so long as it is true to its own nature. That is why, before all else, the truth has to be told whatever the cost. The defence of the Church is never the same thing as the protection of institutions and power structures, even less of powerful individuals.

I owe a debt of gratitude to many, and particularly to those who gave me hitherto unpublished 'inside' information on what journalists call a 'non-attributable' basis. This puts me in a quandary. I am accustomed to indicate my sources, annotating them in an apparatus of footnotes and references. So many of my sources are either non-attributable (on the one hand), or obvious from the text (on the other), that I have decided to dispense with footnotes entirely. I have lodged a copy of the manuscript in the Bodleian library giving all first hand sources and expanding certain passages in the text which have to remain cryptic during the lifetime of those involved. This will be sealed until the year 2040. Since I cannot thank everyone here, I have decided to thank nobody publicly. Those who have helped me in my labours know who they are and how grateful I am to them.

PART ONE

ONE

'Already the Vultures are Circling around this Man'

On Monday 30 November 1987, Derek Pattinson, General Secretary of the General Synod of the Church of England, sent a letter to every diocesan bishop in the provinces of Canterbury and York. It accompanied a copy of the preface to the forthcoming edition of *Crockford's Clerical Directory*, which was to be published later that week. In his letter, Pattinson drew attention 'in particular' to the following passage from the preface's opening paragraph. He quoted the passage in full:

These are critical times for Anglicanism, and now more than ever there is need of an informed and critical account of the state of the Anglican Communion in general and the Church of England in particular. It is not easy for any individual churchman to write such an independent survey in his own name for inevitably it will point to matters which are not for our comfort and it must extend to deal with personalities. It is therefore a fortunate circumstance that there exists a longstanding custom that each edition of Crockford's directory should have an anonymous Preface in which Anglican affairs are subjected to the scrutiny of a writer who is given complete independence.

Some time before, John Miles, the Church House press officer, had made arrangements for copies to be sent to accredited Church affairs correspondents of the Fleet Street press. These were to go out on 2 December, the day before publication; only the Press Association news agency was to get a copy two days before publication (1 December), so that its report could go out over the wire at the same time as correspondents received the full text.

The broadcasting media were excluded from this prepublication distribution: John Barton, broadcasting officer of the Church House

Communications Committee, was so incensed by the contents of the preface that he refused, against the advice of both John Miles and Derek Pattinson, to send it out. Barton was supported in this decision by the chairman of his committee, the Rt Revd John Taylor, Bishop of St Albans. The first inkling the broadcasters had that a major story was breaking was when the Press Association's report was sent out, on the morning before publication.

On Thursday morning the preface was front page news in every national daily except for the Daily Mirror; and in one way or another it remained a major story for some weeks. It is not too much to say that the furore in the press that was to ensue, and the events that were to follow in its wake, are now part of the history of the Church of England. The strains, both in individuals and in the Church as a whole, which were both partly caused by and mercilessly exposed in the searchlight of international press attention, brought about events which showed the Church of England to itself in a way it had never, in modern times, seen itself. The drama of those days will never be forgotten by anyone even remotely involved in them. With the suicide of Dr Gareth Bennett, the drama ended in a tragedy which was not only that of the hapless author of the preface himself, or of those who cared about him, but of the whole Church within which for years the spring activating this extraordinary sequence of events had coiled and tightened. The Church of England lives in its aftermath still.

For the author of this book, the Crockford's tragedy had a particularly personal meaning. Garry Bennett, who for most of his life had shrunk from controversy, had now died of it; the unbearable sadness of that death lay particularly heavily on those of us who had known him. But for me, there was one element in his tragedy which struck close to home. He had himself more than once warned me against the dangers of speaking openly, particularly for a priest whose future in the Church was uncertain. Because of my newspaper articles and my books – for the most part critical of current trends within Anglicanism – I had, he told me, become persona non grata for those in authority in the Church. And he had warned me that this would not be without its effect on my future.

One incident in particular confirmed this perception for us both; for me in a chilling way. After the Eucharist one Sunday at Pusey House, he drew me to one side. I was, he said in gentle but ironic tones, becoming famous. At a recent session of the General Synod, the Archbishop of Canterbury had asked him how things were going at Pusey House, of which Garry was an influential governor, and therefore in some sense my employer. Garry replied that things were going very well under the new principal, Fr Philip Ursell. Dr Runcie had paused before speaking, and then continued simply with an apparent non sequitur: 'What are we going to do about William Oddie?' When it became clear to the Archbishop that I had Garry's support, the conversation moved on. I asked Garry what he thought the Archbishop meant by his question. His eyes twinkled. 'Well,' he said, 'I don't think he had preferment in mind.' I had, he said on another occasion, become 'something of a marked man'.

The following year, he warned me that a particular post for which I had been asked to apply, and which I had been given good reason to suppose would be offered to me, was probably now unattainable, because of the hostile reaction in some circles attracted by my recent book *What Will Happen to God?*, a study of feminist influence in the Church in which I had concluded that certain recent developments – notably the movement for the ordination of women – would, if unchecked, lead the Church away from biblical Christianity. He proved to be a true prophet: among other tactics successfully employed to prevent my appointment, copies of a personal attack on me (implying psychological difficulties over feminism in the Church) by the radical Christian feminist Monica Furlong, were circulated by a senior churchman to the selection committee.

About eighteen months later, after I had left Pusey House, Garry wrote to me (at about the same time, as I now know, that he was being invited to write the *Crockford's* preface) counselling me for the future to avoid controversial writing about the condition of the Church for the sake of my own spiritual peace and tranquillity. He was to pay a terrible price for neglecting his own advice.

The Storm Breaks

But nobody on that cold December Thursday morning was thinking what the consequences of the preface might be for its author. At that stage everyone's attention was focused on its possible effect on the future of one man – the Most Reverend and Right Honourable Robert Runcie, the hundred and second Archbishop of Canterbury, of whose leadership the preface included a brief but damaging analysis.

In fact not everyone in Fleet Street had read the preface in full before they wrote their stories. Speculation in some Church circles about a possible plot against the Archbishop was later fostered by reflections on the unlikelihood of nearly every newsroom in Fleet Street (even the *Sun*, which discovered, remarkably, that it was in possession of a religious affairs correspondent) having without outside help noticed the passage about Dr Runcie straight away, despite the fact that it was buried in a long and scholarly essay on the condition of the Church which could hardly be expected, on the face of it, to provide more than a few rather dull column inches for an inside page.

It may be that such reflections simply indicated the traditionally low view among senior prelates of the intelligence of journalists and the status of the journalistic profession; it certainly reflected their ignorance of the workings of Fleet Street. In fact the explanation for the universal and immediate perception of the *Crockford's* preface as a major news story by all the national dailies, with the sole exception of the *Daily Mirror*, is simple enough. Whether they had read the text of the preface or not, everyone had seen the report sent out over the wire by the Press Association news agency, and received by all the national dailies early on the day before publication.

This was written by the Associate Editor of the Press Association, Reg Evans, who as soon as he looked through the preface understood that here was a news story of major dimensions. Evans, the PA's churches expert, was himself a Christian (not necessarily a prerequisite for ecclesiastical correspondents), and writing the story faced him with a dilemma. As a journalist he was obliged to write the story as he perceived it. He was a senior staff member of the Press Association, and could hardly suppress a story which was in any case bound to come out. At the same time, he was responsible, at the highest level, for advising the Church of England on how to project the most favourable image of itself in the press; Reg Evans is also the chairman of the Church House Communications Committee's Press panel. As a journalist, he was seized by the excitement known to every reporter when it dawns on him that he has stumbled on a major story; as a loyal member of the Church and an admirer of Archbishop Runcie, he was horrified at the implications of what he was now obliged to report.

So it was that on Tuesday 2 December, Reg Evans sat down to write his story. He telephoned his contacts in the Church for speculation as to who might have written the attack; among the suggested names was that of Dr Gareth Bennett of New College, Oxford. He phoned Dr Bennett who issued the first of many denials. 'Absolutely not,' he said, when asked if he was the author; 'what does it say?' When told that it contained criticisms of the Archbishop he replied, 'Well, that's good. But it wasn't me.' Evans said later 'I just didn't think a clergyman would lie.' He ruled Bennett out. He phoned the Bishop of St Albans for his reaction to the preface. As we have seen, as Chairman of the Church's Communications Committee, Bishop Taylor had already backed the decision not to send it to radio and television journalists; now he read a short but very strongly worded statement to Evans who took it down over the telephone. 'This is a cowardly and disgraceful attack', commented Bishop Taylor, 'by a writer who has abused the privilege of anonymity which was accorded to him. Few in the Church of England will have any sympathy with the views he has expressed.' Armed with this reaction, Reg Evans wrote his story, which was sent out the following morning under the headline '"COWARDLY" ATTACK ON RUNCIE IN CHURCH'S WHO'S WHO'.

In view of its importance in the events that followed, the report is worth considering in some detail. Its most noticeable feature, to anyone who has read the whole text of the *Crockford's* preface, is its almost exclusive concentration on the criticisms of Dr Runcie; anyone reading the report without having the text available indeed could draw the conclusion that the 'attack' on Dr Runcie formed the most substantial part of the preface itself. In fact in a very long essay the criticisms of the Archbishop occupy only three paragraphs. This is not to impugn the PA report: newsmen see the question of balanced reporting in a different (and in its own terms, no less valid) way from that in which such questions are approached by scholars. For a scholar, 'balance' means the inclusion of all relevant information, at whatever length is necessary, and the creation of a total picture; for a journalist, it means finding the *story*, that is, the information of immediate public interest, and putting it in a context. The 'context', here, may well not be that which a scholar would think appropriate. A 'balanced' story is one in which differing views are fairly represented.

This difference in perception is obvious enough, but its existence is undoubtedly one of the ingredients in the *Crockford's* tragedy. It simply did not occur to Garry Bennett that his remarks on Dr Runcie which in the essay taken as a whole are made almost in passing would be seen by most journalists and their readers as overwhelmingly the most interesting part of his essay and would be taken as a frontal attack, even an implied demand for the Archbishop's resignation.

The Hunt Is On

Nor did it occur to newsmen, used to reporting the news in terms of power struggles and clashes between personalities, that the criticisms of Dr Runcie were intended by their author not as the centrepiece of his essay but as part of an entire picture, a detail in a portrait of contemporary Anglicanism in which Dr Runcie's primatial style was seen as representative of the condition of the Church of England in particular and the Anglican Communion in general.

For Reg Evans, the story was clear; the Archbishop of Canterbury had been undermined by those whose duty it was to uphold his authority: not only by the author, but by those who had commissioned and then without question published his work. 'An astonishing attack', his piece opened,

on the Archbishop of Canterbury, Dr Robert Runcie, and the way he leads the Church of England, is made today in an official church publication. Dr Runcie is accused of
- 'taking the line of least resistance on each issue';
- 'The desire to put off all questions until someone else makes a decision';
- 'Usually to be found nailing his colours to the fence';
- Preferring as close associates 'men who have nothing to prevent them following what they think is the wish of the majority at the moment';

· Influencing the selection of bishops to prefer men whose careers crossed his own and who often have a BBC religious broadcasting background. The attack is made by the anonymous author of the preface to the new edition of *Crockford's Clerical Directory* – the Church's Who's Who – which is published by the Church Commissioners and the Church's Central Board of Finance.

The report then gave the views of the Bishop of St Albans, quoted above, and continued by reporting the refusal of the Church Commissioners to give the name of the author, 'or even', Evans commented, not without acerbity, 'say how he was selected'. They had simply stated that he was 'a person of distinction in the Church'.

The report went on, with uncanny accuracy, to predict the reaction of the Church hierarchy, and then, equally perceptively, to lay down what, with hindsight, look almost like guidelines for the hunt for the author that was to follow. Only one detail caused minor confusion for some of those inclined to suspect Garry Bennett: the unknown author's obvious support for the Bishop of London, Dr Graham Leonard. There had, in fact, been a very public rift between Garry Bennett and the bishop over Bennett's attack on him, in a radio interview, for his visit to Tulsa earlier in the year, in support of a priest and congregation expelled from the American Episcopal Church. Privately, the rift had been to some extent healed; but for some, including the bishop himself, it lent a certain credibility to Bennett's denials of having written the preface. In all other details, however, Evans's characterization of the author was as accurate as his forecast of likely Church reactions:

Lambeth Palace said there would be no comment from Dr Runcie. But a major row is certain. Bishops, who also come under the writer's lash, will question how the writer was selected and why officials of the church felt unable to interfere when the preface to what is the church's most prestigious and permanent publication was delivered. Although the writer's identity is known only to a few top officials, the style identifies him as a senior academic clergyman involved in the highest levels of Church government, a traditionalist from the church's Anglo-Catholic wing, an opponent of the ordination of women and a supporter of the Bishop of London, Dr Graham Leonard.

The remainder of the report deals at greater length with the criticisms of Dr Runcie and the liberal establishment, and ends with a short section about the attitudes of the preface writer towards the General Synod of the Church of England, the forthcoming Lambeth Conference, and the American Episcopal Church.

By mid-morning on Wednesday, the hunt for the author was on. Academic clergymen all over England were being telephoned and asked whether they had written the preface. Newsmen were hunting up reactions; leader writers were pondering on the significance of the preface for Dr Runcie and the Church of England.

The first media coverage came in some Wednesday evening papers and on radio and television news programmes. The London *Evening Standard* published a story at the bottom of page three with a photograph of the archbishop (captioned 'DR RUNCIE: accused'). The writer, John Passmore, largely followed the PA report but added his own ominous comment: 'the question now', he wrote, 'is how long the writer will be able to hide behind his anonymity'.

There was, however, little sign yet of the extent of the media storm that was soon to break, though it was already clear that the anonymous author himself, and the use he had made of his anonymity, would come under fire from the establishment. The first major coverage was on the BBC's five o'clock radio news magazine, 'P.M.', on Wednesday evening. The presenter's introduction was taken, almost verbatim, from the PA report 'An astonishing personal attack', said the programme's anchor man, 'on the Archbishop of Canterbury, Dr Robert Runcie, and the way he leads the Church of England, is to be made tomorrow in an official Church publication.' John Newbury, then the BBC's religious affairs correspondent, was asked whether there was any precedent for such an assault on an archbishop. His answer did not suggest that he thought a major media event was about to break:

I think you have to understand that *Crockford's Directory* comes out every two years. It always has a preface. It's always anonymous, and it's always iconoclastic. Every two years somebody is given the opportunity for a *cri de coeur*. And under the cloak of anonymity they are able to do that. Back in 1976 they were talking about homosexuality. In 1983, I was interested to see, looking back, somebody was praising what they called the ordinariness of Dr Runcie, saying this may just be what the Church needs. In 1985, the author had a go at the Bishop of Durham, David Jenkins, urging people like him to resign. So it's not an unusual vehicle to use for this kind of stuff.

Newbury went on to say that Lambeth Palace were making no comment on the affair ('they . . . say the Archbishop really can't respond to anonymous criticism. He is giving no interviews, he plans to make no statement'), that *Crockford's* was now published by Church House and, most interestingly of all perhaps, in answer to the question of whether the preface would create a stir within the Church, that

Some people I've spoken to suggest it might actually provoke a backlash of support for Dr Runcie. It is very difficult to say . . . In the past, well, let's go back to 1985, the writer of the preface then urged the Bishop of Durham to resign. David Jenkins. David Jenkins remains the Bishop of Durham today two years later.

The answer given here, it will be seen, is twofold, and does not directly address the question. In fact it answers two different and much more interesting questions. How much support would there be for Dr Runcie? And was his primacy now in jeopardy? It could be that John Newbury's answer unconsciously reflects the anxieties of his contacts within Lambeth Palace itself; it may also reflect their tactics, tactics designed for a situation in which Dr Runcie's position within the Church was perceived as being distinctly vulnerable.

The Backlash of Support

From the beginning, it is clear that Dr Runcie decided to leave his defence to others, himself maintaining a dignified silence. It is difficult to believe that his staff took no steps to ensure that an effective defensive response would be forthcoming from others; perhaps they expected a 'backlash of support' with good information as to who would be providing it in the near future.

At any rate, whether as part of a concerted defence or not, 'P.M.' now broadcast an interview with the Rt Revd Bill Westwood, Bishop of Peterborough, an experienced performer whose speciality is a chatty, informal style of speech, and who is sometimes known as 'the Radio Bishop'. In his answers, he adopted a tactic to be followed widely over the succeeding days: to ignore or sidestep the substantial criticisms of the preface, concentrating on the allegedly underhand nature of the attack, the contemptible character of the attacker, and the impropriety of such criticism emanating from the heart of the Church bureaucracy itself.

This was the first public sign of the recriminations within the Church, not only against the unknown author but also (and with equal vigour) against those who had offered such a unique platform to someone who in the event had used it as he had. The author had produced, not the usual mildly ironic sally about how infuriating (but still lovable) the Church of England was; but a devastating root and branch analysis of the very basis of modern Anglicanism. And he had offered serious criticisms of the leadership of the Archbishop rather than what might have been expected: a few harmless digs within strictly defined limits. The criticisms were the manifestation, said Bishop Westwood in effect, not of the author's genuine concern for the Church, but of his sour and malicious character.

From its inception on that Wednesday evening, the 'backlash' against the author was infinitely stronger, more personal and more intemperate than anything in the preface itself; and, in this first salvo of what might be called the backlash of the bishops, the criticisms themselves were simply ignored on the grounds that in some obscure way (unexplained by Bishop Westwood) their anonymity made any kind of reasoned response impossible:

Well, I think anonymous malice, you know, people hiding behind having no name is always rather unpleasant. What offends me very much is that in former years this was published by a private publisher, that was his business, but this year it's published by the Church Commissioners and the Central Board of Finance who come from the heart of the Church and for them to carry something of this sort I find very offensive indeed.
Q: What about the criticisms themselves?
A: Well, I think that anybody can make criticisms, anybody in a public office like the Archbishop, or bishops, or politicians or anybody are imperfect, they make mistakes, and we all make judgements of them, right and wrong. What is the thing is, if I'm on your programme, interviewed

by you, everybody knows your name, and I know who is getting after me. This, these, they're snide, sort of sour criticisms behind people's back, and my objection to them is not the criticisms themselves, it's a free society after all, but a person under the mask of not being known is doing this . . . in the Church of England we seem to think it's triumphant if we can go around sort of knifing each other all over the place.

The interviewer persisted: what if the piece were signed? How then would Bishop Westwood answer the criticisms, for instance, that Dr Runcie always took the line of least resistance on each issue, and that he put off all questions until someone else made a decision? They were serious criticisms; perhaps they needed to be answered too.

The bishop, however, was not about to answer them. Effectively, he repeated his answer: anonymous criticisms could not be answered. And he added a few hints towards guessing the identity of the perpetrator, *though this was not a question that had been asked.* Again the criticisms were answered by focusing on the personality of the author, and in doing so, Bishop Westwood gave a few remarkably accurate indications about the kind of person the author might be, and even where to look for him.

It is difficult not to infer that he had his own ideas about who had written the preface. He may have derived these from discussions, possibly by telephone, possibly with Lambeth Palace. Certainly, Lambeth had already concluded that Garry Bennett was responsible and, as we shall see, was not averse to spreading the name around. At any rate, Bishop Westwood had his ideas on the identity of the author, and appeared intent on sharing them:

Oh, yeah, but you see if it was [signed], we'd say, oh, that's Charlie who knows the Church very well, and it's a serious thing, and we would meet his criticisms that way. But this man, or woman, well, it's a man, I'm pretty sure, a priest, too, I think, I would say, middle-aged, clever. That sort of person, he is doing all this sort of thing, knowing he is quite safe, and can't be answered . . . A lot of criticisms are just sort of tea-room gossip, you know, Oxford common-room sort of stuff, that sort of spite, and you can't actually answer them. . . .

It's Amazing What a Chap Can Do

In Oxford, Garry Bennett had spent the day, not indulging in senior common-room gossip, but working in his rooms in New College. He had received a number of calls from newspapers, which he had parried by saying, truthfully, that he had not yet received his copy of *Crockford's*. It was already clear that there would be substantial press interest, but he was not at this stage alarmed by the prospect. Certainly he was convinced that, with proper precautions, the secret of his authorship could be kept.

Among these precautions was care in discussing the matter over the telephone. When, shortly before 6 p.m., Father Philip Ursell, one of the tiny group who knew the authorship of the preface, telephoned him in New College to ask if he had heard the 'P.M.' programme, Garry replied by saying that they shouldn't discuss the matter, since the line might not be secure. Instead, the two men arranged to talk after dinner, in the privacy of Dr Bennett's home in the Oxford suburb of New Marston.

Philip Ursell arrived at around 8 p.m. He had the tape of the 'P.M.' programme in his pocket, but when he offered to play it Garry said he would rely on Ursell's account of its contents. Fr Ursell also told him about the following day's *Telegraph* leader on the affair, the writer of which had discussed its contents with him. The leader was to call for Dr Runcie to resign in time for a successor to be installed before the 1988 Lambeth conference. Garry Bennett listened without comment.

Though it was clear enough that there was going to be a considerable stir over the preface, Garry Bennett was by no means displeased at the way things were going. 'It's amazing,' he said to Ursell, 'what a chap can do from his little semi-detached house in Oxford.' Nor, it appears, did he yet have any serious misgivings that his anonymity would be breached. 'Of course they will suspect it is me,' he said later that evening, 'but they will never know for certain.' 'They will never know from me,' Ursell replied; 'Yes, I knew that,' said Bennett. 'That is one of the reasons I told you. I knew I was going to need some support when it was published.'

The two men, both unmarried, talked about the importance for those who live alone of having someone to talk to in such circumstances. Garry talked about the calls from reporters he had received;

both men joked about the ease of starting pressmen along false trails. Ursell had himself started a rumour that the author was the dean of an ancient cathedral in the southwest, which was to be picked up in several papers on Thursday and Friday. The preface was not the only topic of conversation that Wednesday evening; Garry Bennett was chairman of the Standing Committee of Pusey House, and they spent some time discussing the domestic affairs of the House. There were no telephone calls all evening; Father Ursell left about 11 p.m.

For all his apparent confidence, however, Garry Bennett was already beginning to realize that he was in for a rough time. He passed a sleepless and anxious night. The following morning Garry rose at 7 a.m. and walked to the little newsagent's shop where every day he bought his copy of the *Daily Telegraph*. That morning, he also bought *The Times*, the *Independent*, the *Guardian*, the *Daily Express* and the *Daily Mail*. He returned to the house to read his notices. It was immediately apparent to him that the concentration on the short passage about Dr Runcie was almost total, though *The Times* had devoted an entire page to lengthy extracts which gave more of the flavour of the essay as a whole.

The Times also published a major leader which took seriously the entire argument of the preface and which also cast a cold eye over the opportunity of anonymous comment afforded by the preface. 'There is a trap,' commented *The Times*, 'into which the English in particular are prone to stumble, the confusion of decency with Christianity':

Some of the surprise and shock at the tone of the Preface is due to the contravention of these civilized decencies by one churchman, hiding behind the protection of the anonymity which custom offers him. It is a strange custom; and the participation in it of such figures as the First Church Estates Commissioner and the Secretary General of the General Synod, who must bear responsibility for the Preface however much they disclaim it, is an extraordinary indulgence.

Their ultimate defence must be that in a church ruled by such conventions of politeness, only anonymity will allow the painful truth to be heard. It would be healthier if it were not so . . .

Whether or not this was the most appropriate defence of anonymity under such circumstances, it soon became clear enough that some of the leaders of the Church of England were quite prepared to cast aside 'civilized decencies'. Bishop Bill Westwood had now added to his radio interview's contribution to the campaign against the anonymous author with the phrase 'anonymous, gutless malice', reported in *The Times*. He had also approximated one unusual phrase from the Archbishop of York's personal attack (which when Bishop Westwood was interviewed had not been published): 'The piece,' Ruth Gledhill reports him as saying, 'has all the hallmarks of a *disappointed clergyman*' [my italics]. And he added, almost incredibly, in a chilling phrase he must later have regretted using, 'already the vultures are circling around this man'.

At 8.45 a.m. a heart-stopping event occurred. The telephone rang. From the instrument came the unmistakable tones of the Archbishop of Canterbury himself. Garry paused for a moment in an agony of indecision; then he gently replaced the receiver.

The pace now quickened. Back in his rooms in New College, Garry found the pressure on him mounting. Phone calls from press and television journalists on the trail of the anonymous author became incessant. He became more and more uneasy as the day wore on, and decided to telephone Derek Pattinson at his office in Dean's Yard, Westminster, for reassurance. He phoned repeatedly without getting through; Pattinson was in an important meeting. Philip Ursell phoned during the day to see how things were going, but their conversation was guarded because of Bennett's fear of being overheard. The telephone calls from the press continued. By the time Roderick Gilchrist, then Deputy Editor of the *Daily Mail*, telephoned in the late afternoon, Garry Bennett's normally quiet and controlled manner had disintegrated. He was clearly in an emotional state. 'I don't mind telling you,' he said at one point, 'my nerves are shaken. I don't know why everybody is picking on me. I am not the author.' But he did, strangely perhaps, agree to see Gilchrist the following Monday at his rooms in New College, though he telephoned later from his home to cancel the arrangement. By that time his manner was much calmer.

Dr Habgood Steps In

His working day ended at 5.45 p.m., when he ended a tutorial early, so as to be home in New Marston in time for the six o'clock news.

It may have been then that he first heard of the attack on the anonymous author by the Archbishop of York, the Most Reverend and Right Honourable John Habgood, a reaction which immediately raised the emotional temperature of the media coverage and fuelled curiosity about the author's identity.

Dr Habgood's attack had been issued as a personal statement to the Press Association news agency (reprinted in full on page 100) which the Archbishop knew would forward it to every newsroom and every radio and television station in the country. By his own account it was a carefully worded statement; he had had ample time in which to digest the contents of the preface which he had received in typescript two weeks before. In his own defence, he later claimed that he had himself issued it under media pressure, but this is not a statement to be taken seriously. Calls to the Archbishop from the press are filtered by his lay assistant and press secretary, Raymond Barker; and it can hardly be said that 'media pressure' had had time to build up. The statement was sent to the Press Association promptly, on the morning of publication day itself.

Though the full effect of the statement would not appear until Friday morning, television and radio news bulletins had been giving it coverage through Thursday. The first was ITV's 12.30 news bulletin. In the BBC Radio 4 six o'clock news programme, the announcer introduced an item containing several reactions, including those of spokesmen for Dr Runcie, and of the new Bishop of Bath and Wells, Dr George Carey, who had been consecrated by the Archbishop of Canterbury earlier that day. There were no reports of any views supporting the conclusions of the preface, though these certainly existed.

'The Archbishop of York,' the item began, 'has strongly criticized the anonymous author of an article in the Church's directory, *Crockford's,* personally attacking the Archbishop of Canterbury, Dr Robert Runcie.'

The BBC story taken as a whole shows how the whole affair was now beginning to gather momentum, as the juggernaut of the 'backlash of support' – reported by the media but not invented by them – lumbered into action. Dr Habgood's views were later to be reported at greater length, but his attack comes over in this brief account quite strongly enough for there to be already no doubt that things were going to get rough. 'Here,' the announcer continued, 'with more details of the day's developments, is our religious affairs correspondent, John Newbury':

NEWBURY: It's been very much business as usual for the Archbishop of Canterbury. This morning he was at Southwark Cathedral in London to consecrate the new Bishop of Bath and Wells – the Right Reverend George Carey. After the service, Doctor Runcie posed for photographs with the new bishop but refused to answer any reporter's questions. The palace say the Archbishop cannot respond to anonymous criticism. However, Bishop Carey said he thought Doctor Runcie had been a little upset by the article even though its criticisms were unfounded.

CAREY: There are two ways of running a canoe down rapids – one is to go right on the rocks and smash the ship up and the other one is to sail very adroitly and with good navigation. I believe the Archbishop is leading the Church forward very positively, and I back him wholeheartedly.

NEWBURY: It's a mark of how seriously some are taking this matter that the Archbishop of York – the number two in the Church of England – has come out in defence of his colleague. Doctor Habgood said the article was a most scurrilous attack. It was sour and vindictive, purporting to say what went on in private committees.

HABGOOD: If the anonymous author is a member of those groups, then I have to say that he or she has deliberately distorted the truth. On the other hand, if not a member then what we have here is just guesswork.

NEWBURY: The Archbishop of Canterbury spent this afternoon back at Lambeth at his usual staff meeting. I understand the controversial article was likely to be discussed, but those supporting Doctor Runcie have strongly dismissed any suggestion that he might resign.

The affair was reported that evening by ITN's 'News at Ten', but not, curiously, on either BBC TV news or on BBC TV's 'Newsnight' programme, neither of which reported the *Crockford's* affair at all that day.

ITN reported that the Archbishop of Canterbury's friends were rallying round by denouncing the 'attack' on him in the preface: the report singled out the Archbishop of York's adjectives 'sour' and 'vindictive', and the Bishop of Peterborough's phrase 'anonymous, gutless malice'. Like BBC radio news, ITN had been to Southwark, where the Archbishop of Canterbury would not be drawn; he had, he said, gone there to consecrate a bishop; he did not think it was the appropriate time to deal with such a wide range of questions.

Later, Dr Runcie had posed for photographs with the newly consecrated Bishop of Bath and Wells, who told ITN afterwards that
the Archbishop was wounded but would weather the storm.

The anonymous author of the article, continued the ITN commentator, was being well protected as the Church closed ranks. It
was believed that he was an Anglo-Catholic academic. The preface,
she said, accused Dr Runcie of indecision and lacking firm principles. She went on to report the sentence about Dr Runcie's élitist
liberal background, and the anonymous author's 'waspish attack'
on episcopal appointments. ITN then showed a brief but telling
extract from a longer Tyne Tees interview with Dr Habgood. Here,
the Archbishop seemed to be echoing the 'P.M.' interview with
Bishop Westwood the previous day, with its concentration on the
supposedly disabling effect of not knowing the author's name: one
of the damaging things about doing this kind of thing under the
cloak of anonymity, said Dr Habgood, was that it left everybody
'just stuck'. Like Bishop Westwood, Dr Habgood gave no reason
why this should be so. The interviewer asked the obvious question:
did Dr Habgood know the author? There was a long pause; the
Archbishop carefully replied that he could only speculate. Nobody
watching the interview was left in any doubt that he had very clear
ideas on the question: he knew the author, and his feelings towards
him were not warm.

By the time Philip Ursell telephoned that evening, it had become
clear to Garry that the whole exercise had become uncontrollable;
that all his hopes for a radical change in his life, in which his
abilities would be fitly used in the service of the Church, were now
at an end. He had supposed that many would guess at his authorship
but that the affair would be a nine days' wonder. He was not
anticipating what had every appearance of a campaign to disgrace
him once and for all. He made a written note of what he had come
to realize during the course of the day about his position in the
Church. 'I am now right out of the Church of England,' he wrote.
'I shall linger on and not put up again for the Synod.'

His telephone conversation with Fr Ursell was mostly to do with
Pusey House affairs. 'I don't want to talk about *the* subject,' Fr
Ursell told him, 'you must be sick of it.' They discussed the affairs
of Pusey House (to which Garry was devoted) for about half an
hour, discussing the affairs of the library, and touching on the

whole future development of the House, buildings and staff. Garry seemed calm enough over the telephone. But his thoughts by this time were far from calm. There is, indeed, in his diary entry for the day, written that evening, an overtone of real desperation, almost of fear: 'My God', he wrote, 'what a mess, and basically my own fault. I shall be lucky to weather this business through without disaster and some sort of personal exposure.'

The General Secretary Under Fire

The full fury of the storm that Garry feared would break over him if he were exposed was already beating down on another head – that of the General Secretary of the General Synod, Derek Pattinson, who had commissioned the essay and taken the decision to publish it without any editorial interference. By coincidence, the Church of England's Communications Committee had a meeting scheduled for the afternoon of the day of publication of the *Crockford's* preface.

This was the meeting which had prevented Derek Pattinson from taking Garry Bennett's phone calls. It was well attended and those present included, apart from Pattinson, its chairman (the Bishop of St Albans), Reg Evans, David Winter, Head of Religious Broadcasting at the BBC, John Miles and John Barton. The meeting's existing agenda was suspended for later discussion and replaced by one item, the preface and the circumstances under which it had been commissioned. Reg Evans was, perhaps, the most critical of Derek Pattinson, though others joined in the questioning.

It cannot have been a particularly comfortable experience, though Derek Pattinson was by no means bowed down by it. He did not regard himself as the servant of the committee; if anything rather the reverse. He might or might not take its advice if he needed it, but he considered himself in no way vulnerable to its censure.

The criticisms were shared by other members of the committee. Reg Evans led the questioning. He had a list of questions all ready, on a piece of paper, recalled one committee member later. It was, said Evans, incredible that an attack on the Primate of All England should bear the imprimatur of the Church itself. It was as though a white paper had been published including a personal attack on Mrs Thatcher. The press had been mishandled. To refuse to answer questions about the author's identity might have been understandable, but to refuse even to answer questions about who had commissioned the piece was indefensible. The Church had been made to look ridiculous; the affair had already had a far worse impact on the Church's image than the alleged misreporting of the homosexuality debate in General Synod three weeks previously.

The questions rained down on Pattinson's head. Who selected the author? Who saw the delivered text? Was there any consultation over whether or not to ask for changes? Were lawyers consulted? To the barrage of questions, Derek Pattinson's answers were simple, and they formed the basis of his defence throughout the whole affair. He emphasized the tradition of anonymity, pointing out that previous prefaces had also been critical, and that when the Church had taken over responsibility for the publication of the directory it was agreed that the tradition of an anonymous preface should continue. But he also defended the contents of the preface: the criticisms it contained, he pointed out, were no more than were commonly expressed over coffee during sessions of General Synod or in Church House Westminster every day, and in pubs and bars all over England.

Derek Pattinson was not the only member of the committee to be criticized. David Winter and Reg Evans took issue with John Barton over his refusal to send advance copies of the preface to the broadcasters, pointing out that once the decision to publish had been taken, the preface could not be hidden. Attempts to hide it would have led to an even worse press furore, and relationships between Church House and the religious affairs journalists would have been seriously damaged. The uncomfortable meeting went on all afternoon. According to one committee member, as it broke up, Reg Evans said, 'We'll get him. Whoever he is, we'll get him.'

At midnight, Derek Pattinson was at last able to respond discreetly to Garry Bennett's repeated attempts to reach him over the phone. He telephoned Garry at his home in New Marston. He urged Garry to remain firm in his denials; if he could hang on until after the weekend, Pattinson said, the worst would be over, and media interest would start to die down.

The Pressure Builds Up

But Garry was not reassured. He passed a restless night. The following morning he woke early and once more went down to his local newsagents to buy the four quality dailies, together with the *Mail* and the *Express*. The press speculation over the identity of the *Crockford's* author was, he found, continuing, and Garry's was still one of several academic clergy whose names were being bandied about. The others included Professor Roy Porter, Dr Edward Norman, long one of the most effective critics of the liberal establishment of the Church of England, and the august Henry Chadwick, Regius Professor, former Dean of Christ Church, Oxford, and present Master of Peterhouse, Cambridge.

Dr Chadwick provided the first example among senior clergy of the support for the general analysis of the preface that was to show itself after Garry Bennett's death. Having denied his own authorship, he added simply, 'the question is whether the analysis is correct'. It was clear enough that on the present state of Anglicanism he thought that the preface had got it about right.

It must have been clear to Garry Bennett on that Friday morning that most of the press had not yet worked out the authorship of the preface with any certainty, but there were already signals in plenty that certain key members of the establishment had. One of these, as the *Telegraph*'s story that day indicated, was Dr Habgood. The story, by Jonathan Petre, was based on Habgood's long unprompted statement to the Press Association the previous day, but there was a significant addition:

The Archbishop of York, Dr John Habgood, yesterday condemned as 'scurrilous' the attack in *Crockford's Clerical Directory* on the Archbishop of Canterbury, Dr Robert Runcie, and said it should be treated 'with the contempt it deserves'.

Saying he had his 'suspicions' about the identity of the so-far unnamed author, he added: 'The Church would be wise to regard it as an outburst from a disappointed cleric who manages to pinpoint some of the real problems of the Church, but has nothing constructive to offer.'

The remark about Dr Habgood's 'suspicions' was elicited by Petre's questioning; but the fact that he had a particular culprit in mind is already clear enough from the P A statement itself. Petre goes on to report Habgood's defence of Runcie's 'widely embracing style' of leadership, and his view that there was a 'sourness and vindictiveness about the attack which makes it clear that it is not quite the impartial review of Church affairs which it purports to be'. Even before the offical publication of *Crockford's*, Bishop Bill Westwood had dropped heavy hints on 'P.M.' about someone who was 'clever', 'middle aged' and 'a priest', who indulged in Oxford common-room gossip; these remarks had been reported to Garry by Fr Philip Ursell on the evening they were made. Now there were further clues. The anonymous author (whom Habgood implied he had identified) was a 'disappointed cleric' – someone who had hopes, presumably, of office in the Church which had not been fulfilled (Bishop Westwood's phrase had been 'disappointed clergyman'). This was easily recognizable by those even vaguely in the know as a reference to Garry Bennett.

There were still plenty of candidates. Jonathan Petre had a short list of three: Garry himself, Henry Chadwick, and John Lang, Dean of Lichfield. But of these, only Garry was at all feasible. It must now have seemed to Garry Bennett that the identification had in fact already been made by those who counted in the Church, whether it was provable or not, and that this identification was being fed to the press, either in the form of oblique hints like Bishop Westwood's or by 'off the record' identifications.

According to Garry's diary, Dr Geoffrey Rowell tells us, 'a reporter from the *Mail* rang up to offer me £5000 if I was the author and wished to go public with them. He said it was rumoured that an announcement was to be made in the next 24 hours.' But it is unlikely that Garry would have been flustered by this; he knew that the only way an official announcement could be made would be by Derek Pattinson, and it certainly would not have crossed his mind that Pattinson would have told anyone else. Pattinson had himself encouraged him to maintain secrecy the night before this last diary entry. There would therefore, he knew, be no public announcement.

Who Pointed the Finger?

But the leaking of informed speculation in high places was another matter. 'I don't know why you are all picking on me,' Garry had said the previous day to Roderick Gilchrist of the *Daily Mail*. By now Garry had begun piecing together the answer to that question. He knew that the Archbishop of Canterbury thought he was the author; and he also knew that at least one newspaper had elicited this information from Lambeth Palace.

The Times report that Friday morning, by Clifford Longley and Ruth Gledhill, was alarming. 'Yesterday', they wrote, 'numerous theories surfaced as to the identity of the author, and several churchmen suggested each other, followed by general denials all round'; but, the report continued, 'the Archbishop of Canterbury himself was said to be confident he knew who it was, but the Oxford don in question indignantly denied it.'

Even if he had not been informed of the fact, Garry must already have known that Dr Runcie had worked out for himself that he had written the preface. He had good reason to know that Dr Runcie was well acquainted with his personal style: Garry was a regular 'ghostwriter' of sermons and addresses for the Archbishop, and had known him ever since training for the priesthood at Westcott House, Cambridge. There was nothing in the preface that Garry had not already said to the Archbishop's face. He already realized that Dr Runcie suspected him from the telephone call the previous morning which he had not quite had the stomach to answer. Now, he knew that Dr Runcie had not kept his view to himself; but the Archbishop himself was not talking to the press. *How did* The Times *know what Dr Runcie thought?*

Garry had, in fact, been told over the telephone by the reporter concerned that Lambeth was saying it was the Archbishop's opinion that Garry had written the preface, and he made a written record of the conversation. As we shall see, on being told of Garry's death, the Archbishop told two of Dr Bennett's friends that he was sure that Garry had written it. What Garry never found out was that Dr Runcie had not taken the preface as a personal attack; as Dr Runcie also later disclosed, most of the points Dr Bennett was to make in the preface had already been made to his face: this, indicated Dr Runcie, was why he did not see it as an attack. It seems probable that this is precisely what the Archbishop telephoned early on publication day to tell Dr Bennett; if Garry had felt able to take the call, events might have unfolded differently.

However this may be, we know that the Archbishop's opinion on the authorship of the preface was known to some of those around him, and that on at least one occasion, that opinion, attributed to Dr Runcie by name, passed on to a journalist. And so far as unattributable speculation about the author's name was concerned, Lambeth was joining in with the others. It is clear enough that, for much if not all of the press, this was an important source of press speculation.

Those around Dr Runcie – perhaps understandably – were aggressively on the defensive. Apart from the identity of the author, the big story was now the Archbishop's competence and personality. The *Telegraph* even commissioned an article (by me) on the succession to him – how the next Archbishop of Canterbury would be chosen, and who were the likely 'runners and riders'. At this stage, I concluded, Dr John Habgood, Archbishop of York, still seemed the likely successor (an assessment few people would be making two weeks later). For Dr Runcie or against him – and he had his defenders in the press – the battle over the Archbishop had now been taken up by Fleet Street in a big way.

Forgotten, if it had been noticed in the first place, was Garry's long, carefully written analysis of Anglicanism at the close of the twentieth century – by all the dailies, that is, except *The Independent* and – most notably *The Times*, which the previous day had reproduced a whole page of extracts, and which now published another major leader on the condition of the Church, implicitly rebuking those who had failed to read the whole preface and weigh its analysis:

The anonymous Preface to Crockford's is not only about the Archbishop of Canterbury. It is also about a deeper problem – the nature and identity of modern Anglicanism. This the Preface has fully and reasonably discussed. It would be foolish for churchmen to dismiss what it has to say about the problem just because they disapprove of the anonymity with which the Preface assails Dr Runcie.

For most Fleet Street dailies, however, the story was not the underlying condition of the Church of England. The story was Dr Runcie. The *Mail* was the most forthright. In a slashing article under the headline 'For God's Sake, Go!', Paul Johnson's view was that the preface sharply raised the question: 'Can Dr Runcie possibly continue in office?' Whether for or against the Archbishop, however, few commentators seemed to relish the way he had been criticized anonymously. Johnson's attack on Dr Runcie is preceded by a sideswipe at the writer of the *Crockford's* preface. 'It is unhappily characteristic', wrote Johnson,

of the way Anglican bigshots conduct their internal rows that the criticism takes the form of a malicious, anonymous attack by an unknown, but highly placed, assassin.

But, that apart, the broadside is remarkably well-aimed and well-timed – some would say long overdue.

It is true the Archbishop is an 'elitist liberal'. True he is 'peculiarly vulnerable to pressure groups' – chiefly of the Left. True he takes 'the line of least resistance on each issue'.

True, above all, that when he 'does not put off all questions until someone else makes a decision', he is 'usually to be found nailing his colours to the fence'.

Dr Runcie, Johnson argued, epitomized a loss of nerve among Britain's Christian leaders, who were no longer prepared to give the nation moral leadership. 'If change is to come', he went on, '–and who can doubt we need it? – it must start with him . . . he can make way for someone who sees the moral choices facing Britain today in the simple, straightforward terms the public need.'

Over at the *Guardian*, the climate of opinion could hardly have been more different. In a leader which appeared under the headline 'fitting up Dr Runcie', the writer expounded a subtle version of the 'right-wing plot' theory which was now gaining ground in some liberal quarters:

The dynamiting of Archbishop Runcie carried out by an unknown hand in the preface to *Crockford's Directory* constitutes on one level a juicy ecclesiastical furore. . . . But it also deserves to be seen as a significant political event. The assault plainly reflects a body of Church of England opinion to be heard not only at the better heeled lych-gates on a Sunday but in all those everyday forums where Conservative churchmen meet. Its abuse of Dr Runcie is more elegant than most, since *Crockford's* anonymous hand is an unusually silken assassin; but the indictment is wholly familiar. The Archbishop is a fixer, a compromiser, or as people say at Westminster, a wet. . . .

In a separate signed article, the *Guardian*'s religious affairs cor-respondent, Walter Schwartz, was less oblique. The *Crockford's* preface, he said, 'has a tradition of mild-mannered acerbity. But this time it has gone so far over the top that it looks like an orchestrated attack.' The obscure logic of this conclusion was left unexplained.

The Last Journey

For Garry, it was all getting too much. Shortly after 9 a.m. on Friday morning he telephoned Philip Ursell with whom he had been planning to drive to Cambridge where he and John Cowan, a friend and Dean of New College, were to represent the College at the King's College Benefactor's feast. Garry told Ursell, who was going to a similar celebration at Emmanuel, that he was now considering not going at all, that he didn't know if he could face it; the publicity and phone calls were beginning to get him down. Ursell told him he thought he was wrong and that he should go as arranged; to get out of Oxford and away from it all would be good for him. Ursell added that at King's he would be in the company of people most of whom would not have the faintest idea of who he was; furthermore, if he didn't go presumably John Cowan would not be able to go either, indeed they were all depending on Garry to drive them.

Garry agreed. 'Well, perhaps you're right,' he replied, 'I'll see how I feel later this morning and unless I get in touch with you, we will collect you from Pusey House at one o'clock.' The calls from the press began again, and continued through the morning.

At 1 p.m. exactly, he arrived in his bronze Honda Accord at Pusey House with John Cowan. By this time, Garry was on a short fuse. He had already told Cowan that he was not the author. Cowan noted, however, that Garry seemed preoccupied and he was showing irritation over the telephone calls. As they had left the New College lodge in Holywell Street, Garry had turned to the porter on duty to instruct him to block all calls to his rooms and under no circum-stances to give out his home telephone number or address.

At Pusey House Bennett and Cowan were joined by Father Ursell and by Father Stuart Dunnan, one of the priest-librarians of Pusey, Ursell's guest at the Emmanuel feast, which Fr Ursell himself was attending as a former chaplain and fellow of that college. They

47

drove to Cambridge, not by Garry's normal route – down the M40, on to the M25, then North up the M11 – but by Ursell's suggested route: leaving the M25 to take the A1M through Baldock. It was a good-humoured journey; there was some talk about the preface of a general kind, but none of course about Garry's authorship, since both Cowan and Dunnan were unaware of it. The press *suggestions* that Garry was the anonymous writer could hardly be avoided as a topic of conversation; Garry mentioned that the *News of the World* had telephoned to offer him £1000 if he would tell them who the author was, adding, 'Of course if you are the author and are prepared to write an article about it, it would be considerably more'.

On arrival in Cambridge, the four travelling companions separated. Bennett drove first to the studios of Radio Cambridge, where Ursell had agreed to record two interviews 'down the line' about the *Crockford's* preface – one for Radio Wales, one for Radio Four's Sunday religious programme. Garry had been the first choice of the interviewer, Trevor Barnes; he had unknowingly shown impeccable journalistic instinct in both his choices of interviewee. Fr Dunnan was dropped at Emmanuel; then Bennett and Cowan went on together to King's. Cowan remained in Garry's company the whole time; he seemed perfectly relaxed, and the preface was not mentioned.

The following morning, Saturday, Garry bought and read three newspapers: *The Times, Telegraph* and *Guardian*. In *The Times*, the former Bishop of Birmingham added himself to the company of episcopal voices hinting at knowledge of the authorship of the preface; Dr Montefiore claimed also to know his 'ill-intentioned' purpose in writing it. 'Those whose professions have lain in literary criticism', he wrote,

will not find the new preface to *Crockford's* as anonymous as its unsigned status suggests. Its author plainly knew that his critical remarks about the Archbishop of Canterbury would receive widespread publicity. They must be seen as the latest in a series of political statements, ranging from lies in the tabloids to more measured denunciation, all aimed unsuccessfully to date at unseating the present occupant of the chair of Augustine.

Despite the respite he had enjoyed in Cambridge from journalistic and other harassment, Garry was impatient to return to Oxford. He and Cowan loaded their bags into the Honda (Garry's had a news-

paper tucked in to the strap of his luggage, Cowan later remembered), and drove the short distance to the Emmanuel car
park. He had arranged to pick up Ursell and Dunnan at Emmanuel
at 9.30 a.m., but it was only 9.10 when he strode into the small
pleasant breakfast room where each morning bacon, sausage, eggs,
kidneys and other delights await the dons of Emmanuel on chafing
dishes. He was wearing a dark suit and overcoat, and collar and tie
rather than clerical dress. Ursell was reading the *Daily Mail*, which
that morning was running a double spread on the affair. Under the
five column headline 'FIGHT THE GOOD FIGHT' were
photographs of Dr Runcie, Dr Margaret Hewitt – by this time one
of the small list of prime press suspects – and, in a prominent
position, Garry Bennett himself. The caption to Garry's photograph
was 'BENNETT: Besieged'. He seized the paper from Fr Ursell and
sat down to read it.

The article, by Steve Doughty, began by asserting that 'in the art
of political infighting, senior members of the Anglican establishment
are beyond compare', that one of their tactics 'has always been the
discrediting of opponents anywhere in Christendom', and that 'it
was as part of this tradition that the infamous attack on Dr Robert
Runcie was delivered this week in the preface to *Crockford's Clerical
Directory*'. The rest of the article considers various candidates: apart
from Garry Bennett and Margaret Hewitt, the other runners mentioned in the piece are the Evangelical, Roger Beckwith; the Dean
of St Albans, Peter Moore; Henry Chadwick; Edward Norman;
Roy Porter; and (the odd man out) David L. Edwards, the ultra-
liberal Provost of Southwark, a wholly implausible candidate given
his known support for every tendency in the Church denounced by
the preface itself.

Despite this plethora of names, it is clear from the article that
Garry is the prime suspect (it mentions his name eight times). One
reason for this, reported by Steve Doughty after conducting a
survey of opinion in various quarters of the Church, is perhaps
significant, mirroring as his sources do the public attacks on the
unknown author issuing from various quarters over the previous
few days, and particularly, perhaps, the attack of Archbishop Habgood; the word 'disappointed' here may be significant:

The liberals say that the author is a disappointed academic passed over for promotion – which they say fits Dr Bennett and a number of others ignored by the Crown Appointments Commission which chooses bishops. This line attempts entirely to discredit the *Crockford's* piece on the grounds that it is the work of an embittered man . . . or woman.

While Garry was reading this, Fr Ursell had gone to fetch his bag from his room. Walking back across the large open area of grass known in Emmanuel as the Paddock he found Garry coming towards him. He had sent Fr Dunnan and Mr Cowan to the car park to wait for him. Ursell and Bennett walked up and down in the cloisters outside the college chapel. It was clear that Garry was deeply disturbed. 'I don't know if I can take much more of this, you know,' he said, 'it's getting pretty close and pretty nasty.' 'I'd better call round this evening,' Ursell said. 'Yes,' said Garry, 'I think you had. I'm going to need some support.'

But he told Ursell he had decided not to attend the weekly meeting of a small group of like-minded ecclesiastical dons (founded in his Anglican days by Fr Ronald Knox) which forgathers every Saturday in Oxford during termtime and is generally known, to those aware of its existence, as 'the High Church lunch'. Ursell told him that he thought this a tactical error; the other six clergy would inevitably be talking about the *Crockford's* affair, and might assume – since it was an occasion he never missed – that his absence confirmed his authorship. 'No,' Garry replied. 'you can tell them I can't face two large meals in such a short space of time, and that I am tired from the journey.'

They all left for Oxford around 9.30. Garry had been relaxed during his time in Cambridge, Cowan remembered later (they were together the whole time); but now, the irritation he had been showing in Oxford had returned because of what he had read that morning in the newspapers. On the journey back, they went by Garry's route – south on the M11, west on the M25, then up the M40 to Oxford. The talk on the journey was mostly about the different styles of the two Cambridge colleges at which they had been staying; the food and conversation at the two grand occasions they had attended were compared. They arrived at Pusey House at about noon; Garry evinced boyish glee that he had cut about fifteen minutes off the time it had taken them the previous day by Fr Ursell's route.

Home to New Marston

Garry and Fr Ursell took their leave of each other. Garry said, 'I'll see you this evening.' Garry and Cowan drove to New College: right into St Giles; left past the Martyr's Memorial and St Mary Magdalen's Church; left again down the Broad and over the lights into Holywell. At the porter's lodge, Garry picked up his mail, which he put into his overcoat pocket. Cowan suggested that they lunch together; Garry said that he would not, that he would go home. The last words he spoke to Cowan, or to anyone he knew, were these: 'I must get back to feed my cat.'

It makes most sense of the evidence if we assume that this is what he did. But on arrival at his home, he found the cat dead. The food he had put out for it before leaving for Cambridge was untouched. The cat was lying peacefully on the sitting room floor.

Those who have never known the companionship of a cat often suppose them to be cold-hearted, self-centred animals, unlike dogs which are more demonstrative and more openly affectionate. Cats, certainly, are less prodigal with their friendship, and tend to strike up a close relationship with one particular human being. Whether or not the death of his cat was the last straw that broke Garry's resistance to the terrible urge to self-destruction we cannot know. What we do know is that he loved his cat, Tibby. He was a lonely man. The cat was a stray which had elected to live with him; as catlovers know, a relationship with an animal in which it is the animal which has chosen the human rather than (as is normal) the reverse can be deep and tender. Certainly it was so in Garry's case, and there can hardly be any doubt that his reaction to the cat's death was one of considerable grief. Suggestions were later made that he had killed his cat as a calculated prelude to suicide. But the evidence is of natural death and in any case such an act can be ruled out as entirely out of character.

It was probably at this stage that Garry consumed the alcohol, equivalent to two large measures of Scotch, later found by the police surgeon in his system. An open bottle of wine was later found, partly consumed, in the kitchen; he disliked Scotch (the Scotch in his sitting room was kept for friends). It must have been at this time too, rather than earlier in the day, that he took the decision to put an end to his life. When Derek Pattinson returned to his home at six o'clock that Saturday evening, he found a message on his Ansafone from Garry, asking him to telephone urgently. The message had been left at some time after Garry's first arrival home at around 12.45, and probably before he left the house to buy a hosepipe at approximately 2 p.m. If Garry had been expecting Pattinson to return his call, he must at that stage have expected to be alive to receive it.

There is little left to tell but the bare hard practical details which emerged at the inquest. Shortly after 2 p.m., the manager of Carpenter's hardware shop in the North Oxford suburb of Summertown sold a hosepipe. It was sufficiently unusual, at that cold wet time of the year, for him to remember the sale later. The customer, whom he later identified from a photograph as Dr Bennett, was very pleasant in his manner and knew exactly what he wanted – a hosepipe and tap connector. This last item often causes difficulty – there are so many different sizes of tap – but this purchaser seemed to know exactly what he wanted. He was, thought the manager, the ideal customer.

The evidence we have suggests that something like the following sequence of events then took place, though we cannot be sure of the exact time of death. After buying the hosepipe, Garry drove home. Leaving Summertown, he turned left at the traffic lights into the Marston Ferry Road. At the end of the road, he turned right at the New Marston double roundabout, then, a few turnings later, left into Harberton Mead and right into Moody Close, a pleasant cul-de-sac of post-war semi-detached houses. When he reached home, number 15, the last house in the street, instead of parking his car in front of the garage he got out, opened the garage door and drove in.

He shut the garden door behind him and walked into the kitchen with the hosepipe. He removed the plastic packaging, throwing it on to the floor. With a carving knife, he cut off part of the hosepipe, and attached the tap connector to what remained. Picking up a green and white checked tea towel he returned to the garage. He attached the hosepipe to the exhaust pipe, using the tap connector. Then he opened the rear door, wound down the window slightly, inserted the end of the hosepipe, and wound up the window so as to trap the hosepipe. Into the gap on either side of the hosepipe, he stuffed the tea towel. He went back into the house;

perhaps he drank another glass of red wine from the bottle already open in the kitchen; perhaps he went into the sitting room and looked for the last time at the dead body of his cat. Then he walked through the kitchen to the garage. He adjusted the car's passenger seat to a full reclining position. He started the engine; then he got into the passenger seat, and leaned back, his fingertips lightly touching on his lap. Then he closed his eyes and awaited death.

TWO

Dr Habgood and Dr Bennett

About a year after the *Crockford's* tragedy, the Archbishop of York published a collection of essays entitled *Confessions of a Conservative Liberal*. His book included a specially written account of his own part in the *Crockford's* affair (examined in chapter three), but was mostly composed of essays, addresses and sermons for particular occasions, which taken together give a good overall view of the Archbishop's views on Church and society.

A few weeks after the publication of this collection, Dr Habgood was interviewed on television by Jonathan Dimbleby. Before the interview, a brief documentary film was shown on the current state of the Church of England in which one underlying question was whether or not Dr Habgood himself ought eventually to succeed Dr Robert Runcie as Archbishop of Canterbury. Among others, the Labour M P Frank Field gave his opinion on this question:

[Habgood] is totally dominated by what he would, I think, call a liberal approach, which is one of believing that God speaks to us in many different ways, including the society in which we live, and therefore the Church has somehow got to adopt and adapt that outside society into the body of the Church itself; and if you do that, and that's the *only* thing you do, then you are caught by every passing fancy and fashion, and you are very quickly shipwrecked. So for those reasons I would be pleased if he were not appointed. . . .

Christianity and the Spirit of the Age

Field here is not, it will be seen, suggesting that the Church should

54

withdraw from the society which surrounds it, nor is he asserting that the Church has nothing to learn from secular knowledge and activity. But he *is* suggesting that a Church which becomes too closely identified with secular assumptions is intensely vulnerable to changes in social and political fashion. The Church must before all else be identified with the eternal and universal wisdom of God, and its priority in any generation is to mediate that wisdom and show how it may be made real in any human circumstance. The Church must never become the prisoner of the human perceptions of any one period in history, for mankind moves on and yesterday's definitive truth becomes today's collapsing hypothesis. In the words of Dean Inge, 'the Church that is married to the Spirit of the Age will be a widow in the next'.

Field's criticism of Habgood's liberal approach, then, is that it is too closely identified with the ephemeral assumptions of contemporary society. This is a charge which has not infrequently been levelled at theological liberals. Their response tends to be a simple reiteration of the need to communicate with and learn from the society which surrounds them, coupled with the countercharge that the questioner is showing a pietistic refusal to become involved in that society. Sometimes, of course, this is an accusation which is entirely justified. But the mainstream Christian tradition is not one which has, historically, withdrawn from social responsibility or involvement (Frank Field himself exemplifies this). The countercharge, nevertheless, tends to be the same. The charge of secularism evokes a constant response; the criticism is answered by misrepresenting it, and then answering the misrepresentation – one of the many ways, perhaps, in which clerics have learned the techniques of secular politics. This is how Dr Habgood replied to Field's charge in his interview with Jonathan Dimbleby:

. . . what Christians have always done is to enter into a dialogue . . . with a society on the basis of their understanding of the Christian faith, and I was astonished at Frank Field saying that . . . one mustn't learn from what is going on around one; what on earth is the Holy Spirit doing, unless one is learning from what is happening in the world as it is now? But this is not to be taken over by the world. There is a constant process of self-criticism going on and always has been going on all through Christian History.

The problem here, perhaps, is that of deciding to what extent the

Church of England's 'dialogue' with the world around it is truly conducted on the basis of the historic Christian faith. Dr Habgood in one way evades the issue here by talking of a dialogue by Christians with the world on the basis of '*their understanding* of the Christian faith'; for the perennial question for Western Christianity today is how authentically Christian that understanding has remained in any particular case. Is a Christian understanding for Dr Habgood, for instance, one based on a revelation given by God in Christ to all mankind and all ages, and therefore necessarily valid for all societies – if only a way can be found of communicating it? Is the Christian message, for him, one which has something to offer to those who do not yet accept it, or is it valid only for those already convinced of its truth?

To ask the question in this way is not, of course, to deny the particular problems in any given culture of convincing men and women of the truth of the Christian religion. It is simply to ask whether that religion is seen by Christians themselves as, on the one hand, universally valid (in the way that the Christian tradition has until now always insisted that it is) or, on the other, as simply one among a whole range of culturally and historically conditioned options. The suspicion today is that official Anglicanism has settled for a version of Christianity which is comfortable with itself as being simply one option among many, in which claims to any knowledge, however tenuous, of absolute truth are abandoned as ungentlemanly and impractical.

Certainly, this appears to be Dr Habgood's view. In his introduction to a General Synod report produced under his chairmanship, which appeared in July 1987 under the title *Changing Britain: Social Diversity and Moral Unity*, he spelt out his view on this question with remarkable frankness. How should the problems of apparently uncontrollable change be faced 'in a society which is beginning to become self-conscious about its degree of moral and social diversity'? Should the Church give a distinctively Christian response? The answer, says Dr Habgood, is that it should do nothing of the sort:

In trying to give some guidance towards appropriate responses we have chosen to present our argument in a way which we hope makes it accessible to people of different religious convictions, or none at all. If our society is to make any progress towards the moral unity referred to in the title of this study, a broad approach seems unavoidable. We could have contented ourselves with addressing a clear Christian message to any who might care to listen, *and we do not underestimate the value of any such statements from faith to faith. Our choice of a different method reflects our concern to say things which we believe have validity for the whole of our society*. (My italics.)

The implications of such an approach are profound, and they are revolutionary. For, Dr Habgood is not saying that a Christian approach is *difficult* for a non-Christian or pluralist society; in effect, he is saying that 'a clear Christian message' *is not valid* for such a society, and that it is only valid for those who are already Christians. The Christian message can only be conveyed 'from faith to faith' (in whatever reduced sense the word 'faith' must now be understood).

The Changing Britain Debate

Changing Britain was debated by the General Synod on the afternoon of 12 November, exactly three weeks before the publication of *Crockford's* preface. The two opening speakers in the debate, for and very much against the report's approach, were Dr John Habgood, introducing the report, and Dr Gareth Bennett, who was called by the chairman as the first speaker from the floor. The debate may in some ways be seen as a kind of curtain raiser to the *Crockford's* affair itself. For, not only did it pit against each other the principal symbolic antagonists of that grim and confused struggle; in contention here, more quietly but in equally deadly earnest, were precisely the fundamental questions dividing 'traditionalist' and 'liberal' Anglicans which were to arise in a different way as the dust began to settle during the bleak weeks following Garry Bennett's suicide. What is the authority of the Christian revelation as it is recorded in scripture and embodied in tradition? Can it simply be set aside when social and moral issues arise which call on some response from the Church? What is the authority of secular understanding for Christians, and what are the dangers of being intellectually absorbed by such an understanding, once Christian revelation has been confined to communications 'from faith to faith'?

Archbishop Habgood's opening speech shows some awareness

of the vulnerability of his approach, and he defends his report against any who might think it not 'prophetic' enough, in the sense of critically addressing the ills of society from a distinctively Christian standpoint. Here, we see Habgood the 'conservative'; but it is a secular conservatism of the type which consists of making things work the way they are rather than a theological conservatism which returns to first principles. This approach was not acceptable to one member of the working party, Sarah Maitland, who appended to the report a Note of Reservation, explaining why she could not sign it. She was, she wrote, unable to accept the functionalist view of the Church which underlaid the report's arguments. It was not the duty of the Church 'to be the social glue of a society, but to change, to transform'. Dr Habgood attempted to pre-empt such criticisms by explaining his approach:

The trouble with prophetic eyes is that they tend to oversimplify. They prefer sharp distinctions and lurid colours to the more subtle gradations of the everyday world. . . . We decided to concentrate on the necessary complement to prophecy, namely analysis, thereby risking the wrath of those who think that if something is not prophetic it is not really Christian.

It was not, however, as we have seen, the lack of prophetic fire that made the report unChristian; it was the clear decision of the commission itself to avoid a Christian framework of reference. To concentrate on 'analysis' does not of itself preclude the possibility that such an analysis might be a Christian one; that it might be based, that is to say, not only on a purely secular sociology but also on a Christian social theology. Dr Habgood had clearly realized that the non-Christian basis of the report would attract fire; he therefore reminded the Synod of the Christian origins of the term *koinonia*, which the report had adopted as the moral core around which a pluralist society could cohere. *Koinonia*, for the purposes of the report, had been secularized as 'persons in community'. But the word, said the Archbishop,

. . . is there in the background as a reminder that our moral values are ultimately rooted in our relationship with God. Communion in its full religious sense is not something apart from this; and if we want to express symbolically and liturgically the goal of our future society, we do it every time we celebrate the Eucharist. . . .

'There in the background.' But not there as the foundation on which all else rests: 'if we want to'; not 'we want to because we must'. It is an intellectual approach in which man remains firmly in control, and in which God remains firmly in his place, to be invoked if it is thought appropriate (which in a pluralist society will not, it seems, be very often).

Garry Bennett's response to the report was his last speech to the General Synod, and it was probably one of his most unreservedly critical. Garry Bennett's Synod speeches were listened to with great attention, not least because of their restraint and their balance. This speech was in comparison almost fiery in its dismissal of *Changing Britain*. It begins gently enough, but there is soon an ironic note, warning of what is to come:

It is said that after the battle of Waterloo the Duke of Wellington wished to pay off the army chaplains because, he said, he no longer had need of prayers for victory. There is always a danger that when religion comes in to support a basically secular concern you may well miss the heart of the matter, and this report needs our sympathy: the authors have undertaken the difficult task of finding a set or system of moral values without a specifically Christian argument.

He was, he went on, grateful to the Archbishop of York for giving a more Christian introduction to the report than the report would indicate. It had come up with an unexceptionable idea: that value lies in persons, and, more particularly, in persons in community. Who could quarrel with that? But, said Bennett, the report was 'a case study in the way in which the Church of England seems to be becoming more and more locked into a kind of social, educational and economic theory which had its heyday in the 1960s, but which nowadays is increasingly questioned and which is certainly not self-evidently the only Christian theory'. He then turned to some of these secular assumptions of the 1960s, embodied and uncritically accepted by the report's authors.

The first of these was a secular humanistic measure of man, in which the realization of human potential in terms of physical and mental wellbeing was envisaged as the *end* of man. Such a view, said Bennett, might be enough for a political programme, but it was not the essence of Christianity, which is that 'good for man is found not within himself or even within his community, but in men and women redeemed and brought into a new relationship with God'. The report, he went on, continually treated Christian doctrine as an illustration of human activity. Hence, 'the Resurrection is said to be about the potential inherent within each individual'. Bennett's comment was dry and to the point: 'I thought it was about the power of God.' And there had, he continued, been a 'sad secularization' of the term *koinonia* away from its New Testament roots, which he saw as being, if anything, to do with a doctrine of the Holy Spirit.

He went on to criticize the report for its uncritical acceptance of 'the pluralistic premise, the acceptance on more or less equal terms, of a multiplicity of creeds and beliefs, and a looking for some common denominator, no matter how attenuated'. He questioned the report's rejection of Professor Basil Mitchell's call for children to be taught from within a particular religious tradition, and quotes Mitchell in a passage interestingly reminiscent of his own remarks on tradition in the *Crockford's* preface:

[Mitchell's] modest plea is rejected. He believes that 'the young do not learn to think for themselves by being presented with a *pot-pourri* of competing philosophies, but by being introduced to a coherent tradition which they are then encouraged to reflect on critically from within', surely a sensible educational attitude.

The New Orthodoxy

He went on to note the report's bias towards cooperation and against competition (though it had claimed to look at them in a balanced way). Competition was presented as being 'basically self-assertion leading on to polarization and division', and was presented by the report 'with some suspicion in school, society and the economy'. He commented acidly on the report's 'élitist premise that social policy is best left to the experts', and attacked it for its uncritical acceptance of the notion that experts should distribute large scale resources to fund 'generalized schemes of welfare', despite the evidence that in the developing countries such policies had led to dependence and powerlessness and disincentive to growth. Such policies had been described as 'developmentism':

I wonder whether our Church, in its recent choice of expert advisers, has not become over-dependent on developmentists. It is not hard, for example, to detect the distinctive viewpoint of Professor A. H. Halsey in this and other recent reports. I would suggest that this 1960s social theory is becoming a kind of orthodoxy in the Church of England. It is certainly at the root of many of our perceived differences with the present government. . . .

At the end of his address, in the last words he was ever to speak to the Synod, he summed up all his unhappiness with the way the Church of England was going. His words are a rejection of his Church's worldliness and secularism and a call for a return to spiritual priorities. In the last sentence of his last speech he summed up one of the principal themes underlying much of his critique in the *Crockford's* preface. 'I only wish', he concluded,

that there could be a recognition in some of our boards and councils that some of us are waiting for a voice which is radically Christian, sacrificial, and Christ- rather than man-centred.

His call was echoed by other speakers in the debate, on the course of which his influence appears to have been considerable. The sociologist, Elaine Storkey, summed up the anxieties of many, not only in the chamber but throughout the Church. The Church, she said, was attempting to revive the defunct sociological theories of the 1950s and 1960s:

So, why do we not want to revive it? In this again, I would want to re-echo the previous speaker [Garry Bennett]: it is because, I believe, we have something better to offer to the nation, to Parliament, to the people in our churches, than this: we have the gospel of Jesus Christ, and that is not a simplistic thing, but something that will offer us tools for analysis, tools for discernment, tools for the insight that this document, frankly, is not capable of doing. . . . We have something that is the example of the Lord who himself recognized the complexity of the society he lived in . . . and yet witnessed at the same time to the truth. . . . We can observe with biblical eyes, analyse with Christian minds, and we will find then that we have more in common with those of very different values than we have if we start from a functionalist position.

Against this call for biblical eyes and Christian minds, Bishop

Richard Harries of Oxford invoked an alternative and longstanding Christian tradition, that there are generally arguable principles of moral and social conduct which can be arrived at by human reason and which do not require Christian revelation for their acceptance:

Dr Garry Bennett calls for a radical and Christ-centred system of values and so does Mrs Storkey, and both were very eloquent in their plea; but there is another approach which is no less Christian and which is not exclusive of theirs but goes along with it, the approach of this report to try to find as much common ground as possible, to build on those areas that we have in common. In one of our traditions this has been termed the approach of natural law. . . .

In his own response at the end of the debate, Archbishop Habgood picked up this theme. It had, he said, been his lifelong concern to try to talk beyond the boundaries of the Christian Church. 'Of course', he continued, 'we were operating on the basis of the long tradition of natural law. . . . We did not call it natural law because we were deliberately trying to avoid such labels in the interests of trying to be comprehensible to those who do not belong within our tradition. . . .'

How strong is the 'natural law' defence against the accusations made in this debate of secularism and abandonment of Christian values? The question is important, for such accusations underlie much of the critique of the Church's liberal establishment which was already well under way when the *Crockford's* preface was published and which became increasingly insistent in the aftermath of the *Crockford's* affair. If it were a valid argument to say that such 'secularism' is not actually a rejection of Christian tradition at all, but a return to one of its ancient bulwarks, then the whole debate between 'traditionalists' and 'liberals' in the Church would take on a very different complexion.

The Natural Law Defence

There are, mainstream Christian tradition asserts, two sources for our knowledge of God. There is Revelation: God became man in Christ, died and rose again, to reconcile humanity with its creator and to give us the knowledge of that creator we need to become part of His Divine life. We could not have arrived at this knowledge without his intervention in human affairs.

But there is also another source of knowledge about God, which can be arrived at by the use of God-directed human reason. Such truths, it is held, are accessible to non-believers as well as Christians, a fact which made it permissible, for instance, to conduct theology in the categories of Platonic and Aristotelian philosophy. This has its implications for moral theology. As he developed a concept of 'natural' theology, Thomas Aquinas arrived at the concept of a natural moral law. By his own reason, Thomas held, man can gain substantial knowledge of what is ethically good, a knowledge which forms the basis of the natural law, or the law of human nature.

It is a concept which has been more prominent in Catholic thought (some Protestants actually deny it), though it has a clear biblical basis. One of its classic modern expressions is in Pope John XXIII's encyclical *Pacem in Terris*, which pronounces that 'the Creator of the world has imprinted in man's heart an order which his conscience reveals to him and strongly enjoins him to obey. . . .' The encyclical invokes St Paul's letter to the Romans in support of this teaching. Pagans, says Paul, 'who never heard of the Law but are led by reason to do what the Law commands, may not actually "possess" the Law'

but they can be said to 'be' the law. They can point to the substance of the Law engraved on their hearts – they can call a witness, that is, their own conscience – they have accusation and defence, that is, their own inner mental dialogue. . . . (Romans 2:14–15 JB)

Is this, in fact, the approach of the Habgood report in particular and of contemporary liberal Anglicanism in general? There are, it will be seen, several reasons why it is inappropriate to call on the natural law tradition in rebuttal of Garry Bennett's attack on *Changing Britain*.

The most important distinction between the two approaches is that between the objective, the God-given character of Natural Law, and the pluralist and relativist character of social truth as perceived by such bodies as, say, the European Value Systems Study Group (EVSSG), studies by which were a major source of evidence for the Habgood working party. (Dr Habgood, as Garry Bennett points out in the preface is 'the leading theological relativist among the bishops'.) But the existence of a Natural Moral Law is not, in the Christian tradition, a justification to remove God from the equation; it does not justify an absentee clockmaker God who simply leaves mankind to get on the best way it can without him. Though Natural Law does not make God part of its argument, He is, nevertheless, a vital prerequisite for a Christian understanding of it. As Richard P. McBrien puts it,

We exist only within a redeemed order. The difference between natural law and the supernatural law of the gospel, therefore, is not a difference between a law that can be known by reason, on the one hand, and a law that can be known only by revelation, on the other hand. Both 'laws' are rooted in the one source and are grasped within the same redeemed order, whether the persons doing the 'grasping' are Christians or not.

The criticism of *Changing Britain* in the debate was precisely that it did not operate at the level of fundamental moral principles or 'laws', recognizable by men of widely differing religious and intellectual traditions, but of an outdated sociology applied to particular situations. Indeed, Elaine Storkey's assertion that if we observe 'with biblical eyes, analyse with Christian minds . . . we will find then that we actually have more in common with those of very different values than we have if we start from a functionalist position' is an assertion based precisely on the Christian understanding that the natural law has the same ultimate source as the Christian revelation, so that if Christians wish to communicate with non-Christians they do not need to stand aside from Christian presuppositions.

The Embarrassment of the Gospel of Christ

Dr Habgood, who dismissed this speaker with the comment 'we had some fun with Elaine Storkey', believes precisely the opposite. Since the Gospel is full of absolute demands and statements (God being the absolute source of all truth) it is, he clearly believes, embarrassing for modern clergymen who seek to move on what they take to be a wider national stage. Thus, to speak too much of God is thought to be inimical to the Church's influence on society at large. To hold that there is a gospel to communicate, for the lack

of which the world is spiritually dying, is to be naive and obscurantist.

And so, without naming him, Dr Habgood answered Garry
Bennett, with his heartfelt plea for 'a voice which is radically
Christian, sacrificial and Christ- rather than man-centred'. He
wanted, Dr Habgood said, to thank all who had taken part in the
debate. In an aside, he added 'some more than others'. He then
continued his attack on Garry Bennett's ideas, suggesting that they
were simplistic and inadequately directed to the need to communicate with non-Christians. He was not, Dr Habgood went on,
surprised or distressed

... by some of the criticisms that were made of the report early on in the
debate, because I recognize full well, as I am sure many do, that there is at
the moment a mood in the Church which favours everything that is
confident and tends to be slightly inward-looking and assertive. We are
extremely good at talking to ourselves. . . . I am depressed by the naive
optimism which many people have about the extent to which the Gospel
actually communicates with the people who are in the rough and tumble
of decisions in the secular world.

It is a curious view, unknown within the Church at any time
through the Christian centuries until now, at least as an openly
defended position, presented as being the Church's duty. Imagine
St Paul, setting out on his missionary journeys through societies
every bit as pluralist and diverse as our own, consulting some
first century sociologist to find out the current state of moral
'value systems' around the Mediterranean in order to arrive at
and promote a general consensus view designed to achieve
cultural unity.

What Paul did was precisely the reverse: he stood up in public,
proclaimed the Christian view, and in effect told his hearers that if
they disagreed with him they needed to change their minds, a
process known as *metanoia*, or conversion. He believed in being 'all
things to all men in order that some might be saved'; that is, in
identifying with people in their own situation. But he never
supposed that this might mean a modification of the message he
was commissioned to preach. He preached a gospel of love and
personal transformation; and he was very hardline on moral questions. He would certainly not have been invited to have anything to

do with any working party appointed by the General Synod's Board for Social Responsibility.

Dr Habgood, it is important to say, does not hold an idiosyncratic or eccentric view: he is entirely representative of the mind-set of many, if not most, of his episcopal colleagues, and of such synodical organisms as the Board for Social Responsibility. In what does his theological 'liberalism' subsist? He would not, presumably, himself admit that he was theologically less 'Christ-centred' than a traditionalist like Dr Bennett. How would he describe the theological divide between them? In an article which appeared in *The Times* in the month before the Synod debate on *Changing Britain*, Dr Habgood returned to the theme of change. His article is an attack on a lecture which had been given recently in Fulton, Missouri by the Bishop of London urging an end to what Dr Leonard called 'the tyranny of subjectivism'. We shall return to the argument of this lecture in a later chapter. It is enough here to say that it includes a defence of the Christian tradition of natural law. Dr Habgood's attempted rebuttal is a classic example of the gulf in understanding between liberals and traditionalists which leads so often – in practice if not in intention – to argument by misrepresentation; that is, setting up a non-existent opponent and then knocking him down:

There is a . . . difficulty in what the bishop says, in the very idea of 'man and society as created by God'. Are we to assume that this is something given once for all, fixed in a particular period of history, and therefore unchanging and unchangeable, not only in general terms but in detail? . . . In fact the major difference between so-called traditionalists and so-called liberals lies just here. It is not that one is faithful to God-given revelation while the other falls victim to mere fashion, but that there are deep differences of belief about what kind of creation it is that God has made and what he is doing in it. For one the notion that human nature is created by God fixes attention on its givenness. For the other creation is a continuous process, an open-ended adventure set within the freedom given by God which allows the created order to discover its potentialities.

Tradition and Change in the Church

The notion that there is a natural moral law does *not* of course assume that man and society are 'fixed in a particular period in history, and therefore unchanging and unchangeable'; the Bishop of London does not say it or imply it in his lecture, nor has any Anglican traditionalist known to this writer ('so-called' or not) ever done so. The necessity for transformation, personal and social, is indeed a fundamental part of the mainstream Christian tradition. 'In a higher world it is otherwise,' wrote John Henry Newman, that scourge of theological liberals, 'but here below to live is to change, and to be perfect is to have changed often.' 'Tradition' is not a principle enjoining immobility; it is, itself, a principle of ordered change. If we want to understand the Anglican traditionalist's attitude to change we could hardly do better than to read Garry Bennett's essay (reprinted by Dr Rowell) 'Tradition and Change in The Church'. Tradition, says Bennett,

is a living and developing thing as the Christian community responds to changes in human culture and society by developing its theology, liturgy and community structures. If Tradition is a living thing it is the task of theologians, pastors and indeed ordinary Christians to reflect on what it is that the Tradition is intended to guard and preserve and what are the forms which may have to change if the heart of the matter is to retain its ancient meaning and power in a new situation. . . . Tradition is not a code nor a set of binding precedents nor is it concerned with details. It is a series of formularies, structures, liturgies and usages, all of them provisional in form, by which the modern Church tries to remain true to its origins while living a life of witness and holiness in modern society.

The accusation that traditionalists believe in a static view of the Church derives from the fact that they insist that change is subject to certain tests or restraints before it is embarked on: some of these may indeed be unchanging: nevertheless, they are held to be universal in their validity. They do not rule out change and may, indeed, enjoin it, particularly for the purpose of communicating the gospel revealed by Christ in strange or shifting circumstances. But the tradition insists that growth and change are authentically Christian in character, and do not simply reflect ephemeral human knowledge and opinion. Change has to be centred on Christ, who is the same yesterday, today and forever, as he is known within the life of the community of his people.

This brings us back to the debate with which we opened this chapter. For it is the suspicion that the attitude of 'liberals' towards man, society and the Church is *not* 'Christ-centred' in this way which is at the root of Garry Bennett's criticisms of Dr Habgood in his Synod speech (and which can be seen to be at the heart of his argument in the preface itself). Dr Habgood's defence of *Changing Britain*, of course, was that to make Christ central to a discussion of moral values in a changing pluralist society is to introduce a dimension not universally valid *for that society*. How, then, do both men approach questions of change in the Church itself? Is Christ central in this case? Here, we can compare the philosophies of the two men conveniently in the context of a theme close to both their hearts: that of Christian unity. Both Dr Rowell's collection of Bennett's essays *To the Church of England* and Dr Habgood's *Confessions of a Conservative Liberal*, published within weeks of each other, contain essays on ecumenism.

Christ and the Nature of the Church

For Garry Bennett, to begin to achieve Christian unity requires spiritual and theological growth, and a renewed understanding of the nature of the Church. For him,

... the Church, in the sense of the visible, ordered Christian community, is itself a sacrament of Christ's continuing presence and ministry among us. It is more than a convenient assembly of the faithful for religious exercises; it is (as the great Calvin himself asserted) an instrument used by the spirit to accomplish the purposes of God. Indeed, when God communicates himself to men, he does so in a mystery by which things ineffable and unutterable become known in the familiar and the tangible and we are addressed through the things of our ordinary human society and relationships. The gospel of God's mighty acts in Jesus Christ did not at any time exist in a void; it was, and is, a tradition preserved and set forth in an actual historic community. . . . To have saving faith was not to possess a set of opinions or even to have the right theological formulae . . . but it was rather a turning of the whole personality to Christ.

To say that Gareth Bennett was a 'High Churchman' is not to say merely that he liked a particular kind of Church service. He had a high view of the Church. But he was – as his reference to Calvin indicates here – catholic in no narrow ecclesiastical sense. He was deeply concerned for the unity of the Church, not in any merely practical or institutional way, but – to quote C. S. Lewis – at a level 'deeper in'. 'There has been on all sides', Dr Bennett wrote, 'an unwillingness to do the patient theological groundwork which will lift all the participants above their entrenched denominational patterns of thought and practice to a sense of being renewed by being conformed to the One Church which is more than any of its fragmented parts'.

To go from this to Dr Habgood's essay on ecumenism is to perceive precisely the contrast between Bennett's Christ-centred, theological approach and the purely functionalist approach of Dr Habgood that we have already observed in the two men's Synod speeches on *Changing Britain*. There is no mention here of theological groundwork: ecumenism is seen as a purely practical and political matter to do with personal relationships on the ground and institutional schemes to be got through without undue delay. Dr Habgood's essay deals mostly with his own experiences. Here he is, taking up his post as Principal of Queen's College, Birmingham:

When I left Jedburgh, I had the privilege of being Principal of a college in Birmingham which was then an Anglican college, and during my time there we turned it into an ecumenical college. This was through union with a Methodist college in Birmingham, and we also had some participation from the United Reformed Church, and we developed very close relationships with the local Roman Catholic college. This union between colleges took place extraordinarily rapidly. In fact I arrived as Principal in September 1967, and by February 1968 we had a scheme in print. We had to do that for the Methodists because the Methodists gear everything to the Annual Conference and their agenda has to be in print by February at the latest. I have always claimed this for the Guinness Book of Records as the quickest piece of ecumenical negotiation which has ever taken place. We managed it because we left out most of the small print.

One man's small print, of course, is another man's fundamental principle. This is not the place for comment on the results of this particular piece of practical ecumenism, except to say that opinions still differ twenty years later. This is not to say that Dr Habgood's approach has no merit. To say as he does that, though there are barriers, 'meanwhile let us do the things that we *can* do together', has obvious common sense about it so long as it is not all that we do. But what is notable here and throughout the essay is the entire lack of any theological rationale for the ecumenical process. If we compare it with Garry Bennett's essay, we are struck by a very remarkable fact: that in Bennett's thoughts on ecumenism the words 'God' and 'Christ' recur naturally and constantly, almost like the response in a litany; in Dr Habgood's essay, these words hardly occur at all, and then only in passing.

Nothing could more strikingly illustrate the real source of the fundamental theological divide separating the two men. For Dr Habgood, the Church is an institution which is for all practical purposes human and not divine; and its problems are therefore to be solved by human action and human ingenuity alone. Presumably God comes into it somewhere, but he has devolved his functions and left it up to us; man is firmly at the centre. In this he reflects faithfully the firm and consistent anthropocentric bias of the liberal protestant theological tradition.

For Dr Bennett, the Church is a great and sacred mystery, not to be tampered with without devoted intellectual and spiritual preparation, because at the very heart of the Church there is God himself, animating and guiding when we surrender in humble obedience to him. For Catholic and Calvinist alike, the Church is, says Bennett, 'an instrument used by the spirit to accomplish the purposes of God'. It was this vision of what the Church of England ought to be that came more and more to possess him; and it was his realization of what that Church was more and more becoming that led him ever more irresistibly to his personal moment of truth.

THREE

Broken by the Church he Served

Early on the evening of Saturday 5 December, at around six
o'clock, Derek Pattinson returned home from a 'quiet day' – a one
day silent spiritual retreat at the Grosvenor Chapel in Mayfair. He
found a message on his Ansafone. It was from Garry Bennett,
asking him to telephone urgently. He sounded distraught. Pattinson
returned his call immediately. There was no answer; Pattinson
assumed that Saturday (rather than Friday), was the night of the
King's College feast in Cambridge, at which he remembered Garry
had told him he was to be a guest; he decided to phone again the
following day.

A little later, at around 7.15, Fr Philip Ursell pulled up in front of
Garry's house, as he had arranged earlier in the day. As he reached
the end of the cul-de-sac he could see that Garry's car was not
parked in front of the garage, and that the house was dark. Everything suggested either that Garry had not returned home, or that he
had driven away, possibly having forgotten their meeting; he never,
even when the weather was bad, put his car into the garage. As he
turned his car, Fr Ursell noticed that the curtains had not been
drawn, and as it had been dark for at least three hours he assumed
that for some reason Garry had not returned home. His next door
neighbour, Harold Cooper, was outside his house; he said he had
not seen Garry, and that he must be away. But that in itself was
strange. Garry usually told him when he was going away. Ursell
told Cooper they had arranged to meet that evening, that he would
telephone later. So clear in his mind was Philip Ursell that Garry
could not be at home that he did not even get out of his car. He
drove away, puzzled; when he arrived back he telephoned Garry.
There was no answer. He tried again, during the evening, at fifteen

minute intervals. In the end he came to the conclusion that either Garry had stayed with John Cowan, or that he had simply gone away, perhaps for the weekend, to be alone and away from harassment. He thought this entirely in character; still, he was surprised, in view of their arrangement, that Garry had not been in touch. He made his last call around midnight.

Dr Bennett is Missing

The following day, the *Crockford's* furore continued in both Church and Press, as its instigator lay cold and dead in his garage. Looking back, there is an eerie unreality about the two days that passed before Garry's body was found. I myself attended the Pusey House Sung Eucharist that Sunday, expecting to find Garry there. In conversation afterwards, Fr Ursell floated another of his protective red herrings. Would it not be a solution to the whole conundrum of the anonymous authorship of the preface, he suggested, if it had been written by Fr Cheslyn Jones, his own predecessor as Principal of Pusey House who had died earlier that summer? Everything seemed to fit: Cheslyn Jones had been critical of Archbishop Runcie; he had the intellectual calibre necessary to have written the preface; he had exactly the combination of sharp wit and pessimism about the Church of England, together with agreement on almost every single point in the *Crockford's* preface itself; at Ascensiontide, when the preface was dated (though it was delivered later, this was not generally known) Canon Jones had still been alive. Would it not be a mercy if the manhunt could be defused by this highly plausible attribution to a deceased author?

The ironies multiply. In Oxford itself, as elsewhere, the 'backlash of support' for Dr Runcie continued on its now somewhat hysterical course. The Dean of Christ Church attacked the anonymous author from the pulpit of his cathedral, afterwards calling on him to resign (though he was unable to specify from what exactly he *should* resign). Even more implausibly, he called for all copies of *Crockford's* to be withdrawn immediately, and reissued without the preface. 'Is this,' commented the Conservative M P Sir Anthony Grant later, in a letter to *The Times*, 'the "comprehensive liberality" of the Church of England to which the Dean referred on the same day?'

The Archbishop himself continued to fulfil his existing engagements as though nothing were happening. As diocesan bishop of the diocese of Canterbury, he celebrated the Eucharist in the Church of St Mary, Bishopsbourne; in his sermon he spoke of the peace and tranquillity of St Mary's; later he dedicated a chapel there.

At about midday, Derek Pattinson telephoned Garry. There was no answer. He continued to telephone him at intervals throughout the day. Philip Ursell repeatedly telephoned, too, through Sunday and Monday.

By Monday evening, there was real concern at Garry's non-appearance at New College, where entrance examinations were in progress. He had not dined on high table on the Sunday evening, as was his custom; nor had he attended College Evensong. John Cowan decided to go round to Garry's house. He phoned Philip Ursell first to ask if he had seen Garry. When Ursell said he had not, he told him that he would go round to his house later.

When John Cowan arrived in Moody Close, he called on Garry's neighbour, Harold Cooper, who had a key to the house; Cooper usually left food out for Garry's cat when he was away for any length of time. Together, they entered the house by the front door. Garry's suitcase was at the bottom of the stairs; Cowan noticed that the newspaper was still tucked into it. They looked into the dining room and the sitting room. The cat lay dead on the carpet. They went into the kitchen, and then into the garage. In the half-light, they saw, to Cooper's surprise, that the car was there. Then they saw Garry was stretched out in the passenger seat, which had been adjusted to a fully reclining position. Harold Cooper shouted: 'Garry, Garry!' There was a faint smell. They saw that a hosepipe had been inserted through the rear window.

There could no longer be any doubt about what had happened. Cooper called for an ambulance and the police. The police came quickly. At about 9.15, Fr Philip Ursell telephoned for the last time. At last, the phone was answered. But it was by a voice he did not know; the voice of a police officer who broke to him the news of Dr Bennett's suicide.

Stunned as he was by the news of his friend's death, Fr Ursell quickly realized that he must pull himself together; there was a lot to be done. The news would break soon enough, but there were some people who had to be told before it did. There was another

73

problem. Apart from James Shelley, secretary to the Church Commissioners, Derek Pattinson and Dr Geoffrey Rowell, chaplain and fellow of Keble, formerly Garry's assistant at New College, Ursell was the only person who knew about Garry's authorship of the preface. A decision had to be made about whether or not to make an announcement about the identity of the author, now that Garry was dead. Everyone would guess, of course, but should it be left there? Was the anonymity to remain officially in place, at least until events dictated otherwise? Ursell walked down Pusey Street and across St Giles to Geoffrey Rowell's rooms in Keble to discuss the matter. With Rowell, he found Sue Gillingham, Old Testament lecturer at Keble. A difference of opinion soon became evident. Rowell was in favour of an immediate announcement; Ursell believed that an undertaking of silence should be maintained, like the secrets of the confessional, beyond the grave. Geoffrey Rowell thought they should immediately inform the Archbishop of Canterbury of Garry's death; Ursell that, in view of his personal responsibility for the preface, Derek Pattinson needed to know first. They tried his number; there was no answer. Ursell left a message on Pattinson's Ansafone to phone him or Rowell, a message which was not played that night. Then, at about ten o'clock, they telephoned Lambeth Palace, to try to make contact with Dr Runcie. He was not there; he was at Canterbury at a banquet in honour of the Ecumenical Patriarch Demetrios, titular Primate of the Eastern Orthodox Churches, who was then in England on an official visit. Rowell then tried to get through to Dr Eric Kemp, Bishop of Chichester and Chairman of the Governors of Pusey House. Bishop Kemp was in Yorkshire at his cottage; he was not on the phone, and could only be contacted by phoning the cottage next door and arranging for him to phone back. At about 11 p.m., the phone rang in Geoffrey Rowell's room. Philip Ursell took the call. Dr Kemp's reaction was characteristically taciturn: 'Oh. So he did write it.' 'Well,' replied Ursell, 'people will draw that conclusion.' Ursell went home; Geoffrey Rowell and Sue Gillingham went to Keble chapel to pray.

When he got home, Philip Ursell telephoned Lambeth again, and asked that a message should be got to the Archbishop in Canterbury to phone him as soon as possible. At around 11.30 the telephone rang; it was Dr Runcie. He was in a cheerful mood, having just returned from his banquet. Ursell gave him the news. There was a long silence. At last, the Archbishop said, 'Well, I always suspected it was he who had written it, but I never thought there was anything personal in it. He had not written anything he had not already said to me at different times.' This was clearly important for Dr Runcie: he was to say the same thing, in almost exactly the same words, in a telephone call to Geoffrey Rowell the following day. Dr Runcie stayed on the phone for about twenty minutes, comforting Ursell who, he knew, had been Garry's closest friend. He told him not to reproach himself for not having prevented the suicide. He said, 'We have lost a great servant of the Church.' He ended the call with the words, 'All we can do is pray for his soul.'

It was now about midnight. Ursell had one more call to make before he could rest. He telephoned the Bishop of London, Dr Graham Leonard, who was at his house in Witney, to give him the news. Dr Leonard had gone to bed, and was fast asleep. He said little on hearing the news, being full of sleep, except that he still did not believe Garry had written the preface.

As Ursell was telephoning Bishop Leonard, the Archbishop's assistant Christopher Hill was calling Derek Pattinson. He gave him the news, then said, 'I have the Archbishop here; he would like a word.' The Archbishop said, 'We are both mourning the loss of a friend.' Dr Runcie was pastoral and comforting, as he had been with Fr Ursell; he ended the call by giving Derek Pattinson his blessing.

The next morning, Fr Ursell was in his stall in the Blessed Sacrament Chapel in Pusey House at 6.45, to pray for Garry's soul before morning prayer at 7.45 and the daily Mass at 8. When a telephone call came through at around 7.20 from Mrs Eve Keatley, the Archbishop's press secretary, it was taken by Fr Harry Smythe, who wrote down a message for Fr Ursell and took it to him in chapel. 'We believe we can help you. Please telephone Mrs Keatley at home now, or at Lambeth after nine.' Fr Ursell decided to phone Lambeth after nine. Then he broke the news to Fr Smythe, who was deeply shocked and distressed. Then he made one last phone call before morning prayer, at around 7.30 – to the author of this book. I was sitting at my desk when the phone rang. Fr Ursell said, 'Are you sitting down? I have some very bad news for you. I am sorry to have to tell you that Garry has taken his own life.' I remember that, in the midst of my shock, the pieces of the jigsaw came together and I realized that Garry was the author of the preface. We talked for about fifteen minutes, until Fr Ursell had to go to chapel to say the morning office.

After morning prayer, Fr Ursell went to the sacristy, to vest for Mass. White vestments had been laid out, for the Feast of the Immaculate Conception. He put them away again, took out different vestments, and prepared himself for the Mass. Then he went to the altar vested in deepest black, to offer the holy Eucharist for the repose of the soul of Gareth Vaughan Bennett, priest, who in great perplexity of mind had taken his own life; and for the health and sanity of the Church of England, for which he had felt such deep and unrequited love, and whose devoted servant he had been. Before he began the Mass, Ursell told the undergraduate congregation, all of whom had known Garry, about what had happened. He told them that suicide was always a serious matter for Christians – that it was particularly serious for a priest. Then he told them of the Archbishop's words: 'All we can do now is pray for his soul.' As the Mass was celebrated in Pusey House, Geoffrey Rowell was offering the same prayers for Garry's soul at a Requiem in Keble chapel.

A little after nine, Ursell phoned Lambeth Palace. The Archbishop's press secretary had a question for him. Did he mind if the Archbishop disclosed to the Press who had told him about Garry's death? Ursell said he did not.

In that case, Mrs Keatley informed him, there would be consequences: he would be badgered by the press. She advised him to prepare a short statement, not more than two sentences long, so that there would be less chance of reporters getting it wrong. She also advised him not to take any calls himself, but to give the statement to colleagues to read out to any journalists who called. He prepared his statement; then he ran off three copies on his Canon desktop copier, gave one to each of his colleagues, and went home.

The Scapegoat Under Fire

In London, Derek Pattinson slept that night as though poleaxed. He woke late, too late to attend the daily Eucharist at St Matthew's,

Westminster, as he often did. He went straight to work at Church House. One of his first problems was to deal with the new situation created by Garry's suicide. He faced the same problem that Philip Ursell and Geoffrey Rowell had discussed the previous evening. Could he, or should he, continue to refuse to disclose the authorship of the *Crockford's* preface?

Hindsight makes the disclosure seem not only inevitable, but almost unnecessary. Now that the chief suspect had killed himself, was it not plain for all to see who had written the preface? In fact, at the time, it was not necessarily obvious at all. Certainly some, like the Bishop of Chichester, had immediately assumed Garry's authorship on hearing the news; but the Bishop of London, a straightforward and trusting personality, still believed Garry's denials. So, at first, did Fr Jeremy Sheehy, chaplain of New College, who told *The Times* that he still did not believe that Dr Bennett had been the author of the *Crockford's* preface. But he added that 'the pressure of the finger pointing at [him] may have been a factor in his death.' This *Times* report goes on to record that 'in spite of his repeated denials, many in the Church who knew him suggested he must have had a role in the affair, *possibly without realizing that he was contributing material which someone else would use.*' (My italics.)

At the time, then, the matter was by no means obviously closed. It might well have lingered on as one of those questions to which everyone thinks he knows the answer, but about which (until the inquest) some element of doubt would have remained. In the event, Derek Pattinson's decision to disclose Garry's authorship of the preface was dictated by events. The previous week, he had received a letter from Roderick Gilchrist, then deputy editor of the *Daily Mail*. It asked him to pass on a letter to the author, offering him a platform in the *Mail*, so that he could explain his position. It also offered a generous payment, (the amount of which was unspecified) to go to the Church, a designated charity, or any other recipient of the author's choice. Derek Pattinson had forwarded the letter with a handwritten covering note which read 'Dear Garry, I think you should see this for yourself'. But he himself had not read the letter. When asked later, at the February General Synod, why he and James Shelley, the secretary to the Church Commissioners, had felt it necessary to pass the letter on at all, he answered (not unreasonably) that

We were directed by our feeling that we are not in the position of censoring other people's correspondence. What was in the letter the *Daily Mail* sent to Dr Bennett, I do not know.

To another questioner he commented that he 'would have been astonished . . . if [Dr Bennett] had decided to respond to the *Daily Mail*'s invitation.' It was not, in fact, the *Mail*'s only attempt at getting the invitation through. Gilchrist had also written direct to Garry who he was personally convinced was the author after having spoken to him twice on the telephone on the day of publication. The letter forwarded by Pattinson was found by the police among unopened mail Garry had collected on Saturday morning from the New College Porter's Lodge. Gilchrist, not unnaturally, assumed that the Oxford Coroner would take immediate possession of this letter if it had been found. In fact, the Police forwarded it some weeks later to Geoffrey Rowell, who in his turn gave it to the Coroner. Gilchrist did not know; but he decided to float a trial balloon. He phoned Derek Pattinson, telling him he had heard that the Coroner was in possession of the letter he had forwarded to the anonymous author; this letter had been found among Dr Bennett's things. Pattinson realized that whether this was true or not he had no alternative but to confirm that Garry was indeed the author, and said that he would probably be putting out a statement to that effect.

The letter addressed to Garry by name had been sent by courier: a motor cyclist had roared up the M40 in black leather to deliver it in person. He was too late; Garry was already on his way to Cambridge. The letter was found after his death in his rooms by the chaplain of New College, Fr Jeremy Sheehy, and returned unopened.

The official admission of Garry's authorship of the preface was issued jointly by Derek Pattinson and James Shelley on Tuesday evening:

In view of statements attributed to the Oxford coroner's staff, the Secretary General of the General Synod and the Secretary of the Church Commissioners have this evening confirmed that they invited Dr Bennett in February 1987 to write the preface to the 1987/8 *Crockford's Clerical Directory*.

In accordance with the *Crockford's* tradition, the preface, as published, was the text as he gave it to them.

If there was a slightly defensive tone about the second paragraph of the statement, it was not to be wondered at. It was now only two days until the scheduled meeting of the General Synod's Policy Subcommittee at Addington Palace. Without any consultation with Derek Pattinson as General Secretary (an unprecedented step), Archbishop Habgood's office had just announced that he would be taking the chair during the committee's discussion of the responsibility for the publication of the preface.

Press reports that he would insist on taking the chair during the committee's discussion of the *Crockford's* preface had until now been denied by Dr Habgood as 'speculation'. Now the speculation appeared to be borne out. Since the author himself was dead, press attention became centred on the alternative scapegoat, Derek Pattinson, who, with James Shelley, had invited Dr Bennett to write the preface, and who had published it without editorial intervention. Habgood would be after Pattinson now; that was the story.

It was not an entirely outlandish suggestion, to be dismissed out of hand as irresponsible 'press speculation'. Certainly, it is what Derek Pattinson himself assumed, and it is what he told the Archbishop of Canterbury; he felt that the Archbishop of York was working against him. There was, without doubt, a question mark over his continuation in office, and not only in the minds of the press; he now became the central *dramatis persona* of the *Crockford's* tragedy.

But first, just for a moment at least, the pressure was relieved by an episode of rather splendid Ealing comedy. On Wednesday morning, Derek Pattinson woke at his usual time, and went to the early morning Eucharist at St Matthew's, Westminster. As he knelt in his pew after the celebration, making his thanksgiving for Holy Communion, the Bishop of London's chaplain told him that a large crowd of pressmen was besieging the entrance to his block of flats; he should under no circumstances go back home for breakfast yet. The vicar of St Matthew's also saw the crowd of journalists from his window; they were, he observed, standing not far from a local store. He had a brainwave. He telephoned the manager of the store, and asked him to give a message to the Press Association representative. He was, the message said, to return immediately to the office. The PA already had all the photos and copy they needed. The message was delivered, and the ruse worked like clockwork.

The journalists all left; if the P A was going to put out a story with photographs, they would be able to write their own stories from that. Derek Pattinson walked unmolested to the safety of Church House.

The Establishment Closes Ranks

But the attention of the press was not, for Derek Pattinson, an unmitigated source of amusement. The appetite for the spectacle of heads rolling had been whetted, though it was not the newspapers who had first started looking for scapegoats. The tone of the reaction of some senior clergy, not only to the content of the preface but to the fact that it had been commissioned by someone whose duty it was to keep things running smoothly, had been sharp. What more natural than that there should be resignations? The Dean of Winchester, the Very Revd Trevor Beeson, seemed to be after at least two resignations. In a letter to *The Times*, published the previous Saturday (Garry read *The Times* that day, his last day alive) the Dean had suggested that if the Permanent Secretary of the Cabinet and the Permanent Secretary to the Treasury had allowed Mr Edward Heath anonymously to publish a savage attack on the prime minister in an official government publication 'it might be assumed that these two civil servants were either inept or disloyal. They would either have to give a very good account of themselves or they would have to resign.' The suggestion was obvious enough. The Dean looked forward eagerly, he continued, 'to the response of the General Secretary of the General Synod and the First Church Estates Commissioner'. He got no change from the First Estates Commissioner, Sir Douglas Lovelock, who was having nothing of such talk: in a letter to *The Times*, published immediately underneath Dean Beeson's, he vigorously pre-empted any suggestion of personal responsibility. He did not know who the author was; he played no part in such things; it was nothing to do with him.

It was not Sir Douglas, however, who was really in the sights of those who thought like the Dean of Winchester; it was Derek Pattinson. He it was who would have to resign if anybody did.

Certainly, *The Times* apparently thought he should. It devoted a long first leader to the *Crockford's* affair on the morning of the Policy Subcommittee's meeting to discuss the way in which the preface had been commissioned. Among other magisterial utterances, Derek Pattinson was shaken that morning to read the following barrage of cross-examination:

Did Mr Pattinson not realize a hunt for the anonymous author was inevitable? Once it began, he surely had a further duty to advise Dr Bennett on his defences. Did he advise him to lie, or warn him not to? Or does he accept no responsibility whatever for how Dr Bennett reacted to the pressure, the growing atmosphere of suspicion, deception, and acrimony, and his consequent and eventually fatal isolation from the support of friends? If Mr Pattinson has no good answers to these questions, he should resign.

Mr Pattinson had no intention of resigning. Nor, with the benefit of mature reflection, does it seem at all right that he should have. *The Times*'s conclusions may have been understandable enough, but they do not stand the tests of further reflection and knowledge of the facts. Apart from anything else, the widespread assumption that the convention of anonymity had led to Garry's 'fatal isolation from the support of friends' is quite simply untrue. He had constant support from his closest friend, who took care to spend a good deal of time with him during those few days, who had been with him shortly before the suicide, and who was due to visit him only hours after he actually killed himself. As for the 'growing atmosphere of suspicion, deception and acrimony', what, Pattinson was surely justified in asking, did he have to do with these? It was not he who had directed pressmen towards Dr Bennett with 'deep background' suggestions that 'if I were you I would ask Dr Bennett'. Nor was he responsible for the growing atmosphere of acrimony. That had been established by the senior clergy who one moment were talking of the comprehensive liberality of the Church of England, and the next were calling for resignations – of the author (whoever he was) from his job (whatever *that* was); of the First Estates Commissioner; most insistently of General Secretary Pattinson. The hysterical atmosphere had to do partly with the fact that there was a press hunt for the author, but it had far more to do with those who had given the hunt its spice by their vindictive attitude to the author – and their heavy hints as to his identity.

The assumption that the whole furore was foreseeable was very damaging to Derek Pattinson; for though it was generally accepted that Garry Bennett, being an Oxford don, was necessarily utterly unworldly (a useful concession which could also be used to discredit the preface) Derek Pattinson was, or so it was said, the very opposite – someone at the heart of things who knew exactly what to expect but who went ahead and commissioned the preface anyway.

Both these assumptions, which have now become part of the mythology of the affair, are wide of the mark. Garry Bennett was by no means an unworldly clerical don. He knew the life of the parishes and kept in close touch with the many clergy he had appointed to New College livings, visiting them regularly and taking a close pastoral interest in their affairs. Nor was he cut off from the world outside the Church. He was 'switched on' to the media; those who visited him when the television news was on kept quiet until it was over. Nor was Derek Pattinson a worldly and devious Sir Humphrey, sitting in Church House, Westminster at the centre of a network of power and manipulation, like a spider in the middle of a web. Certainly, he was General Secretary of the General Synod, and tended to be where decisions were made in the boards and committees of that misty and labyrinthine entity; but not everyone would agree that the General Synod represents the reality of the Church, or any other reality for that matter.

The real fact is that nobody could have foreseen the intensity of the atmosphere that developed almost immediately on the publication of the preface. The accusation that a man of Derek Pattinson's experience should have known what would happen does not stand up. When he had taken delivery of the typescript at the July Session of the General Synod (it is dated 'Ascensiontide' but was actually delivered late), the atmosphere was generally quiet. There were no great controversies, not ones at any rate that had attracted press attention. By December, the atmosphere had been wholly transformed by the debate, during the November session of General Synod, on the sexual ethics of the clergy. The Reverend Tony Higton, a prominent Evangelical, had sought some kind of declaration from Synod that 'appropriate discipline' would be applied to erring clerics. Faced by a barrage of television lights and popping flashbulbs, Synod members were picketed by gay liberationists as they arrived for the debate. By the end of a perfunctory morning's discussion, in the judgement of many, the bishops (and particularly the Archbishop of Canterbury) had successfully avoided the issue.

The popular press went to town with a series of appalling 'queerbashing' headlines which still beggar the imagination. The murkier end of Fleet Street can hardly ever have been nearer to self-parody. 'Holy Homos Escape Ban', trumpeted the *Star*; inside it concentrated on the scandal of the 'revolting revs' in a theological college. The *Sun*'s contribution to this tide of anal alliteration was 'Pulpit Poofs Can Stay: Church Votes Not to Kick Them Out'. The rather more upmarket *Daily Mail* wrote of the 'Scandal of the Gay Vicars', and described the Synod's overwhelming support for the Bishop of Chester's gently worded compromise amendment as 'a classic fudge'. There was an ugly atmosphere, a feeling among the leaders of the Church that the press was out to do anything it could to discredit the Church of England and that open discussion of the Church's dirty linen had played into their hands. The stage had been set, not only for the press to pounce on the criticisms of the Church's leadership in the *Crockford's* preface (only three weeks later) but for that leadership to react with extreme irritability against anyone else rocking the boat.

But when Derek Pattinson had first read the *Crockford's* preface the previous summer, all that was in the unimaginable future. His first reaction, in his room on campus at York University (the venue for Synod meetings in the Northern Province), was that the preface was pretty strong stuff in places but by no means beyond the parameters of the *Crockford's* tradition. Strong criticism of arch-bishops of Canterbury, as we shall see, was by no means unprece-dented. He was, in any case, not at liberty to make any changes. Garry Bennett had thought very carefully before accepting the commission: Pattinson, indeed, had had to make a special trip to Oxford before he had finally agreed, which he did on the solemn understanding that no changes of any kind would be made and that his anonymity would be strictly maintained. Since these conditions were precisely those which had always prevailed in the past, the General Secretary saw no obstacle to giving that undertaking in this case. He had kept strictly to precedent. He could, he felt, not have foreseen the atmosphere of hysteria; nor could he have foreseen that Garry Bennett (who, though quiet in his manner, also gave the impression of a certain toughness and resilience) would so quickly founder in the storm he had provoked. To have *The Times* call for his resignation was deeply disturbing; and he felt its injustice keenly.

Dr Habgood Comes Under Fire

But if Derek Pattinson was shaken by *The Times* leader, what must have been the reaction to it of the Archbishop of York? In two biting paragraphs *The Times* summed up what was a growing opinion, held not only by many in the press but also by the public in general: that the intolerable pressure under which Dr Bennett had cracked was exerted in no small part by the general reaction of the Anglican establishment, and by the particular reaction of one of its leading members. It was precisely the same individual, furthermore, who was due that day to play a continuing part in the *Crockford's* saga by taking the chair at the standing committee's inquiry into how it came to be commissioned in the first place. 'It would be seemly', thundered *The Times*,

if, in presiding over such an inquisition as this, the Archbishop of York, Dr John Habgood, were also to acknowledge that his own contribution to the public debate on the preface was at fault. It was, at least, a failure of charity. Not apparently knowing the author, and unable therefore to estimate his words (or for that matter the truth of what he was imputing), he described the preface as scurrilous, sour and vindictive.

He thereby helped unwittingly to propel the tragedy towards its final curtain. So, to greater or less degree, did those at every level of the Church who pointed a finger of suspicion at Dr Bennett, for the benefit of each other or of inquiring journalists, once they knew he had denied responsibility. If he felt they were speaking from knowledge rather than guesswork he must have felt utterly betrayed, indeed deliberately entrapped.

In the event, it was not the Archbishop of York who presided over the meeting of the Policy Subcommittee. There had been a growing feeling that Dr Habgood was not a dispassionate observer; some members of the committee made their views known that he should step down as chairman. At a meeting of the two archbishops and a small inner cabinet before lunch, it was decided that Dr Runcie would take the chair at the meeting. It was evidently a time for mending fences. The press were out in strength at Addington Palace. Derek Pattinson had arrived with a set smile; to the awaiting forest of microphones, he simply said 'I'm very good at saying nothing, you know'. Inside Addington Palace, the two archbishops advanced on him together, and each took one of his arms. 'Derek,' said Dr Habgood, 'I'm not working against you.'

The meeting of the full committee, fifteen members and seven staff, began after lunch. It soon became clear, from an apparently insignificant procedural decision, that Derek Pattinson's position was safe. As he opened the discussion of the *Crockford's* affair, the Archbishop of Canterbury, as chairman, said that it might be necessary at some point in the proceedings for Mr Shelley and Mr Pattinson to withdraw. Everyone saw the point: they would have to withdraw if the question of their resignation was to be discussed. An influential member of the House of Laity, Mr Oswald Clark, said, 'Is that really necessary?' It became clear that the meeting thought it was not. Thus simply, one matter before the committee, at least, had been settled.

The real question underlying the committee's deliberations was whether to discuss the preface simply as a publishing event, the arrangements for which required explanation; or as an analysis of the condition of the Church of England which itself needed to be discussed and if necessary answered. Those who only wanted to discuss how it had all come about tended to think that the preface was self-evidently unjustifiable. But it was clear that there was a body of opinion on the subcommittee which thought that the preface had got it about right. 'There was no way,' one member said to me, 'that we were going to allow Derek Pattinson to take any blame, since that would be to accept that what the preface said did not need saying.'

In the end the committee agreed to issue a statement expressing their confidence in Derek Pattinson and James Shelley, having accepted that there was no question about Garry Bennett's suitability to have been asked to write the preface. But no discussion was allowed about the content of the preface. It was decided that there would be the opportunity for a fuller discussion, both of the content of the preface and of the arrangements for its publication at the February meeting of the Synod. The text of a statement, prepared in draft before lunch, and amended by the full committee, was agreed. This was to be read out to the press by the Archbishop of Canterbury; it was decided that no questions would be allowed in order to obviate the possibility of the kind of misrepresentations which would cause further inflammation of the situation. After three and a half hours the meeting came to an end. The agreed statement was as follows:

1. The Committee expresses its very great grief at the tragic death of one of its members, Dr Gareth Bennett. His views were well known to the Committee which had valued greatly his contribution to its discussions and his personal friendship.

2. The choice of the author of the *Crockford* Preface and the procedure for publication were the responsibility of Mr Derek Pattinson, Secretary-General of the General Synod of the Church of England and Mr James Shelley, the Secretary of the Church Commissioners, who gave Dr Bennett an assurance of complete anonymity. In that and all other respects they acted strictly in accordance with precedent.

The Committee expresses its total confidence in the way these officers handled the whole matter.

3. The Committee deplores the various pressures to which Dr Bennett had evidently been subjected following the Preface's publication.

One member of the committee was not prepared to leave it at that. The Evangelical priest David Holloway, who had called for a discussion, not simply of how the preface was commissioned but also about whether or not its analysis was true, insisted on making a personal statement to the press. He called for radical change in the Church of England if it was to avoid disaster; and he insisted that if people were to read the preface in its entirety, they would see that Dr Bennett 'was not making a personal attack on Dr Runcie but on the predominantly liberal leadership that he heads'.

Dr Habgood Does it Again

The aftermath of Garry Bennett's death now moved into a new phase. On the morning of Saturday 12 December, two days after the Addington Palace meeting, Archbishop Habgood went to the BBC's studio in York, to give a radio interview 'down the line' to Sue MacGregor in the 'Today' programme's studio in London. The interviewer began with a statement of what, by now, had become the obvious: 'The *Crockford* preface – and its author Dr Gareth Bennett – is unlikely to go away for some time.' She reminded listeners of the results of the Policy Subcommittee's meeting the previous Thursday; she reminded them too of Dr Habgood's contribution to the affair in his statement to the PA. The Archbishop, she said, had 'described the *Crockford* preface before its authorship was known as "scurrilous, sour and vindictive".' Did he still think it was scurrilous? In his reply, the Archbishop for the first time used a defence which was to become familiar. He had been quoted out of context:

Dr Habgood: Well, obviously, a person's death does make a difference and when one knows what one's talking about, one might perhaps have used different language, but I do want to make it clear that I did not use the word 'scurrilous' of the article as a whole. I referred specifically to the charges and the charges in the article against the Archbishop of Canterbury and myself were very serious ones, basically they were a charge of conspiracy and lack of integrity and it seemed to me that that sort of charge did need a vigorous riposte.

It was not the normal practice, Sue MacGregor pointed out, for *Crockford's* prefaces to be signed; should an exception have been made in this case? The Archbishop said that the question of anonymity was very difficult; it had been thought a risk worth taking. Nobody, he said, would have questioned the choice of Dr Bennett 'as an appropriate person to write that preface, though, when we read it, we were obviously deeply surprised and hurt by its contents'. 'You also', replied the interviewer, 'felt the contents were written by somebody in a vindictive mood?'

Dr Habgood: Well, I think when criticism of this kind becomes very personal which this was, then vindictive is an appropriate adjective. I don't want to press it and I don't think it's worth going back over those particular adjectives now we have the sadness of Dr Bennett's death.

Sue MacGregor now elicited from Dr Habgood an answer which produced, both within the Church and from the press, a reaction of such anger and disbelief that in a book published nearly a year later, the Archbishop felt it necessary to include an essay on the *Crock-*

ford's affair in order to set the record straight as he saw it: with what effect we shall see. 'What the preface has done, of course', said Sue MacGregor, 'is . . . expose a huge rift in the Church of England; and that in itself can have come as no surprise to you?'

The effects of Dr Habgood's reply were to confirm the interviewer's analysis, but in effect he ignored the question. The unavoidable impression is that when he came to the BBC studio in York, the Archbishop had his own fish to fry. He now seized his opportunity:

Dr Habgood: Well, I think you have to remember that around this there has been an enormous amount of media 'hype' and this is the sort of thing which in gentler days would have been accepted as [a] sort of scholarly criticism, but when the thing was personalized, when it was taken up in a very very big way by the media, when the media has been screaming out that the Church of England is about to disintegrate and so on, then obviously, reactions become different and I do think it needs to be recognized that the media pressure on Dr Bennett does seem to have been a major factor that led him to his tragic death. Obviously, a great deal is going to have to come out at the inquest, but I think it's not generally known that in his car there was a letter from a newspaper which was offering to pay £10,000 to a charity which he could name for him to write an article about the preface and I do think that kind of pressure on a sensitive academic who was not used to press exposure must have been very great indeed.
Sue MacGregor: Are you saying, in effect, that the press had a hand in Dr Bennett's suicide?
Dr Habgood: Well, I think that has got to be left for the inquest but since so much of the criticism at the moment has come back on the Church . . . I think the other side of it must be recognized.

The interview now returned to more predictable themes. Was the Church changing too fast? What about the ordination of women? The leadership of the Church, said Dr Habgood eirenically, admitted that there were 'fears, particularly among the Catholic constituency and this is why the leadership of the Church has to try to be so very gentle and cautious in endeavouring to make sure that everybody's voice is heard and that the Church is held together'.

It was, however, too late for such talk from Dr Habgood. Quite simply, too many doubted the sincerity of one who had behaved with such haste and such contempt toward the author of the preface and who now talked of being 'gentle and cautious in endeavouring to make sure that everybody's voice is heard'. As *The Times* had charged, 'not apparently knowing the author, and unable therefore to estimate his words (or for that matter the truth of what he was imputing), he described the preface as scurrilous, sour and vindictive'. He himself, indeed, had in effect admitted the justice of this charge by conceding at the beginning of the 'Today' interview that 'when one knows what one's talking about, one might perhaps have used different language.' But instead of unambiguously accepting his share of whatever blame was going, he now sought to offload any responsibility. Nobody wanted him to grovel; but some sort of statement of regret, not necessarily of penitence, would have achieved what was necessary. It could even have been conditionally phrased – 'I may have used unfortunate language; if I have contributed in any way to the pressures which led to Dr Bennett's death, I am sorry' – that, or something like it (particularly if it had been followed by silence), would have defused an explosive situation.

The Agony is Prolonged

Instead, Dr Habgood detonated the explosion, and then carried on lobbing hand-grenades. Dr Habgood's high profile self-defence throughout the whole affair was in strong contrast, generally noted, with Dr Runcie's total silence. Now, he took to writing letters to the newspapers. In a letter to *The Times*, which appeared on 18 December, he took issue (without mentioning it) with the leader which had appeared on the morning of the Policy Subcommittee meeting the week before. Strangely he did not confront the leader's substantial criticisms of his contribution to the affair but confined himself to a single point. He had not called the whole preface 'scurrilous' at all but only the charges levelled against Dr Runcie and himself. 'May we hope', Dr Habgood concluded, 'that adjectival detachment will be recognized as a dangerous journalistic disease and receive prompt treatment?'

If this letter was merely puzzling to many, another aroused stronger feelings. A Synod member and former MP, Peter Bruinvels, had accused Dr Habgood of 'spearheading a total witch-hunt' against Dr Bennett, and of 'accusing the author of a scurrilous and vitriolic attack on the Archbishop of Canterbury'. In a letter to the *Daily Telegraph*, the Archbishop rebutted charges of spearheading a witch-hunt (we shall consider his defence shortly) and rightly said that the phrase 'scurrilous and vitriolic' was Mr Bruinvels's own. He then expressed the hope that Mr Bruinvels could be 'persuaded to refrain from further comments until the inquest establishes what can be known about Dr Bennett's mind at the time of his death'.

This letter aroused a stinging rebuke from a fellow of Gonville and Caius College, Cambridge, Dr J. P. Casey. The actual words used, said Dr Casey, were 'scurrilous, sour and vindictive'. The last two words were particularly wounding, constituting a 'personal attack' (the usual phrase for the preface's criticisms of Dr Runcie) on Dr Bennett himself, clearly implying that he had personal motives for his criticisms – 'perhaps disappointment at being passed over for episcopal preferment?' Dr Casey's final paragraph evokes all the heat and passion of that extraordinary time:

Dr Habgood did undoubtedly lead the witchhunt. He has since been most anxious to impress his views upon the media. It is no use his telling Mr Bruinvels to keep quiet until the inquest establishes the true cause of Dr Bennett's death, when he himself regaled listeners to 'Today' with his confident speculation that media pressure was responsible. It is difficult not to suspect that he is now chiefly concerned to divert attention from his own unpleasant role in the affair. His intemperate and unfair comments on the preface were made by someone with blood in his eye. Is he now trying to wash his hands?

The 'Today' interview had stirred up a new hornet's nest. It had, indeed, become difficult not to suspect that Dr Habgood was now, in Dr Casey's words, 'chiefly concerned to divert attention from his own . . . role in the affair'. He had accepted no responsibility for the tragedy; and in his radio interview, he produced his alibi: the letter in the suicide car, which – it was clearly implied – had contributed directly to Dr Bennett's decision to kill himself. The press (and, as we shall see, one newspaper in particular) was predictably unamused. But the most serious effect was on the clergy and laity who had felt Dr Bennett was speaking for them, and who had been utterly horrified by the 'backlash of support' in general and Dr Habgood's contribution to it in particular.

His attempt to fasten blame on the press now produced its own backlash. *The Times* reported some of the reactions. 'If the press had been greeted with greater urbanity and a sense of proportion by those in high places,' said the Anglo-Catholic Synod Veteran, Canon Brian Brindley, who had been present at the Policy Subcommittee two days before the broadcast, 'they would not have pursued the hunt so vigorously and with such tragic results'. One churchman was particularly outspoken. 'My experience of the press', said Canon George Austin, 'is that they have behaved very responsibly. I believe Dr Habgood is trying to divert attention from his earlier remarks, which were quite indefensible. What he said about the preface must have added to Dr Bennett's distress'. Asked whether he thought Dr Habgood's chances of succeeding Dr Runcie at Canterbury would be affected, Canon Austin was forthright: 'Habgood cannot possibly go to Canterbury now', he said. 'The attacks on Dr Bennett have made me ashamed to be a member of the Church of England'.

In more dispassionate tones, *The Times* had come to the same conclusion about the prospects for Dr Habgood's future. In the latest of a series of weighty and thoughtful leaders, the paper now pronounced that

Dr Habgood's high profile in this sad affair will not have enhanced his reputation. His interventions stand in marked contrast to the bearing of the Archbishop of Canterbury, Dr Robert Runcie, whose quiet and dignified manner throughout will have won him new admirers. Dr Runcie is the older and wiser man. In spite of Dr Habgood's many gifts and his already dominant role in the Church of England, he has not yet proved himself sufficient of an ecclesiastical statesman to guarantee his automatic translation from York to Canterbury when his time comes.

The Times made it clear that in its view that time ought not to be allowed to come. Dr Runcie had it in his hands. If he retired soon, Dr Habgood's appointment would be more likely. If, however, he served until the latest permitted time for his retirement, the Church, and the prime minister, would have to turn to younger men. 'If', the leader continued, 'Dr Runcie's reflections on the *Crockford's* affair, and on the argument of the preface itself, give him a second wind to offer the church more leadership, both more prolonged and more decisive, that would undoubtedly be for the good of the church.'

The Mail *Strikes Back*

But there was one Fleet Street paper where there was little inclination for any such relaxed and urbane judgements. The *Daily Mail's* reactions to the Archbishop's 'revelations' about the letter in the suicide car were to assume that he was referring to one of their own letters to Dr Bennett. After the broadcast, they attempted to speak to Dr Habgood on the telephone. Failing in this, they sent a reporter to Bishopthorpe, to wait for the Archbishop to emerge, a process known in the trade as 'doorstepping'. The *Mail* doorstepped the Archbishop, as he recalls in his own essay on the preface, 'for most of a day in order to pass me a message, as I left for an evening engagement in Lancashire, that I had made "a very serious charge", and to elicit the reply that I had said nothing about the *Mail* at all'.

The following day, Monday 14 December, the *Mail* ran a furious leader. This needs to be quoted at some length, since it contains not only charges against Dr Habgood, the justice of which have to be examined as scrupulously as possible, but also a defence of its own actions during the affair, which were themselves to be the object of counatercharges from Dr Habgood. These too require careful scrutiny. The leader began by asking whether media efforts to identify the anonymous author could have contributed to Dr Bennett's death:

Of course they could.
   This was an appalling and totally unforeseen tragedy which we must all regret.
   Like other newspapers, together with radio and TV, the *Daily Mail* strove to solve the mystery. We offered the author a press platform to both defend his views and reveal his identity. There was also the offer of a 'generous' fee to go to a church charity if he so wished.

It was, the leader continued, through the good offices of the Church itself, in the person of Derek Pattinson, that Dr Bennett had first received this offer. The *Mail* had reported the truth about this:

But the truth, it would seem, is not enough for Dr John Habgood, the Archbishop of York. He must needs embellish it with hearsay.

In a Radio 4 interview he declared that media pressure 'must have been a major factor' leading to the tragic death. With gratuitous innuendo, His Grace talked of a letter offering £10,000 from a newspaper (which he will not or cannot name). He said the letter was found with Dr Bennett's body in his car.

This newspaper can only speak for itself. At no time and in no way was a figure of £10,000 or any other specific figure ever mentioned directly or indirectly by the *Daily Mail* to Dr Bennett.

We do not know what was found in Dr Bennett's car nor do we know what was in the poor man's mind in the hours before he died.

What we do know is that the fiercest and the fastest and most crushing attack on the writer of the *Crockford's* preface was delivered by Dr Habgood. He called it 'scurrilous' and 'vindictive'. Furthermore it was the same Archbishop of York who headed the inquiry determined to find out how the preface came to be written.

Could such an attack and prospect of such an inquisition have played their part in helping to destroy Dr Bennett's peace of mind?

Of course they could.

Of an Archbishop in the wake of this deeply upsetting death, it may be said that Dr John Habgood has been more ready to point the finger at others than to bare his own soul.

How much of this indictment can be sustained? It falls broadly into two parts: firstly, the charges and the countercharges connected with the mysterious 'letter in the car'; secondly, the charges (by no means levelled only by the *Mail*) to do with Dr Habgood's statement to the PA and his subsequent, allegedly 'inquisitorial', behaviour, and its possible effect on Dr Bennett's frame of mind at the end.

Did the letter in the car actually exist? As we have seen Roderick Gilchrist of the *Mail* sent two letters; he assumed that the Archbishop was referring to one of these, but knew that if he was he had got his facts wrong. The Archbishop had said the letter offered Dr Bennett £10,000 whereas the letter sent by the *Mail* said nothing whatever about any sum of money. Gilchrist sent a local stringer to Bishopthorpe to doorstep the Archbishop. He waited in his driveway throughout Sunday 13 December before making fleeting contact as the Archbishop got into his car.

The Letter in the Car

He was not the only journalist that day who was curious about the letter. One churches correspondent, telephoned Dr Habgood's press secretary, Raymond Barker, to try to pin the elusive document down. His question was simple enough. Was the Archbishop absolutely sure that the letter existed? Barker's reply was glacial. The Archbishop, he said, was not in the habit of speaking without checking his facts.

The following day, Monday, one of Father Philip Ursell's colleagues at Pusey House took a telephone call. Ursell himself was at New College, helping to arrange Dr Bennett's funeral the next day. Would his colleague please make sure he got an important message? Would Father Ursell please call the Archbishop of York's press secretary urgently at Bishopthorpe? On his return, Philip Ursell returned Raymond Barker's call. Barker's question was simple enough. Had there in fact been any letter, offering £10,000, in the car? Ursell told him there had not, but that a newspaper (he did not know which one) had offered him £10,000 by telephone.

The *Mail* also made offers by telephone. One of these seems to be recorded in the last entry in Garry Bennett's diary: 'A reporter from the *Mail* rang up to offer me £5000 if I was the author and wished to go public with them. He said it was rumoured that an announcement was to be made in the next 48 hours.' This entry is something of a mystery. Both Roderick Gilchrist, who directed the *Mail*'s coverage of the affair, and Steve Doughty, who reported it, spoke to Garry Bennett by telephone, and admit that they made offers of generous but unspecified sums for Dr Bennett to go public. They are both quite clear in their minds that they made no mention of £5000, or of £10,000, or of any other sum; nor did they say anything about an impending announcement. There seems to be little reason to doubt that no sum was specified by the *Mail* if those concerned say so; they admitted the offers from the outset, and if it was wrong to make such offers at all (a debatable question) it was no worse to specify any particular amount. One explanation could be that Dr Bennett was confusing the *Mail*'s unspecified offers with offers from other quarters. There were, it is clear, several of these. Philip Ursell thinks it quite possible that in Garry Bennett's somewhat confused and overexcited mood the diary entry recorded the name not of the paper that actually made the offer of £5000 but another. The same could be true of predictions about 'an impending announcement'. Dr Bennett had no reason to doubt that his name would not be divulged by any of the four men who actually knew who had written the preface. But informed speculation was another matter. He did know that the Archbishop of Canterbury thought it was him, and that Lambeth had told *The Times* so. The highest authority in the Church had worked it out, and Lambeth Palace was already putting his name about to journalists. He was getting offers from newspapers. He must have wondered how many of the other suspects were. In fact, so far as I have been able to discover, he was the only one.

This is not quite the end of the affair of the 'letter in the car', though it probably would have been had not Dr Habgood decided to revive it, in order 'to put on record what I know, so that when the whole story is told some of the more obvious mistakes and misinterpretations can be avoided'. Here, then, is Dr Habgood's account of how he came to speak about the offer over the air. He had, he said, come to the conclusion that since Dr Bennett was 'well used to ecclesiastical controversy', media pressure was a more plausible explanation of the suicide. He referred to two pieces of evidence for this impression:

The first was an informal remark by a leading member of the press that they would not rest until the author was found. . . . The second was a statement by one of Dr Bennett's close friends whom he had told about a £5000 offer from an unnamed newspaper for an article on the preface, with a promise to increase it to £10,000 if he would admit his authorship.

Given an invitation to comment on the matter on a live radio programme, I decided to refer to the £10,000 and to question the current explanations of Dr Bennett's suicide, which were then hardening into a widely canvassed orthodoxy.

Dr Habgood appears to be mistaken: the 'close friend' referred to here is presumably Father Philip Ursell, and the 'statement' must be the one he made in his telephone call to the Archbishop's press secretary at Bishopthorpe which we have just discussed. No other close friend, in a position to know such details for certain from first hand knowledge, was contacted on the Archbishop's behalf, or made any statement on the matter. On the strength of that statement, says the Archbishop, he decided to bring up the matter of the £10,000 offer in his broadcast on the morning of Saturday 12 December. *But, as we have seen, the telephone conversation in which the 'statement' was made did not take place until two days later, on Monday 14 December.* It was, in fact, a call made in order to check the allegation Dr Habgood had already broadcast. *The allegation was that the offer was contained in a letter actually found by the body, thus implying that it was directly and causally linked with the suicide itself.* In Dr Habgood's revised version, the letter simply disappears.

When reviewing Dr Habgood's book *Confessions of a Conservative Liberal*, in which Dr Habgood's account appears, I pointed out the strange disappearance of the letter in the suicide car. *The Mail on Sunday*, for which the review was written, telephoned Bishopthorpe to check my facts before publishing them. The Archbishop's press secretary firmly denied that Dr Habgood had said anything about a letter. *The Mail on Sunday* then acquired a transcript of the broadcast. The paper also carried out a further piece of research on Dr Habgood's book. At considerable expense, borne by the Archbishop, two pages of the book had sizeable passages pasted over with new material. According to the publishers these patches would be impossible to remove. *The Mail on Sunday*, however, achieved this feat. One of the original versions thus revealed is not without interest to this inquiry, and I publish it here for the first time. As one example of the kind of extreme and intolerable press pressure Dr Bennett had to endure, Dr Habgood offered the following:

... I am told that one well-known journalist spent three-quarters of an hour in a telephone call to Dr Bennett during which he warned him [falsely] that the Archbishop of Canterbury was about to reveal his identity.

The revised telephone call, considerably less convincing as a motivation to suicide, reads as follows:

... I am told that one well-known journalist spent over half an hour in a telephone call to Dr Bennett. Such intense press interest in him may well have aroused fear that his identity was about to be revealed.

As with the letter in the car, a highly coloured allegation has been toned down (on this occasion, in the nick of time) after belated further inquiries.

Was There a Witch-Hunt?

The second part of the *Mail's* counterattack took the form of the serious charge against part of which Dr Habgood had defended himself in his radio broadcast and in his letter to the *Telegraph*. Dr Habgood, said the Mail, had levelled 'the fiercest and fastest and most crushing attack' on Dr Bennett, and he had spearheaded the inquiry into how the preface had been written. 'Could such an attack', asked the *Mail*, 'and the prospect of such an inquisition, have played their part in helping to destroy Dr Bennett's peace of mind?' Dr Habgood's answer to the charge of leading an inquisition is given in his book. 'One curious twist to the story', he recalled later,

so far as I was concerned, was a newspaper speculation that I would be leading an investigation into the affair at a meeting of the General Synod Policy Sub-Committee which was to take place a few days after the publication of the Preface, and which Dr Bennett had himself been due to attend. (He had in fact sent his apologies before the Preface was published.) The implication of this speculation was that fear of this confrontation was one of the factors which had led him to take his life. The story was pure invention.

Dr Bennett, certainly, could have had no fear of a personal grilling by the Policy Subcommittee; as Dr Habgood rightly says, he had already indicated that he would not be present. The reason had nothing at all to do with the preface; he was to have been involved in the conduct of entrance examinations at New College all that week. The announcement that Dr Habgood was to chair the committee's inquiry into the publishing arrangements was not made until two days before the meeting itself, and after Dr Bennett's death. There is no reason to doubt that the story that Dr Habgood had demanded to chair the meeting, so that he could personally conduct an inquisition, was – as he said at the time – 'pure newspaper speculation'. It must be added, however, that in view of the press speculation about Dr Habgood's intentions, it seems extraordinary that he should have been asked to replace Dr Runcie as chairman, and in the whole catalogue of blunders that make up this extraordinary affair this is by no means the least. But there is no evidence that Dr Habgood was responsible for this, though he would certainly have been wiser to have declined the invitation; nor was he directly responsible for speculations about an institutionally conducted witch-hunt.

The story, as he said later, 'was pure invention'. But it was not without plausibility; and this plausibility had been supplied by Dr Habgood's initial reaction to the preface. And it was this, more than any committee meeting, that many people had in their minds when they thought of him as 'spearheading a total witch-hunt'. His reaction, together with the reaction of certain other members of the hierarchy, contributed to a general atmosphere in which such accusations became inevitable: and he was the most senior contributor.

All those involved made exceedingly derogatory judgements about the author's conduct and character, judgements far more stinging and uncharitable than anything in the preface itself. Garry Bennett, as we have seen, read all the newspapers in which these remarks were reported. (I have taken care only to quote from newspaper reports which I know he read. He went specially to the newsagents to buy the four quality dailies and the *Express* and *Mail* in Oxford on the Thursday and Friday; and in Cambridge on Saturday, he bought *The Times,* the *Telegraph* and the *Guardian*, and read the *Mail* at Emmanuel). We may be quite sure that he would have read their reporting of reactions to the preface thoroughly. Whether or not he was 'used to ecclesiastical controversy' (my own experience is that it is always deeply unpleasant), the 'backlash of support' was quite unprecedented and its cumulative effect, building up in his mind between Thursday and Saturday lunchtime, would have been very considerable even on the most battle-hardened veteran. Garry, however, was not by temperament a pugnacious controversialist, though as we can see in his life of Atterbury he sometimes admired those who were.

Nor was he indifferent to other people's opinion of him. He must have expected extreme annoyance: he did not expect, nor did he deserve from fellow churchmen, a reaction of such virulent personal contempt. The Bishop of St Albans called the criticisms of Dr Runcie 'a cowardly and disgraceful attack by a writer who has abused the privilege of anonymity which was accorded to him'. But as well as expressing anger and contempt, most episcopal attacks also implied knowledge of the perpetrator's identity in a way which made the hunt for that identity easier for the press. In an interview given to *The*

Times, Bishop Bill Westwood spoke of the author's 'anonymous, gutless malice' and added that the preface 'has all the hallmarks of a disappointed clergyman'. In his radio broadcast, he had hinted at knowledge of his identity: 'it's a man, I'm pretty sure, a priest, too, I think . . . middle-aged, clever. That sort of person. . . . Oxford common-room sort of stuff, that sort of spite. . . .' It could hardly be a more explicit indication of the author's name. To *The Times* he hinted that the author's identity would be discovered, and that it would be the worse for him when it was. 'Already', he said, in an astonishing remark published in *The Times* two days before Garry Bennett killed himself, 'the vultures are circling around this man'. Bishop Hugh Montefiore wrote an article in *The Times*, which appeared on the day of his death, claiming that the identity of the 'ill-intentioned' author was no mystery to him: 'those whose professions have lain in literary criticism', he wrote, 'will not find the new Preface to *Crockford's* as anonymous as its unsigned status suggests'. Dr Habgood himself told the *Telegraph* that he had suspicions about the writer's identity; his press statement itself clearly implies knowledge of this identity and throws out a few hints as to where journalists might look. (The statement, it should be recalled, was made to the Press Association, and not picked up by them from some declaration to Church people.) One hint was particularly pointed; the anonymous author, said Dr Habgood, was a 'disappointed cleric' – someone, clearly, whose hopes of office in the Church had not materialized. This was a clear pointer to Garry Bennett whose frustrations were well known and whose lack of preferment, to those who appreciated his qualities, had for some time reflected ill on those responsible for such matters.

'Sour, Scurrilous and Vindictive'

Dr Habgood's attack on the author was made in a long statement, not all of which was reported. Since the Archbishop later claimed to have been quoted in a way which distorted his intention, it is here reproduced in full. One thing is clear from the full text: that the attack on the author of the preface is overwhelmingly the most powerful part of the statement, and that anybody with the professional advice available to the Archbishop should have known that this would be seen as 'the story'. It is very hard to avoid the conclusion that this is what he intended; and if he did not intend it the inference that he did is hardly a culpable one. The Press Association put out the following statement on the morning of Thursday, 3 December, that is, on publication day:

There is a sourness and vindictiveness about the anonymous attack on the Archbishop of Canterbury which makes it clear that it is not quite the impartial review of church affairs which it purports to be. At the heart of the attack is a claim to know what goes on at private meetings of a key sub-committee and of the Crown Appointments Commission which recommends the names of bishops to the Prime Minister. If the anonymous author is a member of these bodies, then he or she is guilty of deliberately distorting the truth. If not a member, then he or she is writing with assumed confidence on the basis of guesswork. Either way, the cloak of anonymity puts those who try to answer scurrilous charges in an impossible position, and I hope the public will treat this abuse of privilege with the contempt it deserves.

Accusations about lack of leadership are easy to make, but in a body where there are few effective sanctions and which depends upon consensus, a widely embracing style of leadership may in the long run be the most effective. A recent church report said 'Clergy, particularly bishops, are familiar with the call to "give a lead" in circumstances where it is quite clear that a lead in only one preferred direction would be welcomed'. The anonymous author is careful to say nothing about the direction in which he himself is looking for a lead. In fact the entirely negative tone of his whole Preface is one of its most disturbing features. I think the Church would be wise to regard it as an outburst from a disappointed cleric who manages to pinpoint some of the real problems which face the Church of England and the Anglican Communion, but has nothing constructive to offer about the way ahead.

This was not, the Archbishop wrote later (in his essay on the Crockford preface) 'a hasty response'. He had had the text for a fortnight, and had become aware of

the extent to which much of the Preface's argument was cumulative. In trying to pinpoint the central defect of Anglicanism, the author explored and rejected a number of possibilities, and in the end focused on the leadership, and in particular on the way in which Church of England Bishops have been selected.

The passage about the operation of the Crown Appointments Commission was central to the preface's argument, wrote the Archbishop: the most destructive criticism 'concerned this supposed lack of integrity in the conduct of the Commission'. If he had left it unchallenged, this charge would have diminished confidence in the work of a vitally important body.

It is difficult to comment on the justice of Dr Bennett's analysis of the workings of the Crown Appointments Commission without being privy to its activities. Bennett himself had clearly been talking to someone who was a member of it (members and former members tend to give widely differing accounts of its activities, so far as they can be induced to say anything), and attended one meeting, after he had written the preface and before his death. His friend, Father Philip Ursell, has said that he said nothing to him to indicate a change of mind, and is sure that had actual experience invalidated his comments he would have said something to him. Here, however, we are concerned with the justice of Dr Habgood's response. It has to be said that it is difficult to see how it can be claimed that the question of the appointment of bishops in England is the lynchpin of the preface's criticisms of the Church of England in particular and modern Anglicanism in general. Far more central is Bennett's analysis of 'the decline of a distinctive Anglican theological method' (discussed on pages 116–18 below). This, Bennett calls *'the most significant change'* (my italics) in modern Anglicanism, and he goes on to analyse 'its effect on the coherence of the Communion'. Dr Habgood says that Bennett 'explored and rejected a number of possibilities' (thus focusing on the appointment of bishops). But Bennett did not 'explore and reject' this one; on the contrary, he built the preface on it. Dr Habgood entirely ignores this, and talks instead of Bennett's attempts to 'pinpoint the central defect of Anglicanism'. But this is precisely what the preface does not do. What it *actually* does is pinpoint the defects of an ecclesial organism within which 'Anglicanism' has, in his view, ceased to be the theological motivating force.

Nor, surely, can it be said that the existing system of appointing bishops is in some way beyond criticism. Undermining confidence in it was certainly part of Bennett's aim; and many would say an admirable aim. Whether or not he got the reasons for its widely perceived inadequacy right is another matter; but he was scarcely the first to express lack of confidence in the results of its work however its decisions are arrived at. Nor is it at all obvious that Bennett's analysis constitutes 'scurrilous charges' of 'lack of integrity'. If Garry Bennett gave the wrong answers (and it is perfectly permissible for anyone to speculate on such matters), he asked questions which need to be asked: 'Who, in fact, does manage the system and what kind of an episcopate has it created?' Dr Bennett's real crime was to state the crashingly obvious: that 'behind the secrecy . . . a complex power-game is played out with momentous consequences for the Church of England'. His description of what he believed to happen behind closed doors has been challenged by members of the commission. But they hardly amount to 'charges'; rather, they are a description of the 'group dynamics' of committee decisions which will be familiar to anyone who has had any involvement in such decisions. One final comment seems inevitable: that secrecy may be in the interests of those interested in exercising power in the Church, but it is hard to see how a little more openness in the process of selection could be in any way harmful to the rest of us.

The real question to be answered here, however, is this: was Dr Habgood justified, because of the passage in the preface containing Dr Bennett's speculations about the Crown Appointments Commission, in saying that there was 'sourness and vindictiveness' about the criticisms which made it 'clear that it [was] not quite the impartial review of church affairs which it purports to be'? Was he justified in saying that he hoped the public would 'treat this abuse of privilege with the contempt it deserves', a hope which necessarily extended this contempt to the author himself? Was he right to dismiss the charges by imputing the personal motives of revenge (this is what 'vindictiveness' inescapably implies) of a 'disappointed cleric', who used the preface to get his own back on Dr Runcie for his own lack of preferment? Were the media so very wrong after his death to present Dr Bennett as being (to quote Dr Habgood's mocking summary of their coverage) 'a misunderstood prophet who had dared to criticize an all-powerful establishment, been savaged by it, and died in despair at a Church which rejected him'? Was this really, again in Dr Habgood's words, so very 'psychologically implausible'?

What Sort of Church Does This?

Certainly it seemed entirely plausible to this writer at the time, steeped as I was in the same recent press reports that Garry had so painfully worked his way through during the three days that intervened between the publication of the preface and his cold and lonely death in a concrete garage. I now know more than I did: that by the evening of the first day, he had come to feel that he was finished in the Church of England; that he had preserved in his diary a small nugget from the nightmare of exposure and disgrace that now threatened him. After the inquest in which that diary entry was read out, as we all walked out into the street, someone said, 'What kind of Church is it in which someone can have such terrible fear of exposure after simply speaking his mind?' One of the journalists covering the inquest answered, 'What sort of a Church is it in which you need to be anonymous in the first place?'

They are dreadful questions to which there is a dreadful answer. For though the press could encompass the exposure, it had no power to bring about the rejection and coldness which would have followed it. I felt then, as a priest of the Church of England, and I shall always feel, that he died because an institution which is supposed to mediate to the world the love and reconciling power of Christ had itself become 'sour and vindictive'. Just how sour and vindictive it would be to him, he had already seen. 'Already the vultures are circling around this man', a bishop of his own Church had told *The Times*.

Why not forget it all? Why not allow the wounds to heal over? The answer is that when a wound heals without having first been cleaned out, it becomes septic. The divisions within the Church of England have at their roots the feeling that those who swim against the tide have been 'marginalized'. It was one message of the preface itself, and Garry Bennett's death was to be the ultimate symbol of that marginalization.

So it is fitting that the memory of those days should not fade, at any rate, not yet. Self-knowledge is the beginning of wisdom. It is also, for Christians, the beginning of penitence. We need to know what we are capable of and the *Crockford's* affair showed what the Church of England was capable of. Memories are short: but this is one memory which should be indelible, for those who forget their mistakes are doomed to repeat them.

Everybody remembers, so it is said, what they were doing when they were told of the death of President Kennedy. Two men could not have been more different; but for many members of the Church of England, there is now another moment like that, perpetually remembered, as though frozen by some strange photography of the mind – the moment they heard of the death of Gareth Bennett. It was one of those moments after which nothing is ever quite the same again.

After I heard the news, I took my small daughter to school, then, with my wife, I walked until my mind was clear again. Then I went home and wrote an article for the *Daily Telegraph* with which I now conclude this chapter – not, I hope, out of self-indulgence, but because the response to it has been, over the months, not only a comfort to me but a revelation. Wherever I have been since, in England or in North America, someone has mentioned it and has told me that I spoke for them. So I return now to my own personal photograph of that terrible moment, for I have good reason to know that I recorded widely held feelings about the modern institutional workings of liberal Anglicanism which have not yet been taken seriously, and which will not be assuaged by soothing words and a few strategically placed 'conservative' appointments. Things, of course, are more complicated than they seemed to me in that moment; nevertheless, what I thought I saw then, I still believe I saw truly in all essentials. And now the rewriting of history has begun, by those who for a time remained silent but now have returned to the battle, sneering at Garry Bennett's legacy, all the while speaking of peace and reconciliation and the 'comprehensiveness of the Church of England'. It is important that we do not forget how it really was; for it is a characteristic of the human mind that those who have lost their memory are psychologically incapable of moving into the future.

Broken by the Church he Served

From the Daily Telegraph, Wednesday 8 December 1987

Yesterday morning I walked through the Oxford University Parks. It was a crisp clear morning of stunning beauty. Every twig and every blade of grass was etched in frost; the sun shone blindingly through the willows by the Cherwell. I was trying to come somehow to terms with the death of a friend who had taken his own life. Across the river were the fields through which, every morning, Garry Bennett walked to his rooms in New College, where for nearly three decades he had been a fellow. It was a morning to raise the spirits of the most depressed. But it had come too late for him.

And I thought of the Church of which he and I were priests. Of how it could be that it had come to this: that for speaking what he and very many others believed to be the truth about the current state of the Church of England, he should now lie cold and dead. For now I knew that he was indeed, as so many had surmised, the anonymous author of the *Crockford's* preface which had aroused such a vitriolic response.

Reading the preface again, one is struck by two things. Firstly, that the supposedly 'vindictive attack' on Dr Runcie is actually nothing of the kind. His remarks on the Archbishop occupy only a few paragraphs in a very long essay; and his undoubtedly critical remarks are balanced by others more positive. Dr Runcie, he wrote, is a 'notable holder of the primacy'. He referred to the Archbishop's 'intelligence, warmth and . . . formidable capacity for hard work'. His speeches and addresses he characterized as 'thoughtful, witty and persuasive'. Secondly, even the critical remarks have to be seen not as personally dismissive, but as part of a wider analysis. He deeply believed that the Church of England had lost its way. And he saw Dr Runcie's primacy as reflecting rather than causing this loss of direction. But he and Dr Runcie remained friends; and it will be a source of consolation to the Archbishop that it was he who gave Dr Bennett his last communion when he visited Pusey House on the Sunday before these tragic events.

He was devoted to the Church of England, and had been for some time pessimistic about its present condition. But it was the violence of the backlash against his essay that brought him to such despair, and particularly the injustice of the accusation by certain senior prelates (which was picked up and parroted obsessively by the rougher and less principled newspapers) that he was a 'disappointed' man who in a 'sour and vindictive' way had indulged in a 'cowardly' attack on the Archbishop of Canterbury. The lie stuck; and on Saturday it became too much to bear. He was not, I believe, guilty of the sin of self-murder; rather, 'the balance of his mind', in the old formula, 'was disturbed' by the intolerable pain (magnified and sustained by the popular press) of the deep injustice done him by fellow churchmen, in language infinitely more hurtful and violent than any he had used in his preface.

It is undoubtedly true that he was disappointed that his gifts had not been better used by the Church. Those who knew the quality of his mind and the sincerity and depth of his faith had expected that the kind of senior position in the hierarchy suitable to a scholar priest of his distinction – Durham, perhaps, or Winchester – would long ago have been offered him. But he was certainly not bitter: and the notion that he could ever be accused of the squalid meanness of seeking revenge for lack of preferment would (until it happened) have seemed incredible to him.

Garry Bennett is dead. Nothing will bring him back. But it is important that he should not have died for nothing. What needs now to be placed under scrutiny is the context in which his tragedy unfolded. For it has to be understood that this is no isolated act, whose significance is confined within its own boundaries. Garry Bennett's life and death are representative of something that has happened to the Church of England. His death was the product of a terrible and loveless rejection; a rejection which in less finally tragic ways has been felt by many others who have spoken out against current tendencies within the Church.

The Church of England has a reputation for comprehensiveness and tolerance. This reputation is now, it has to be said clearly, totally undeserved. Those who do not accept the beliefs of the liberal modernist establishment now ruling the Church of England have been (to use 'liberation' theology jargon) 'marginalized'. Granted, the odd low-key Anglo-Catholic or Evangelical slips through on to the bishop's bench. But very few priests who do not toe the line (particularly on certain contentious issues) will be allowed into positions where they can influence events.

I offer one story (among many in a substantial collection) to illustrate the kind of thing I mean. The position of principal of a theological college was advertised sometime during the last three years (I am being deliberately imprecise). A priest with ideal qualifications applied for the vacancy. He had several degrees, including an Oxford doctorate. He had taught theology at university level. He had been a parish priest so successful that his church had to be enlarged to hold the congregation. A substantial number of vocations to the priesthood emerged from this congregation. Some weeks after applying, he received a telephone call from the bishop who was chairman of the college governors. The bishop was complimentary; he had, he said, rarely seen such ideal qualifications. But there was one thing he needed to know. What were the priest's views on the ordination of women to the priesthood? The priest said he was against it, but was strongly committed to women's ministry. Not only did he not get the job: he was not even called for interview.

Such stories are not isolated incidents; they are the norm. Few of the laity realize how far the rot has set in. The illiberality and the political ruthlessness of the so-called 'liberals' of the Church of England have now become a profound scandal. And the latest manifestation of this scandal has been the backlash against the *Crockford's* preface.

No one who actually reads the preface can be in any doubt that its real target is not the Archbishop of Canterbury. Rather, it is a profoundly intellectually impressive analysis of what is wrong with the Church as a whole. It is a portrait of a Church whose unrepresentative leaders have turned against Scripture and Tradition as their chief guides and now rely principally on the ephemeral wisdom of the passing age; men who now have to maintain their position not by persuasion but by political manoeuvres and the stealthy exercise of power. It is evident that after the *Crockford's* preface hit Fleet Street the tactic of the liberal establishment was to distract attention from its analysis by concentrating on the comparatively insignificant portion of it dealing with Dr Runcie, and by creating an artificial scandal over this supposedly 'disgraceful' and 'scurrilous attack'.

One newspaper last week quoted me as saying that there would be a witch-hunt over the *Crockford's* preface. I was right; and the witch-hunt has now claimed its principal victim. Now, this year's preface must be read, marked, learned and inwardly digested (rather than being misrepresented). Its lessons must be absorbed and not turned into a 'nine days wonder'. Many of the best minds in the Church of England accept its analysis: there was no shortage of feasible candidates when the press were hunting for the author.

There needs now to be a great revolt against the ruling dispensation within the Church of England. Garry Bennett's preface could be its manifesto. At the very least it will be his monument: the monument of a brave, distinguished, and prayerful priest whose heart in the end was broken by the Church he served.

PART TWO

FOUR

The Theology of Pontius Pilate: Anti-dogmatism and the Growth of Intolerance

What is truth? said jesting Pilate, and would not stay for an answer.
— Francis Bacon

The attention of the press during the *Crockford's* affair was not centred entirely on questions of personality: Who wrote the preface? Who commissioned it? Was Dr Runcie really (to recall one elegant *Daily Mirror* headline) 'a wimp'? Did Dr Habgood lead a witch-hunt? The underlying problems of the Church of England were also seriously considered by some in the media even while the controversy was at its height, and in the weeks and months after Dr Bennett's death they became the focus for a real debate within the Church. In the media *The Times* led the field. Already, by the day after publication, it had moved beyond the criticisms of Dr Runcie. The headline of its first leader on Thursday 4 December was 'The Deeper Problem'. The preface, it said, was not only about Dr Runcie; it was about 'the nature and identity of modern Anglicanism':

To accuse Dr Runcie of indecision raises the question: what is he supposed to be decisive about? The problem is not that there are too few answers. It is that there are too many. Anglicanism has lost the single identity which flowed primarily from uniformity of worship and from the doctrines stated or implied in that worship – doctrines contained in the Book of Common Prayer.

... the removal of the one central pillar, a Book of Common Prayer imposed throughout the Church by an Act of Uniformity, has left the Anglican credal and liturgical edifice standing with no visible means of support, liable to collapse under its own weight. It is that which alarms the anonymous writer of the *Crockford's* Preface above all; and it is serious enough for even a good and loyal churchman to employ any and every means at his disposal to try to get the Church to address itself to so grave a peril.

The preface, it became more and more perceived, was a serious analysis of the malaise of the Church of England in particular, and of Anglicanism, at least in Anglo-Saxon countries, in general. It became clear as the weeks passed that the backlash against it was not only provoked by the 'attack' on Dr Runcie. The preface had opened out the debate on the nature and prospects of contemporary Anglicanism for an audience which had previously been thought incompetent to be involved in it, giving a focus to a general unease among many who had felt their feelings to be ignored. This was far from welcome to those who had dominated the debate for twenty years: the *Crockford's* affair revealed as much as anything else the icy élitism of the liberal establishment.

The Prague Spring of 1988

Bennett's general analysis was now dealt with in one of two ways. On the one hand, it was dismissed as too obvious to warrant real attention; obvious but 'negative' and therefore to be ignored. Those responsible for the Church's leadership, it was implied, were well aware of the problems, and had been wrestling with them for years. On the other hand, Bennett's criticisms were, to use his own ironic borrowing from the vocabulary of liberation theology, 'marginalized' by representing them as supported only by a class of Anglican malcontent to be found on the 'fringes' of the church.

It became obvious at an early stage, however, that the preface was more than an isolated dissident's protest. In a Gallup Poll of the clergy, taken about two weeks after publication, it emerged that of those who had read the preface and were prepared to comment (about 75 per cent of those asked), about twice as many supported its broad analysis as rejected it. This was particularly significant in view of the clear loyalist swing among the same sample group behind Dr Runcie himself. The clergy sampled demonstrated a very consistent orthodoxy on such questions as the Resurrection and the Virgin Birth, and the authority of Scripture and Tradition.

The liberals, for the moment, seemed on the defensive, and they remained so for some months to come. In the wake of the February Synod, indeed, it was possible for an article to be published by a commentator as well-informed as Clifford Longley of *The Times*, under the headline 'Now that Liberalism has Lost'. 'Before Dr Bennett's shocking death', wrote Longley on 22 February,

the Anglo-Catholics and the liberals were bombarding each other with roughly equal effect. Then suddenly the liberal guns fell silent, and the conservatives had it all their own way. When the issues finally came to the Synod earlier this month, Dr Bennett's dissenting protest had mysteriously transformed itself into the consensus.

Longley then quoted Canon George Austin's 'neat demolition' in the recent Synod of the view that liberalism in the Church occupied the moderate middle ground in Anglican churchmanship. 'Church-manship', wrote Longley,

is too easily regarded as a simple spectrum with Anglo-Catholics at one end, Evangelicals at the other, and liberals in the centre, he argues. Hence, a liberal is assumed to be a more acceptable leader to the greatest number. Canon Austin has proposed as an alternative truer geometry, a triangle with liberal, Evangelical, and Anglo-Catholic at the three corners.

The headline 'Now that Liberalism has Lost', though some had their doubts, did not seem extravagant in the atmosphere of the time. There was something like a 'Prague Spring' for conservatives. One of them was appointed to the Deanery of St Paul's, for years a redoubt of 1960s' liberalism; Canon Austin, the hammer of the Archbishop of York, was appointed to high office in a bold stroke, by the Archbishop himself. This appointment was greeted with cynicism by some; the Archbishop, they said, was trying to mend his fences. Others, more charitable, saw it as a sign that the Archbishop was a bigger man than they had supposed. But most saw it as a portent, as a sign that a real and permanent shift had taken place. For Garry Bennett's supporters it seemed for a time that he had not died entirely in vain. One of them, on leaving New College chapel after Dr Bennett's Requiem, had been heard to say that he had just attended what would be seen in years to come as either the funeral of the Church of England or the beginning of its Resurrection, depending on whether 'they' had learned the lesson of the preface and its terrible aftermath. And, for a time, it really seemed as though they had.

Dr Habgood Strikes Back

The post-*Crockford's* advance of the conservatives, however, had not been accepted within the liberal ascendancy, whose silent retreat had been merely tactical. Dr Habgood might, during this period, have appointed one of his critics over the *Crockford's* affair to high office, but he was far from having undergone a change of heart or of mind. This was his lofty dismissal of the preface in *Confessions of a Conservative Liberal*, written a bare five months after Garry Bennett's death:

When the ugliest passions and distortions have been cleared out of the way the question still remains, Why did this donnish and predominantly negative analysis of the state of Anglicanism arouse such a response?

This fundamental question was not answered, by Dr Habgood at least. He went on to say, in effect, that the problems addressed by Dr Bennett were familiar enough to the Church's rulers, and that those who found his analysis fresh and thought-provoking were simply showing what outsiders they were:

Unkind cracks at the Archbishop of Canterbury can produce media headlines, but there has to be something more substantial if an essay is to be labelled 'prophetic' and 'profound'.

I find these adjectives puzzling. Dr Bennett wrote well and much of his analysis was acute and touched on real, if familiar, problems. For many readers such a trenchant exposure of them was clearly new and exciting, but for those of us who had been wrestling with these same problems for years there was disappointment that the author had gone no further than making complaints, and had failed to use his considerable theological skill in advancing the arguments constructively.

Dr Habgood's counterattack against the ideas of the preface constituted a chilling demonstration of indifference to the feelings of many ordinary Anglicans, who had responded so strongly to the preface not – as Dr Habgood implied – because the ideas it expressed were new to them, but because at last they had been voiced from a platform and in circumstances which made it impossible for them to be brushed aside in the usual way. In the preface, Bennett had found a missile which had pierced, for a time, even the massive complacency of the Church's ruling caste. Now, they were asked to accept that 'the author had gone no further than making complaints'.

Could the *Crockford's* preface of 1987 really be dismissed as easily as that? If that were so, how was Dr Habgood's own question to be answered: *Why did it arouse such a response?* Could this reaction really have been evoked by a mere list of complaints, which conveyed no positive countervailing vision of the Church? It began to appear almost that there were two texts; or two kinds of Anglican between whom there was an absolute breakdown in communication: those, on the one hand, who broadly accepted the new liberal and bureaucratic status quo – conceived in the 1960s, now apparently immovably entrenched; and those, on the other, who did not accept it but who did nevertheless have a real and positive vision of what the Church should be, a vision which they recognized as the basis of the criticisms in the preface. The first group simply did not perceive the preface's spiritual and theological foundations, either because they could not or because they would not.

Certainly Dr Habgood's reading of the preface, on his own evidence, seems to have been selective. Even at the time, his concentration on the brief passage in the preface on the workings of the Crown Appointments Commission when everyone else was talking about the specific criticisms of Dr Runcie, seemed somewhat eccentric. How did he read the text as a whole? This is how Dr Habgood later summarized the preface's argument:

The Preface [he wrote] had three main strands:
1. A critique of the Anglican Communion for avoiding hard questions about authority;
2. Criticisms of the General Synod and its committee structure for failing to provide a coherent policy for the Church of England;
3. The identification of a powerful liberal establishment determined to upset the traditional balance of the Church.

Not discussed in Dr Habgood's essay was the real keynote theme of Bennett's preface which implicitly permeates his whole argument. That the woes of Anglicanism had to do with a crisis of identity; that the crisis had to be addressed theologically; and that until the foundations of Anglicanism had been made firm again (rather like those of York Minster) the builders' work was in vain that builded it. The entire analysis depends on the theological context, which Dr Bennett establishes clearly in the preface, but which Dr Habgood fails to address. It may be, indeed, that he does not even mention it; it is not entirely clear to what he is referring in his casual aside that it 'managed to put sharply and succinctly what many people knew already, but failed to offer any real help in suggesting viable alternatives'. This dismissive judgement is offered of what Dr Habgood regarded as 'the best part' of the preface.

The Decline of Classical Anglicanism

Is it in fact true that Bennett offers no viable alternative to late twentieth century Anglicanism? Only if we dismiss the possibility of returning to our own roots, and of learning from tradition. Anglicanism has lost direction, the preface says in effect, because it has ceased to *be* Anglicanism:

Of all the changes that have taken place within Anglicanism over recent decades, *the most significant* is the decline of a distinctive Anglican theological method. [My italics.]

This seems, at first, the kind of statement which confirms the ordinary Anglican in the pew in his view that academics are cut off from real life. To him, more visible developments (whether he approves of them or not), like the virtual disappearance of the Book of Common Prayer, seem far more significant. The average church-goer is well aware that the services have all changed and that there seems to be more politics in public statements by bishops than there used to be; he probably has a feeling that the Church has opted out of giving a lead in questions of personal morality. But that something called 'theological method' has anything to do with the current malaise of the Church is an idea not widely entertained.

Nevertheless, the disappearance of the prayer book and the

collapse of the traditional Anglican way of doing theology are intimately connected. Prayer and doctrine are closely bound up in the Anglican tradition: *Lex orandi, lex credendi.* The ordinary Anglican has never had a markedly speculative bent; nevertheless, the way a Church does its thinking about God in the end tells us what kind of Church it is; here we will read its character, however dry and overintellectual such an approach may at first seem. It may be, indeed, that the very fact that Anglican theology has in recent years taken such matters out of the normal ambit of ordinary believers says more about Anglicanism's current sickness than anything else.

For, in the end, thinking about God and praying to him are only seen as radically different activities when something has gone wrong; when they separate out completely (as in much modernist theology) what has occurred is something like the curdling of mayonnaise. Thus, when Bennett reminds us in the preface of the familiar triangular formula identifying the Anglican method as 'giving attention to Scripture, Tradition and Reason to establish doctrine', he goes on to emphasize that this is no merely cerebral activity: 'the context of such theological study', he insists, 'was the corporate life of the Church and the end was to deepen its spirituality'.

This tripartite balance of Scripture, Reason and Tradition was the special product of history, a fact which has rooted Anglican thinking about God firmly in the ways in which Anglicans have actually known Him in the unfolding story of His Church. The emphasis on Scripture has been guarded particularly by Evangelicals; the emphasis on Tradition by Catholics. Human reason, in its proper place, has been recognized by both alike, and as an autonomous principle has been specially stressed (together with human experience) by theological liberals. The classical Anglican churchman derived his theology and spirituality from all of these principles (though his understanding of the word 'reason' would have been very different from that of a modernist) and would not even have bothered to separate them in his mind. 'Our special character', wrote William Temple in 1930,

and, as we believe, our peculiar contribution to the Universal Church, arises from the fact that, owing to historic circumstances, we have been enabled to combine in our one fellowship the traditional Faith and Order of the Catholic Church with that immediacy of approach to God through Christ to which the Evangelical Churches especially bear witness, and freedom of intellectual inquiry, whereby the correlation of the Christian revelation and advancing knowledge is constantly effected.

The view of theology reflected by this classical approach to Anglican divinity, says Bennett, still appears in official Anglican reports and archiepiscopal addresses. But its last real exponent was Archbishop Michael Ramsey, 'whose many scholarly studies represent a last stand before the citadel fell to the repeated assaults of a younger generation of academics'.

The 'essential characteristic' of this new generation, says Bennett, is its dislike of combining the role of theologian and churchman, and its wish to study the Fathers of the Church and Scripture itself not for their power to evoke or enrich faith, but simply as the raw material for a scholarship exercised in an unashamedly secular fashion. The process is effectively and concisely summed up in one of the chapter titles of J. L. Houlden's book *Connections* (1986), 'The Alienation of Theology from Religion', and it is a process of which, it is clear, Houlden himself firmly approves. This 'alienation' has, we may observe, a great deal to do with the decay in Western theology of an understanding of faith as being itself a means of perception (and therefore as necessary for theological reflection as the faculty of sight for a painter). For Houlden, faith is the enemy of objectivity. Thus, 'theological study and religious commitment' are seen by him – self-evidently it would seem – as 'psychological contraries'. This is, it needs to be said, a modern understanding, until the present age unknown to the Christian tradition (though of course fundamental to the atheistic humanist view of religious belief).

Living Amid the Ruins

This in itself would, for Houlden, be no argument against any such perception. His book *Connections* is, of course, cited by Bennett in the preface as representative of modernist theology precisely for its rejection of the notion of 'living in a tradition', and for its approving description of the way in which the modern Church has been distanced from what until the present age have been thought to be its necessary prescriptive sources. 'It would seem', Bennett comments in a memorable passage, 'that modern man must live amid the ruins of past doctrinal and ecclesiastical systems, looking to the scriptures only for themes and apprehensions which may inform his individual exploration of the mystery of God'. And he goes on to comment, surely accurately, that 'it is doubtful whether such views, explicitly stated, are acceptable to most modern Anglicans.' It is necessary to add further, perhaps, that the ruins are the result, not of structural collapse but of revolutionary military bombardment. Classical Anglicanism has been displaced from Anglican seminaries not because it was intellectually exhausted but because it was, in effect, forcibly excluded.

It is easy to see why this retreat of classical Anglican divinity – the most obvious sign of which is the reluctance by the Church's leaders either to define doctrine or to insist on any particular belief in those they ordain to the Church's ministry (except, in some provinces, belief in the ordination of women) – should have brought in its wake such widespread uncertainty and loss of morale. For it was a doctrinal method which could operate at any level of intellectual attainment; it was as viable in the parishes as in the universities.

Unlike what has replaced it as the intellectual staple of the clergy, it was capable of sustaining a popular teaching, and nourishing a popular piety. The Lambeth Quadrilateral, one of its classic formulations, was no mere formal document; its claims to be an authoritative statement derived from a real sense that the Church is the guardian of a revelation which it is compelled to make real for its people, not by superior packaging but by discerning real and viable first principles. Take the following, from Bishop Walter Carey's little book for lay use, *The Church of England's Hour* (1946). Carey sees the Church's ineffectiveness as deriving not from any incapacity to cater for modern needs but from its failure to be itself. What that self consists of is not for him in doubt; there is no identity crisis here. Carey's teaching is based on the Lambeth Quadrilateral, which he calls here 'the four fundamentals':

I think we clergy are often very *ignorant and confused*. I was and am. First we are either ignorant of or afraid of our own principles by which we entirely stand or fall. The four fundamentals (Bible, Creeds, Apostolic Ministry, and Sacraments) are often treated as if they could be ignored or waived or bartered away for some sentimental reason. They cannot be so treated. Ignore or betray *any* of them and the Church of England, Catholic and reformed, is dead and scripture violated. It is unprincipled and therefore doomed. Let no bishop or priest or layman make any mistake about that.

The 'four fundamentals', for Carey, *'and their full content* [my italics] – come to us from Christ and from the authority of that living Christian organism, the Catholic Church'. The hearty confidence of such as Bishop Carey may have generated a teaching manner which today can, at times, seem slightly comic; but it is not easy to be sure that less robust episcopal demands, or a more tentative theology, are as capable of bringing salvation to modern man in his confusion. Certainly, Bishop Carey makes no concessions to the intellectually squeamish:

I think Rugby football is such a good photograph of the Christian religion: a coach to advise, a captain to lead, an enemy to beat, rules to keep, boundaries to keep within or else all fun goes out of the game; discipline, obedience, efficiency, skill – all that is common to both.

It is easy to smile at such unselfconscious certitudes. But if Anglicanism, forty years later, is suffering an identity crisis, it is because Anglicans – whether in the university, the seminary, the rectory or the pew – no longer know what they believe or what they are. The notion that any irreducible minimum of faith (let alone of discipline) is required of them has largely disappeared except in certain kinds of parish which increasingly operate as refugee centres.

The problem is that this uncertainty appears actually to be thought desirable by those whose responsibility it is to lead the Church. The very search for certainty is itself represented as a sign of immaturity, and there is a particular mistrust of those who – like C. S. Lewis – are successful in making viable for our age the notion of a received tradition which does not need radical reconstruction. Lewis has been a mainstay, not only for lay Christians seeking intelligent Christian nurture in an age of intellectual confusion, but also for many of those who have had to undergo the official processing provided by Anglican theological colleges and seminaries, but who were determined nevertheless to hang on to their faith.

It is precisely Lewis's intellectual success in defending the notion of a revelation which still has real concreteness and authority that makes him dangerous to those who need to make the current uncertainties seem somehow desirable, in the name of some vague notion of intellectual integrity. Lewis's crime is to suggest that there is any such thing as certainty to be had, even in a limited way, and even after such a rigorous intellectual pilgrimage as his own. For the liberal churchman, the search for absolutes is of all things to be avoided. 'Has it occurred to you', said Dr Habgood in a television interview in December 1988, 'that the lust for certainty may be a sin?' Jesus, he said, upsets our certainties; this is the meaning of the Christian life. Precisely so. He upsets all our human certainties. But Jesus does not say that there is no certainty, or that we should not search for such things. He upsets our human certainties by putting His own certainties in their place. One way of putting this is to say that he replaces merely human wisdom, shifting and uncertain, by revelation. 'I am the way, the truth and the life', He said. 'I am', not 'I may turn out to be, once all the alternatives have been considered'. 'He who *believes* in me shall have eternal life.'

Anglicanism, of course, has always been wary of too elaborate or definite a doctrinal structure to safeguard such belief. It has nevertheless always been clear enough as to what the essentials consisted of; and it has seen the necessity for defining them clearly and economically. 'There is ... general agreement', wrote Archbishop Cyril Garbett of York in the 1940s, 'that some statement of belief is necessary. No society whether religious or secular can hold together unless its members are united by some common convictions and aims. A Church with no statement of faith could not exist.'

A Pattern of Belief

What is at stake here is, of course, more than some mere checklist of assumptions required for membership. Certainly, the Creeds, for example, have been seen as a kind of yardstick of belief. Bishop Charles Gore, for all that he is now regarded by theological liberals as being one of them, insisted that his clergy believe in all the articles of the Creed:

We must be very gentle with scrupulous and anxious consciences. We must be very patient with men under the searching and purifying trial of doubt. But when a man has once arrived at the steady conviction that he cannot honestly affirm a particular and unambiguous article of the creed, in the sense that the Church of which he is a member undoubtedly gives to it, the public mind of the Church must tell him that he has a right to the freedom of his opinion, but that he can no longer, consistently with public honour, hold the office of the ministry.

But Gore is talking here about something more than any merely intellectual assent. It was only possible to regard the Creeds as a touchstone for the exercise of priesthood because they were more than a set of theological propositions. Another dimension was also involved, nearer the heart of the origins of priesthood itself. And to understand what that means, to enter into that dimension, we have to be part of the living spiritual tradition of which the Creeds are both the expression and the safeguard. It is a tradition in which the spiritual life and intellectual understanding were inextricably bound up, not 'psychological opposites', but mutually necessary parts of a unified enterprise. Here is Michael Ramsey addressing young men about to be ordained priest. He is speaking as one who believes that certain doctrines, handed down, must be assented to; but in no dry or obscurantist spirit:

We have given to us the pattern of belief set out in the Creed, from 'God the Father Almighty' right through to 'the resurrection of the body and the life of the world to come'. Do not treat the doctrines of the Creed as a string of impersonal items, like a row of bricks picked out of a box. Treat them as doctrines of Christ, as so many aspects of the mystery of which he is the centre. Thus the Father Almighty declares his almighty power most chiefly in showing mercy and pity – in the mercy and pity of Christ's Incarnation. Again, the Holy Catholic Church is Christ's family, Christ's household. The Communion of Saints is the company of those who reflect Christ's glory, and heaven is the enjoyment of Christ's radiance. See Christian doctrine in this way, and it will make all the difference to your study of it. Study gets very irksome if you think of it as adding more and more items of knowledge to your bag. Think of study rather as being refreshed from the deep sparkling well of truth which is Christ himself. Study in this way does not stuff our already over-stuffed minds. Rather does it refresh us with new understanding and wonder. I love the phrase in the Ember collect 'replenish them with the truth of Thy doctrine'.

To pass from Michael Ramsey to Houlden's *Connections* is to perceive the decline, not simply of spiritual vitality but also of understanding, that has occurred with the collapse of the classical Anglican approach. It is also to understand the gulf between theologians and the faithful that opened up with the advent of the new generation of theologians in the 1960s, a gulf which coincides with a new sense that the Christian revelation is increasingly inaccessible now that the formularies which had always been the basis of teaching, as in the catechism of the 1662 prayer book, have been declared non-definitive.

For Houlden, for example, the Creeds may be seen as 'useful pointers, in certain contexts, to that which lies deeper'. But they are emphatically not what they are for Michael Ramsey, a 'pattern of belief' which is *given to us* by God through His Church. The Creeds for Houlden are a 'propositional expression of belief' which 'began either as a summary of belief, useful for purposes of baptism where such a summary was required, or as a set of defining articles to stand by in case of challenge or uncertainty'. And he continues by asserting that '*the continued usefulness of this kind of expression of belief is now restricted to the former role*' (my italics).

This stands in sharp contrast to the attitude of Gore, who we have seen using the Creeds precisely as 'a set of defining articles to stand by in case of challenge or uncertainty'. Gore's understanding depended on the traditional Anglican notion that there were certain beliefs that could be regarded as essential, to be distinguished from those that were inessential, mere accretions which had – correctly or incorrectly – been inferred from the original deposit of faith. And those essentials were knowable, and had been defined in objective form. The Creeds, for example, were, for Gore, expressed 'in terms which are deliberately unambiguous'.

Gore eighty years ago, and Archbishop Garbett forty years ago, could argue from the background of 'a general agreement that some statement of belief is necessary' and the assumption that without some such defined understanding the Church could not exist. This 'general agreement' has certainly declined among theologians, but it is still widespread at a popular level – among those, that is to say, who would find it difficult to understand how it could be that Christian doctrine has become an academic speciality governed only by secular intellectual disciplines and ambitions. For them, Christian 'doctrine' (i.e. teaching) is given by revelation and guarded by tradition; it is articulated for their own generation by the Church of which they are members. The business of the leaders of the Church is – or so they suppose – to say what Christian doctrine actually consists of, and how it affects them.

The Refusal of Clarity

For those who determine the theological attitudes prevailing among the Church's leaders today, however, this widespread assumption is an embarrassment, and those who continue to show such expectations are shown scant respect. Demands, for instance, that the Doctrine Commission of the Church of England's General Synod should actually see it as part of its function to define doctrine – to produce, in Archbishop Garbett's words, 'some statement of belief' – are treated with ill-disguised irritation by the new establishment that has grown up to defend the new uncertainties.

Those who do expect clear teaching from their teachers are patronized as neurotic and unreflective, unable to cope emotionally with the necessary uncertainties of the life of faith. Hence, the chairman of the Commission, introducing its 1987 report, felt it necessary to rebut 'those who depend for their own sustenance, temperamentally as well as mentally, on something very cut and dried. Those with a leaning towards fundamentalism', he loftily asserted, 'will feel let down'.

More than one member of the Commission, nevertheless, confided to this writer at the time that they did feel there was a need for doctrine to be defined, and that the report was somewhat remote from the current needs of the Church. One of them was Gareth Bennett himself, who, although his name was appended to the final document, had in fact ceased to attend the Commission's meetings some time before in disillusion.

Nevertheless, by the standard of reports issued by the Commission over previous decades, that published in 1987 was already showing distinct signs of a growing pressure from the grass roots for something more continuous with Anglican – and Christian – tradition. Its assumptions were certainly very different from those of the most famous Doctrine Commission report, *Christian Believing*, produced in 1976 under the chairmanship of Professor Maurice

Wiles. This was a collection of essays which faithfully represented the cultural relativism which by then had come to dominate Anglican theological reflection. The report was widely felt by ordinary Anglicans to be unacceptable, and the then Archbishop of Canterbury, Donald Coggan, made sure it never reached General Synod for open debate. The Commission itself was disbanded and reconstituted with a new membership.

But this belated rearguard action could not stem the tide; it was all too little, too late. The underlying assumptions of *Christian Believing* have continued to determine the intellectual formation of the Church's leaders up to the present day. As Bennett puts it in the preface,

... the movement in theology which it represented was not thus to be set aside. English faculties of theology are now part of an international scholarly enterprise which has moved steadily away from the churches. . . . If Anglicans once did their theology through a study of the historical experience of the Christian community that seems no longer to be the case. . . . While such a tendency is understandable in theological faculties in modern universities, its effect is most notable in Anglican theological colleges which have now trained a whole generation of priests with a minimal knowledge of classical Anglican divinity or its methods. Clergy without a sense of there being some authority in the historic experience of the Church may well come to think that theology is the latest fashionable theory of theologians.

Two years after he had produced *Christian Believing*, Maurice Wiles contributed, with others of his school, to a now notorious collection of essays entitled *The Myth of God Incarnate*. Both for its supporters and its detractors, the consequence of the essayists' conclusions could, in the words of Professor Adrian Hastings, 'hardly be other than the necessity of winding up historic Christianity, with a minimum of pain to all concerned, as unacceptable to the modern mind'.

To live within a given historic tradition, this school of thought assumed, is not only spiritually immature, but intellectually dishonest. It is to narrow the mind and to refuse to accept the multi-faceted nature of Christian truth and the challenge of modern knowledge; it is also to reduce God to our own intellectual capacity for defining him.

Such assumptions, however, could not be sustained, or even

argued plausibly for very long, outside the remote academic fast-nesses where they originated; certainly, they have attracted little support when openly expressed. It has been clear even to relatively uninstructed minds that to live within the assumptions of the biblical revelation has not in fact historically led to a tradition which has extinguished the intellectual quest for truth: modern science, Galileo notwithstanding, is an essentially Christian phenomenon. As the nuclear physicist Dr Peter Hodgson puts it, there is 'a living organic continuity between the Christian revelation and modern science; Christianity provided just those beliefs that are essential for science, and the moral climate that encouraged its growth'. Nor has the Christian tradition down the ages done other than nurture, more deeply than any liberal modernism conceivably could, the spiritual quest for a God who is seen as being infinitely beyond our-selves.

It is, of course, necessary to say that no human language can ever do justice to the bottomless mystery of God. But it does not follow that because we must say this we can say nothing definite about Him at all, or that to define what we believe is to 'depend ... temperamentally on something very cut and dried'. Nor does a coherently delineated faith preclude tolerance and intellectual liberty. For most of the last three hundred years, indeed, 'Anglican Comprehensiveness' actually did exist within clear doctrinal bound-aries. As the Lambeth Conference statement of 1948 puts it, 'the co-existence of ... divergent views within the Anglican Com-munion sets up certain tensions; *but these are tensions within a wide range of agreement in faith and practice*' (my italics).

Catholics and Evangelicals within Anglicanism might have differed, sometimes bitterly, over the meaning of Church and Sacra-ments; but they were held together at a much deeper level by an unspoken and unquestioning faith in the incarnation and resurrec-tion of Christ. Anglicans accepted as authoritative Holy Scripture as understood by the Councils of the Undivided Church and embodied in the historic Creeds. No Anglican Divine suggested that his faith should be, in the words of the Doctrine Commission Chairman quoted above, 'cut and dried'. Nor did they suppose that God was anything but the greatest of all mysteries. But neither did they think it wise or seemly to propose, for groups or individuals, unguided tours into total theological uncertainty.

Excessive theological certainty is, of course, just as bad as uncertainty. It is arguably more dangerous, leading to bigotry and sectarianism and religious wars. Uncertainty as a way of life, however, is ultimately debilitating. Modern Anglicanism is suffering from an advanced case of what we might call the Hamlet complex. Its 'native hue of resolution ... sicklied o'er with the pale cast of thought', it meanders fitfully at large on endless unmapped journeys of exploration, towards the ultimate catastrophe attending all those who cannot make up their minds.

It is, surely, not to claim anything outlandish or extreme to say that if white Anglo-Saxon Anglicanism (Africa and the East are a different matter) is to regain the spiritual authority it has manifestly lost, it needs to rediscover what it is and what it believes. 'Religious tolerance' cannot mean refusing to define doctrine in case anyone feels left out. And yet the 1987 Doctrine Commission report (for all its comparatively traditionalist tone) assumed precisely that. The Church, it pronounced, should not attempt 'a doctrinal definition to which all can consent, *for some would always be unable to assent and would then risk being "unchurched"*' (my italics). These were not views with which Garry Bennett was happy to be associated; and as we have seen he withdrew from the Commission's work.

The Roots of Liberal Exclusiveness

The refusal to define doctrine should not be confused with the 'comprehensiveness' of the Anglican tradition. Anglicanism has been able to comprehend both Catholics at one 'extreme' and Evangelicals at the other, not because it has *not* defined doctrine, but precisely because it *has* defined enough doctrine for all to agree that they are held together in loyalty to the fundamentals. It is simply not adequate to say, as the liberal apologist John Whale does, that 'definition divides'; it also unites. *It is also necessary to insist that the refusal to define doctrine is itself doctrinally definitive.* It necessarily excludes the traditional mainstream Christian (and Anglican) understanding of the Church's authority to know and define the truth of the gospel. It thus constitutes a clear and, despite appearances, rigidly intolerant ecclesiology which has as a matter of observable fact tacitly justified the increasing exclusion from positions of influence within the Church of England of those who do not accept it. To refuse doctrinal definition is not to be inclusive of those (probably the majority of Christians) who believe that truth must to some extent be defined. It is definitively to relegate them to the position of a kind of theological underclass; hence, as we shall see, the rise of politically ruthless 'liberal' élites in certain Anglican churches. If 'definition divides', it is by no means so divisive as Mr Whale's version of Anglican inclusiveness. Nor have its results ever been so dreary or dispiriting as Mr Whale's resulting vision of the future. This, from his book *The Future of Anglicanism*, is how he hopes it will be:

Because of certain attributes of the parent Church of England, [Anglicanism] is already unhostile to departures from doctrinal orthodoxy. Alongside doctrinal orthodoxy it will increasingly accommodate the idea of a God who does not act, and a unitarian God at that. It will be explicitly uncertain about an afterlife, and unassertive about the exclusive rightness of Christianity as against other faiths.

In the Church of England, at any rate, old forms of worship will continue to lose ground to the new, and perhaps a little faster than is wise. Old churches, meanwhile, will go on being sold for secular purposes like garden centres, or demolished, or incorporated into secular buildings; but perhaps more slowly than is wise.

These forecasts, says Whale, 'have an element of wishfulness in them'. His own, perhaps; but how many others will be drawn to so drab and attenuated a hope?

Comprehensiveness (another word for toleration), as the 1948 Lambeth document insisted, depends on the existence of agreement on essentials; and that means that those essentials must be articulated. It is *not* 'fundamentalist' to say that no society, religious or otherwise, can survive without a sense of its own identity, or be inclusive without being to some extent exclusive; such assumptions are the very basis of any soundly conducted sociology. And by such elementary tests of coherence, contemporary Anglicanism fails utterly. It is possible today, like the Revd Don Cupitt, to declare disbelief in the objective existence of God and to remain as a 'practising clergyman' (his own description) of the Church of England. In the final analysis, a Church in which it is possible to believe anything is one which will end by believing nothing very deeply. It is also, as we shall see, a Church in which the seeds of intolerance will find fertile soil. For there is no one more detested by those for whom truth is always provisional than a person who believes it has been revealed; nobody who hates knowledge, however dim, of the absolute more than someone who believes all knowledge is subjective or relative. There is nobody more distasteful to the theological modernist than the Evangelical who believes in religious conversion.

The doctrinal collapse of institutional Anglicanism in the 1960s and 1970s, without doubt, was one of the principal factors leading to a prevailing atmosphere of crisis in the 1980s. It would hardly be too much to say, indeed, that some parts of the Anglican Communion – most obviously perhaps the Episcopal Church of the USA – reached a kind of eleventh hour. Never had the threat of schism and disintegration within the Anglican Communion been so real and so pressing.

The most immediate perils had, on the face of it, to do with one particular question: the ordination of women to the priesthood and to the episcopate. But major upheavals in the Church rarely have as their fundamental cause some particular controversy, even one as vitally important as the integrity of the ordained ministry of the Church. That is not quite how things happen. Rather, a particular controversy crystallizes for a particular time some deeper problem of faith.

The problem for Anglicans throughout the closing decades of the century has become more and more acute as it has become more clearly defined. It involves nothing less than the question of how they are to think about the very nature of the Church, and beyond that, and even more fundamentally, about the nature of the faith itself; what might be called the doctrine of Doctrine. What is the Church, and what does it believe? By what authority does it believe it? How does it minister to individual souls, and to human society as a whole? What are and what ought to be the effects of the surrounding culture on the actual content of our belief? What *is* the content of that belief?

The relationship of defined Christian teaching, as traditionally understood, to the needs of modern society, is generally perceived to be problematical; for the modernist theologian it is so problematical that the tradition itself has to be dismantled as the only realistic means of dealing with the apparent incompatibility of twentieth century man and a tradition deriving from events which took place two thousand years ago.

Dogmatic and Pastoral

We can see this particularly vividly, perhaps, in the field of moral and pastoral theology. The problem was neatly illustrated by one of the announced themes for discussion by the 1988 Lambeth conference: 'Dogmatic and Pastoral concerns'. For, in the context of today's theological assumptions, there is something unusual here. 'Dogmatic' and 'pastoral', we can say, are two words which are not in these days often seen together. And this is not simply because they are perceived as describing two distinct areas of theological endeavour; it is also because they have taken on certain emotional overtones, indicating human attitudes seen as incompatible. The word 'dogmatic', we might say, is understood in today's theological atmosphere as almost synonymous with words like 'unpastoral', 'hard', or 'insensitive'. To be pastoral in this sense means before all else to be undogmatic, to accept people as they are without the notion that it might be better if they were different – a notion deriving from some clear doctrine about what mankind is supposed to be and to do.

This belief that there is a necessary tension between the pastoral on the one hand and the dogmatic on the other, has rarely been seen more dramatically expressed than in the placards that in 1987 greeted the Pope – a man of profound pastoral instinct and unceasing pastoral activity – held aloft in San Francisco by militant gay activists, on which was written in large clear lettering the simple slogan: 'CURB YOUR DOGMA'.

For Anglicans, there is of course nothing new in tension as such. Anglicanism has always had, almost built into it, a whole series of theological tensions. The most obvious of these, perhaps, has been the tension between the Catholic and the Evangelical visions of the Church. This has been a tension sometimes destructive, but often immensely creative. It has produced much of the finest of Anglican thought and spirituality.

The kind of tension that Anglicanism, in common with much of

Western Christendom, now has to face is of a new kind. The word 'dogma' has conveniently surfaced in Anglican discourse in the unlikely context of a Lambeth conference; and one useful way of perceiving this new tension is by seeing it as one between a dogmatic understanding and an anti-dogmatic understanding of Christianity. It is as well here to understand what we mean by the word 'dogmatic', since as we have seen it has become in popular parlance synonymous with intolerance and inflexibility.

The term has, historically, been used most by Roman Catholic theologians. Some would add that this has been during a particularly intransigent period in Roman Catholic theology, and it is certainly true that it has been used as a regular part of the theologian's vocabulary only over the last hundred years or so, falling into some disfavour in the aftermath of the second Vatican Council; in 1975, the Jesuit Fr Gerald O'Collins felt the need to defend the concept, in a book entitled *Has Dogma a Future?* It might be as well, therefore, to refer to a definition of the word by an Anglican theologian who cannot be accused of either intransigence or obscurantism, Professor John Macquarrie. 'A dogma', he writes,

> would seem to have at least three distinguishing marks: it has its basis in . . . revelation; it is proposed by the Church, as expressing the mind of the community on a particular issue; and it has a conceptual and propositional form . . .

A dogmatic approach, it will be seen, assumes several things about the nature of the Church and the Faith. It assumes, firstly, that the faith has a universal and objective character. It has been revealed by God to all men, and its relevance therefore is not to any particular cultural or historical setting but to all cultures and all ages. Secondly, it assumes that the Church has the capacity authentically to discern the revelation. Thirdly, it assumes that the revelation can be expressed in a form which conveys its universality and objectivity.

Historic Anglicanism has been rooted in such an understanding. We might say, indeed, given Anglicanism's record on intellectual liberty and its reluctance to insist on more than the irreducible minimum of doctrines, that it has been one of Anglicanism's great historic vocations to demonstrate how undogmatic a dogmatic approach can be. There is no contradiction here. Anglican freedom, like many other freedoms, has depended on the maintenance of secure and inviolable boundaries. When a priest was ordained by the rite of the Prayer Book Ordinal, he knelt before the bishop, who solemnly asked him this question:

Will you be ready, with all faithful diligence, to banish and drive away all erroneous and strange doctrines contrary to God's word; and to use both public and private monitions and exhortations, as well to the sick as to the whole, within your Cures, as need shall require, and occasion shall be given?

It is, or was, an oath also taken by bishops at their consecration. The response is simple: 'I will, the Lord being my helper'.

The oath itself originally depended on a simple attitude to Christian doctrine, which was shared by all believers without exception. It was supposed that there had been a revelation of God in the person of Jesus Christ, and that this revelation was definitive. It was a revelation open only to those with faith, and it was radically different, both in content and nature from any mere human understanding. 'We received not,' says Paul, 'the spirit of the world, but the Spirit which is of God . . . Which things also we speak, not in words which man's wisdom teaches, but which the spirit teaches . . . Now the natural man does not receive the things of the spirit of God; for to him they are foolishness.' [1 Cor. 2.4f. . . . 14–16]

This Pauline attitude is essentially that of mainstream Christianity down the ages, and it is inherited and affirmed by historic Anglicanism: Christian doctrine is given by God and taught by his church: it is at enmity with the wisdom of a fallen and man-centred world; and it is vital for our soul's health that we receive this truth and defend it and ourselves from human error. It is an attitude asserted in collect after collect in the Book of Common Prayer. Here is the collect for Saint Mark's day:

O Almighty God, who hast instructed thy holy Church with the heavenly doctrine of thy Evangelist Saint Mark: Give us grace, that, being not like children carried away with every blast of vain doctrine, we may be established in the truth of thy holy Gospel.

There is such a thing as truth; we, as fallen beings, are most apt, like children, to be carried away from it by the latest flashy novelty; but by the grace of God (and not by our own merit) we may be preserved from our own tendency to error, and brought into a right relationship with God.

Carried Away With Every Blast

Here, in extreme contrast, is an example of what I have called an 'anti-dogmatic' attitude to Christian truth, quoted from Bishop John Shelby Spong's book *Into the Whirlwind*:

Slowly but surely it is dawning on the leaders of Christianity that the Church faces a tradition-rending frontier. We are being forced to make a decision. We can withdraw from life ... or we can step outside the certainties of the past into the churning relativities of the present to grapple with the increasing uncertainties of the future. This is a critical moment in Christian history. If we can risk stepping over this line, we will have to lay aside forever the cherished claims of the past that the Church possesses the ultimate and unchanging truth of God.

The assumption here is that there is no such thing as a universal and objective truth (the corollary being that there never has been, and that any such understanding within Christianity has in fact been imposed by political coercion); that there is therefore no such thing as divine revelation except through a responsiveness to one's own cultural circumstances; and that the ephemeral perceptions of one's own time and culture have an absolute priority over any insights from the past, whose claims to universal significance are simply meaningless:

If we Christians, willingly or unwillingly, are engulfed by this tide of modern life, it is quite clear that the Church as we know it will be in jeopardy. Yet anyone who breathes deeply of the intellectual revolution or the knowledge explosion of our day must surely be aware that no other alternative is possible.

Is it credible to suggest that the Christian Church can confront this world armed with the claim that in our holy book, which was completed before A.D. 150, the unchanging eternal truth of God has been captured for all time . . ?

Leaving on one side the question of whether this is a fair or accurate representation of mainstream Christianity, it is obvious enough that between those who do and those who do not believe in the biblical revelation as it has been traditionally received, there is a tension of a kind previously quite unknown within the Christian dispensation. The results of this tension have so far proved almost wholly negative, during a period in which older tensions are approaching resolution.

It has, for instance, become clear that the possibility exists of a real synthesis between Catholic and Protestant insights, a synthesis which denies the true nature of neither, properly understood. It has not so far emerged whether it is possible for there to be anything but a total intellectual and spiritual warfare between the assumptions of a man-centred secularist modernism and those of a supernaturalist revealed Christianity which is enshrined in Scriptures understood as divinely inspired and a tradition which is accorded real authority. In a 'dialogue' between David L. Edwards, one of the liberal ascendancy's leading ideologues, and the distinguished Evangelical John Stott, Stott summed up his disagreement with Edwards in terms which make it clear that they are not divided in a way easy to resolve. The dialogue itself was conducted in a way which tellingly indicates how Edwards' school of thought regards those who disagree with liberal assumptions, even when they are attempting to convey the impression of tolerance and respect: the book consists of alternating chapters by the two men, with Edwards first attacking Stott's beliefs, and Stott defending himself, with no response by Edwards to Stott's defence: a significant example of 'dialogue' liberal style. The conclusion persists throughout that the two men believe in what, for all intents and purposes, are different religions. In an epilogue, Dr Stott summed up the differences:

. . . wherein lies our basic disagreement? It seems still to belong to those two subjects of traditional debate – authority and salvation. Indeed, the fundamental questions in every religion are the same: by what authority do we believe and teach what we believe and teach? . . . is it unfair to say that your final criterion for truth is 'modern opinion', whether your own or others? It certainly seems to me like that, and explains why you feel able to set aside biblical teaching, e.g. on the cross, on miracles and on homosexuality.

Dogmatic and Anti-dogmatic

So far, the tension between the theologies represented here by Provost Edwards and Dr Stott (whatever the civility with which the debate may be conducted) has been, for Anglicanism, destructive to the point of real crisis. We need, therefore, to examine more closely what is involved in what I have called dogmatic and anti-dogmatic Christianity. We can conveniently define our terms by considering two passages from the literature sent out in 1987 to the bishops of the Anglican Communion in preparation for the Lambeth Conference the following year. Both passages refer directly to the Lambeth theme of 'Dogmatic and Pastoral concerns'. Here is the first:

The Church needs to have its faith right. It is not simply that credal orthodoxy is important for its own sake. The faith we hold
  · determines our understanding of and relationship with God
  · shapes our worship
  · gives direction to our pastoral and evangelistic practice
  · affects our relationships with other churches and other religions
  · influences the way we live out our christianity in daily life.
This is why it makes sense to bring together dogmatic and pastoral concerns in one section of the agenda for Lambeth 1988.

This is a clear expression of a dogmatically understood Christianity: 'the Church needs to have its faith right'. There is such a thing as credal orthodoxy; on a right understanding of our faith depend our relationships with God and with man, and the conduct of our daily lives. Belief, for the author of this passage, comes first; everything else depends on it. And the strong implication is that belief is in something objective, not dependent for its truth on cultural circumstance. We need to have our faith *right*, not simply attractive to this or that particular cultural market. In contrast, here is the second passage:

Many parts of the Church are feeling a crisis of faith. Some respond by demanding a more forceful reaffirmation of our traditional doctrinal formularies. These will continue to have their distinctive place as norms of the expression of the faith. But they do not meet all our contemporary needs. They are often couched in thought-forms which we no longer employ; they may reflect cultures which are alien to the Church in some parts of the world; they do not always take account of developments in human knowledge and experience; and they may not answer new questions which have arisen since they were formulated. Within the Church these

classic formularies continue to have unique significance; but they may
need to be restated if they are to have a cutting edge in the world.

We need to say, of course, that at a certain level, a great deal of this
is self-evidently true. We do need, for each new age, and in different
cultures, to find appropriate forms of expression. But it also needs
to be said that this is not a necessity discovered for the first time by
the liberal theology of the modern period. The Church has always
faced this problem. Suddenly to say that we now have it for the first
time is plainly untrue. To say to a tradition which includes – to pick
out a handful of names almost at random – Paul, Ambrose, Gregory,
Augustine, Anselm, Aquinas, Hooker, Newman, Chesterton, and
C. S. Lewis, that the great saving truths of the Christian religion
'may need to be restated if they are to have a cutting edge in the
world' is to attempt to teach your grandmother to suck eggs on a
scale not hitherto contemplated in human intellectual history; always
assuming, of course, that to restate does not mean to reinvent.

The great doctors of the Church have always restated the faith
for their own time. None of them, however, would have count-
enanced the proposition that developments in human knowledge
could alter the substance of what was being taught, or in any way
modify the revelation once for all delivered. This is itself challenged
by the anti-dogmatic school, even though this school may admit
that the Fathers and mediaeval doctors *intended* to defend a universal
and objective faith. Nevertheless, it is claimed, the content of
Christian teaching has varied *substantially* at different periods of the
Church's history and in different cultural circumstances.

How true is this contention? Certainly we can say that there have
been variations of emphasis in response to particular contemporary
pressures. Nevertheless, what needs to be held up as remarkable is
the astonishing degree of unanimity to be found between those who
have handed on the tradition over the centuries in such different
historical and cultural contexts. To take one obvious example:
there has at no time until the present been any real dispute as to the
authority and objective character of the Nicene creed.

In this process of handing on, the traditional formularies of the
Church – most notably the Creeds – have been central. This was not
because it was thought that any such summary of belief could ever
contain the fullness of faith: but it *was* supposed that the truths they

embodied were both true and indispensable, and that without these truths there was no starting point for the journey. The Creeds retained their unquestioned authority until the modern period, not least because they authentically and evidently represented a reality which was of God and not of Man; this reality was beyond our understanding, but we could know something of it through God's own self-disclosure in the person of Christ. And because it was of God, it made demands for growth and for change, for us to adapt to the revelation, never for the revelation to be adapted to us.

Mankind Come of Age

This sense that the truth in its fullness is given and objective is very strongly felt by many, and probably most, ordinary Christians. Though we may know little of God, we can nevertheless through his own self-revelation reliably know something. And so, much as they may despise such simple pieties, theologians who think in the way the writer of our second passage thinks, very often find it necessary to pay lip service to this instinct.

Thus, according to the writer of this passage, we find that the traditional formularies of the faith 'will continue to have their distinctive place as norms of the expression of the faith'. What this means is not easy to determine. An assertion like 'the traditional formularies will have their distinctive place' says nothing about how important that place is, or how many other 'norms' will be jostling for position beside them.

And the word 'distinctive' says nothing about how *definitive* these formularies might be. The shape of a bishop's mitre is certainly 'distinctive'; but it is possible still to have a very high view of his office even if it is considered that the shape of his hat is not only distinctive but ridiculous.

Similarly, when the passage goes on to say that 'within the church these classic formularies continue to have unique significance', it is as well to remember that, like the word 'distinctive', the adjective 'unique' says nothing at all about the value of the noun it qualifies. We might compare the sentence 'the creeds have unique significance' with the sentence 'the three stooges have unique significance'. Both are equally true and equally self-evident. A particular well-known priest dislikes babies, and for some reason has them constantly brought to his attention by their doting parents for his admiration. He is a kind man; he is also honest. He has therefore devised a standard brief utterance, which he delivers on such occasions with great sincerity: 'My word,' he says, 'that *is* a baby.' 'My word,' says this author, 'that *is* a Creed.'

You know that he has not got the point of the Creeds, just as the priest has not got the point of babies, from his next sentence. He has just told us that the Church's traditional formularies – and this certainly refers to the Creeds before all else – will continue to have their distinctive place. Then he goes on:

But they do not meet all our contemporary needs. They are often couched in thought-forms which we no longer employ; they may reflect cultures which are alien to the church in some parts of the world; they do not always take account of developments in human knowledge and experience; and they may not answer new questions which have arisen since they were formulated.

It is difficult briefly to do justice to the misapprehensions this passage contains. What seems to be involved here is a major shift in the way such statements are perceived. Let us look briefly at the central section of one of these formularies. It needs no identification:

He suffered and was buried, and the third day he rose again according to the scriptures, and ascended into heaven, and sitteth on the right hand of the Father.

It is the very heart of the Christian religion. It is emphatically not simply one way among many in which that religion might be expressed. It needs a great deal of explanation; but then, it always did. And of course, the way in which it has had to be expounded has had to change; but it has never been anything less than a total challenge to and defiance of all merely human assumptions. It has always been a stumbling block, a madness, to any normal secular ex-pectation.

The modernist school often explains its discontinuity with pre-vious theologies by saying not only that modern man has come of age and therefore cannot be expected to rest content with the simplicities of earlier theologies, but also that new problems arise in our period which did not arise before. We have just considered some of the criteria to which, as a result, the Creeds are now subjected. In response, we might pose certain questions, about the short passage from the Nicene Creed quoted above. How, precisely, does the death and resurrection of Christ not meet our contemporary needs as it did meet the needs of previous generations? How is this particular passage from the Nicene Creed couched in thought-forms we no longer employ, in any sense that to talk about a man dying and rising again ever was a 'thought-form' generally employed except in wholly exceptional circumstances? How, exactly, are the contents of the Nicene Creed alien to the Church in some parts of the world in any way which demands that the Creed, rather than human culture, needs to be adjusted as a result? What new questions have arisen to which answers ought to be adducable from some new creed of a kind which ever were supposed to be answered by the Creeds we already have? Further, what new developments in human knowledge and experience invalidate any part of them?

One answer sometimes given to this last question is that modern science has persuaded us that virgin birth and bodily resurrection are impossible. But the whole point of the virgin birth and the resurrection is precisely their impossibility. No one ever thought they were anything else.

Here, we approach the crux of the matter. To God all things are possible. We are not asked to hold within our grasp an understanding of the mystery of his love for mankind: we are bidden simply to reach out and touch the mystery with the farthest tips of our fingers. And the willingness to be satisfied with what we are given is in fact part of our basic spiritual equipment; it is part of the basic humility that alone makes faith possible. A faith which came within the ambit of our unaided human comprehension – or, indeed, within the comprehension of our culture – would be simply not worth having. We need in our faith what John Keats called 'negative capability': the *capacity* for being in uncertainty and doubt without the irritable stretching out for certainty and proof. 'A man's reach', wrote the poet Robert Browning, 'must exceed his grasp or what's a heaven for?'

It is here, perhaps, that we can identify one fundamental source of the present crisis of Western Christianity. For, the longing for a heaven beyond what we now know and can grasp, the deep knowledge that now we see as through a glass darkly but then face to face – the yearning from a sense of our own present imperfection, which has always been the basis for true Christian faith – has long since leaked away as a central directing principle from the milieux inhabited by the rulers and teachers of liberal main-line Christendom. And this leakage has a great deal to do with the growth of the notion that we are, in the end, dependent on ourselves alone for our understanding of God.

The Theology of Negotiation and Ambiguity

There exists, then, a tension between a Christianity which is given and objective and which it is 'important to have . . . right' on the one hand, and a Christianity whose expression and content are constantly at the behest of culture and circumstance on the other. It is a tension between a dogmatic Christianity, beyond our grasp but offering at least something we can know with certainty, and an anti-dogmatic Christianity which is perpetually remade to be accessible to culture and conformable to human intellect, and which regards certainty of any kind as being a sign of immaturity, even of neurosis.

The tension can often be seen enacted in controversies between particular groups. But it is increasingly becoming itself institutionalized, thus repeating one of the perennial patterns in Christian history whereby, for good or ill in any particular case, dangerous tendencies are, it is hoped, neutralized by absorption. Faced by the increasing polarization of Anglicanism, a new technique is emerging, in which different views, whether incompatible or not, are asserted as ingredients of a new synthesis. This can, of course, be fruitful and necessary: the insights, for instance, of 'Bible Christians' and 'Sacramental Christians' are never contradictory, unless either Bible or Sacrament is understood in a distorted way; this kind of synthesis of apparently contradictory emphases is one of the great achievements of the Anglican genius. But when divisions are based on real intellectual incompatibility, the effect of yoking contrasting beliefs together by violence is to produce what is not so much a new synthesis as a kind of surrealist intellectual montage, a Daliesque theological landscape, in which the blasted branches of a residual orthodoxy have draped over them the shifting forms of modernist revision. This new theological technique was strikingly on display at the 1988 Lambeth Conference. I have already quoted, from the preparatory conference documents, two passages embodying clearly incompatible views. In fact these two passages come from the same document. Not only that, the second passage follows immediately on from the first. The document has two signatures at the bottom of it (this may explain something) and it is the official letter sent to all the bishops of the Anglican communion to introduce the Lambeth theme of 'Dogmatic and Pastoral Concerns'.

Anglicanism has moved, we may observe, into a period in which theological utterance from official quarters has to be, as it were, negotiated so that all viewpoints are catered for, no matter whether they are inconsistent with each other or not. As Garry Bennett pointed out in the preface, Archbishop Ramsey was the last real exponent of classical Anglicanism; nevertheless, he noted, 'such a view of theology still appears in Anglican reports and in archiepiscopal addresses'. This was strikingly borne out at Lambeth in an address delivered by Archbishop Rayner, one of the co-signatories of the letter quoted above, who gave a lengthy exposition of the classical Anglican view of a theology based on scripture, reason and tradition, before moving on to expound a 'pluralist' view (which we shall shortly examine), wholly incompatible with it and entirely at odds with the Anglican notion of a comprehensiveness based on agreement on essentials.

To the traditional theological specialisms, it seems, we must now add another: the theology of negotiation and ambiguity, a theology fashioned for a world in which the truth is something we are always looking for but never finding. Like Pontius Pilate, so many of today's Anglican theologians constantly ask the question 'what is truth?'; like him, they take good care not to stay for an answer. It is a theology in which nothing means quite what it appears to mean, in which everything has to be adapted if it is retained from the past, rather like some of the Regency terraces in London which have been totally gutted by developers. Outside they are early nineteenth century; inside they are high-tech office buildings. Similarly, traditional structures and theological language are still there in today's Church; it is impractical because of conservationist pressures to get rid of them entirely. We have the Creeds; but they have been gutted and redefined. They are no longer, with the bible and the sacraments and the apostolic ministry, 'fundamentals'; they are now simply 'part of our heritage of faith'. Having been emptied of conviction and meaning, they have been retained as decorative features so that if accusations are made of loss of theological identity they may be indicated as standing intact. In just the same way the great cannons which swayed the battles of former years, emptied of their thunder, stand in museums and on the battlements of ruined fortifications.

Perhaps the most striking example of this technique in recent years, though one which shows that it has to be used discreetly if it is to escape detection, has been provided by the Rt Revd David Jenkins, Lord Bishop of Durham, who claims to believe 'passionately' in the Resurrection of Christ. The fact that he strongly disbelieves it in any sense that the Church has understood it for the last two thousand years becomes irrelevant. Words now mean what the individual theologian decides they will mean. The Bishop of Durham is not lying; he just means something different from what the Church means.

The Closing of the Anglican Mind

The difficulty, of course, is that the very notion that theology has to do with a truth to be defended against the errors to which natural man is naturally prone is deeply antipathetic to modern Western secular culture. And white Anglo-Saxon Anglicanism has become deeply secularized, that is, committed to the assumptions of the *saeculum*, the present age. It is natural that the ingrained modern suspicion of any idea of truth as being something absolute, 'once for all delivered', has saturated our theology too. Truth is provisional; and it has to do, not with eternity, but with the here and now. It follows, perhaps, that the recovery of a sound theology must begin with a critique of our own culture. The problem for believers in the existence of absolute truth who live in the advanced industrialized nations of the West, has been brilliantly spelled out in an important book, *The Closing of the American Mind*, by Allan Bloom. This is how Bloom sees the problem, from the perspective of a university teacher:

There is one thing a professor can be absolutely certain of: almost every student entering the university believes, or says he believes, that truth is relative. If this belief is put to the test, one can count on the student's reaction: they will be uncomprehending. That anyone should regard the proposition as not self-evident astonishes them, as though he were calling into question $2 + 2 = 4$. These are things you don't think about. The students' backgrounds are as various as America can provide. . . . They are unified only in their relativism and in their allegiance to equality. And the two are united in a moral intention. The relativity of truth is not a theoretical insight but a moral postulate, the condition of a free society, or so they see it. . . . The true believer is the real danger. The study of history and culture shows that all the world was mad in the past; men always thought they were right, and that led to wars, persecutions, slavery, xenophobia, racism, and chauvinism. The point is not to correct mistakes and really be right; rather it is not to think you are right at all.

Now it is fairly clear that just as a revealed religion like Christianity poses difficulties for the relativist, so a thoroughgoing relativism is difficult to argue wholeheartedly for even the most radical of Christian theologians. Unless, that is, he is prepared to go as far as the Revd Don Cupitt and to blow his cover by denying the objective reality of God himself. If God objectively exists then so does absolute truth.

Even the liberal theologian, then, is tied in some way to the notion that there is such a thing as absolute truth, though he may say that it is not accessible. Relativism is not therefore conveniently arguable (though it is openly defended by some, most notably by Bishop John Spong). Dr Habgood, for instance, writes of

the movement of critical thought itself, away from certainty about anything into an all-pervading kind of relativism. On such a view, what we think we know is relative to who we are, where we are, and the culture we have assimilated and the society we belong to. There can be an African or Chinese understanding of reality, say, which is just as valid as the one which seems natural to us as part of Western culture. . . .

Nevertheless, he continues,

An undivided mind looks in the end for an undivided truth, a oneness at the heart of things. And this isn't just fantasy. The whole intellectual quest, despite its fragmentation, despite its limitations and uncertainties, seems to presuppose that in the end we are all encountering a single reality, and single truth. It may be incredibly mysterious or wonderfully simple. But ultimately, beyond the imperfections of our knowledge, beyond all the relativities, it is what it is. I think that if we gave up believing that there is some ultimate truth, ultimate reality in this sense, then we would be in danger of losing the notion of truth altogether.

In general, then, it is not necessarily true of liberal theology to say that it is wholly relativist, though relativism does often seem to be a hidden, perhaps unconscious, assumption never far from the surface and often weakening the vision of ultimate truth expressed here by Dr Habgood. The instinctive relativism of contemporary Western society, so clearly anatomized by Allan Bloom, has deeply affected its theology too. Nevertheless, since God objectively exists, the only coherently arguable stance, even for a modernist theology, is to safeguard its suspicions of an objectively delivered revelation by insisting on the essential *subjectivity* of our own *response*, and to make the *response* – rather than the revelation itself – the focus for theology. I can appropriately illustrate this approach by quoting from another document prepared for the 1988 Lambeth Conference by the Inter-Anglican Theological and Doctrinal Commission (to whose work Dr Habgood looks for the reestablishment of theological coherence within modern Anglicanism). The work is entitled *For The Sake of the Kingdom*, and the committee that produced it has seventeen members. God, it will be recalled, did not send a committee; this is how the members of this one approach the problem of objective truth:

The scriptures and the creeds never speak apart from a context . . . hence our understanding of them is always conditioned – by culture, by social structures and attitudes, by a given world view. On the other hand, the scriptures and the creeds speak in many contexts, both in the history of the church itself and in the various cultures and societies of the contemporary world; and it is this fact which, in the end, can set them free from the narrowing and distorting effects of any particular way of reading them.

Now, of course, we have to say again that this is partly true. There is, in fact, no such thing as a wholly and absolutely objective response to objective truth. We have to know through our own perceptions; and these are unique. Not only that; it is certainly necessary to say that our own response to the mystery of our salvation in Christ needs to be enriched from other traditions of thought and spirituality, which will frequently point to deficiencies in our own understanding.

What is Truth?

But this passage is saying more than that (as is so often the case in modern theology, it is necessary to discover the hidden subtext). It is saying that from within any particular perspective, *we cannot free ourselves from our own subjectivity*; that we can never have enough self-knowledge to disentangle the object of knowing from the means of knowing it, or the context in which it is known. Indeed, in some versions of the modernist response, it is only the context which confers meaning; hence we speak of contextual theology. And what this particular Anglican document is saying is that we are actually trapped within the context of our own perceptions. Essentially its message is that of the Christian atheist Don Cupitt, that 'we are [completely] enclosed within the limits of our own humanity, bound by history, culture and language, and able to see the world only from a human point of view which is itself perpetually shifting. We can have no absolute knowledge. . . .'

And so, to return to our Lambeth document, since our understanding 'is always conditioned' our only means of knowing anything is to add our own distortions to everyone else's in the hope they will balance out. What we end up with, according to the Inter-Anglican Theological and Doctrinal Commission, is not relativism (which is philosophically unarguable and in any case is getting a bad name) but something else which *is* arguable, and has the added bonus of being almost universally supposed to be a good thing and not a bad thing: not relativism, but *pluralism*. There is indeed, say the authors of *For the Sake of the Kingdom*,

a 'sovereign' truth, something beyond our fashions and fancies, but . . . it is to be known only in the continuation of active human encounter. It is this that we mean to point to when we speak of 'pluralism'. If relativism denies that the notion of truth has any comprehensive meaning, pluralism, in the sense intended here, testifies to a truth more comprehensive than all our particular standpoints. And in Christian terms, to the extent that we remain bound in a narrow loyalty to our given perspective, imagining it to be final, 'objective' or 'scientific', we keep truth, life-giving truth, at a distance.

What does this actually mean? There is, once more, a surface level at which it is clearly true. It is, of course, undeniable that we each see only a corner of the mystery, and that we need to think and pray within the fellowship of the Church for precisely that reason.

But that is not the underlying meaning here. It is clear, for instance, that those who are accused of remaining 'bound in a narrow loyalty to [their] given perspective, imagining it to be final, "objective", or "scientific" ' are not the biblical critics, who have had such an immense effect on the teaching of the faith in this century and who have consistently made claims, now more and more seen to be spurious, that their scholarship is 'final', 'objective' and 'scientific'. Those targeted here are those who, in all humility, and knowing well how little of God they know, are attempting against the odds to remain faithful to the living tradition of faith they have received, a tradition whose foundations they profoundly believe are laid down by God and may not be adapted by men, even though the timeless and unchanging gospel must be taught in the language and categories which emerge from perpetually changing human culture and circumstance. And that tradition through the ages has insisted that (however dimly) we may truly and unmistakably know as much of the truth revealed in Christ as each can bear; *and that however various our perceptions that truth is the same truth for us all.*

Of course it is necessary to say that the ancient formularies of the Universal Church do not encapsulate the endless mystery of God. We cannot put God in a bottle. But that does not mean they are not true, or that the understanding of faith they so fleetingly summarize is anything less than entirely essential. A navigation chart of the Atlantic Ocean does not even begin to plumb the mysteries of those mighty waters; but the chart is, nevertheless, entirely true. A navigator who follows it will successfully cross the Atlantic; one who decides to enter into dialogue with the passengers to ascertain how they see the problem *may* succeed in steering his ship to the Statue of Liberty, but the chances are overwhelmingly against it. We may not comprehend the mysterious seas; but we do know something about them. We may understand almost nothing about God, but we do know something; and Jesus came to reveal it in His person. The creeds are the navigator's charts of that absolute, objective and indispensable knowledge. Without it, we are lost, hopelessly out of our depth. Without it, we shall drown in our own pride.

A dogmatically understood faith, then, insists that, though we may know little, and that imperfectly, we do know something about the truth God came to reveal to us. In sharp contrast, what I have called the theology of negotiation and ambiguity insists that truth is not in this sense knowable at all. Again, I quote from *For the Sake of the Kingdom*:

We do not come to see 'truth' as an object; we do not arrive at a high ground from which to comprehend the whole work of God [no one of course ever claimed that we did]. . . . The Holy Spirit, who guides into all truth, may be present not so much exclusively on one side of a theological dispute as in the very encounter of diverse visions held by persons or groups of persons who share a faithfulness and commitment to Christ and each other.

In other words, we cannot know the truth and nor should we try to; the word 'truth', indeed, has to be placed in sanitizing quotation marks. ' "What is truth?" said jesting Pilate, and would not stay for an answer'. He could, of course, have had one had he been searching for it: 'I am the way, the truth and the life', said Jesus; 'he who believes in me shall never die'. But then, how are we to know that He really said it? Is it not an inevitable part of the pluralist attitude to truth that, though of course in one way the gospels are true, in another way we cannot believe a word they say? What is truth? I have called this 'pluralist' Anglican theology the theology of negotiation and ambiguity; it might better be called the theology of Pontius Pilate.

In the end, it is vital to note that this theological pluralism, which has nothing in common with traditional Anglican comprehensiveness, is deeply intolerant in practice, however much it may wash its hands of overt claims to infallibility. In fact, the claims to real pluralism are entirely spurious. How could it be otherwise? How can there be a pluralist theology which embraces a point of view which says that we are hopelessly confined within our own conditioning, so that theological truth is ultimately unknowable, and which also embraces a point of view which says precisely the opposite: that scripture and the tradition of the Church in fact enshrine an objectively knowable revelation? If Anglicanism is a way of doing theology in which scripture, God-directed reason and tradition are balanced, then Anglicanism is effectively abolished by what is claimed here as pluralism: if this is pluralism, it is a curiously selective one.

The Tyranny of Subjectivism

But of course, what we are really talking about is not pluralism but subjectivism. And subjectivism is an essentially intolerant mental attitude. Essentially intolerant, since no view which depends on the imprisonment of individuals and groups within their own respective subjectivities has the possibility for resolving disagreements. As the Bishop of London said in a lecture delivered in Fulton, Missouri, 'discussion about [disagreements] becomes impossible for there are no criteria to which appeal can be made in common discourse. There can be no more on the part of the subjectivist than the restatement of what he considers self-evident truths . . .'

Nowhere do we find any more striking confirmation of the intolerance of subjectivism than in the behaviour and utterance of many of those who support the ordination of women. There is no more telling contemporary example of a widespread assumption that a particular course of action is based on 'self-evident truths'. Traditionalists have become used to being informed that 'there are no theological arguments against it'. They may rehearse the arguments repeatedly; but they will still be told, not that their arguments are bad, but that they do not exist. Certainly little is heard at such moments of the sentiments, quoted earlier, that 'the Holy Spirit, who guides into all truth, may be present not so much exclusively on one side of a theological dispute as in the encounter of diverse visions. . . .' For the woman-priest lobby, truth is very much on their side, and those who oppose it are simply not to be taken seriously, except as misguided, and prob- ably – according to the Bishop of Durham – neurotic, political opponents. They are, to employ a suitably totalitarian expression, non-persons; and since their opposition springs from their own psychological hang-ups, they are to be wholly ignored. The ordina-tion of women, says Bishop Jenkins, should be encompassed 'at almost any cost'.

There are many and various ways in which opponents of women's ordination in particular (and of the liberal modernist revolution in general) are made into non-persons. We will examine the American experience in the next chapter. Institutionalized intolerance in England is more subtle; but it exists, nevertheless, and with results just as terrible in terms of blighted human lives. Canon George Austin explained something of the process to the General Synod, during the debate on the *Crockford's* preface:

Anyone who has challenged the views of the liberal establishment is aware of the sequence of events which follows – and it has happened to me many times. First of all, the friends who gave support and encouragement suddenly are not there, and that is part of my guilt in relation to Garry's tragic death. One can readily understand why this happens. Then, when a reasoned argument is offered, instead of a reasoned response it produces vulgar abuse from those who ought to know better – and Garry had his share of that. Because that goes unrebuked by our Church leaders, and seems sometimes to be encouraged by them, it is then taken up by the lesser fry, and to it they add distortion, often accusing us of stating the very views that we have specifically denied or denounced – and that has happened to me many times. Worst of all, as with Soviet dissidents, we come to expect the suggestion of mental instability: we cannot be against women priests for theological reasons, the integrity of which must be acknowledged, but because we feel threatened by women or have sexual hang-ups. I dismissed as bizarre the suggestion made to me after Garry's death that people would now say he was unbalanced. But it happened and, frankly, it was at this point that I felt soiled and ashamed to be a member of such a Church.

The present political struggle within Anglicanism reflects in many ways what happens when those who have captured the intellectual citadel find themselves challenged. Counter-revolutionaries have always been treated with special detestation by those who have newly attained power. The *Crockford's* tragedy, which happened too suddenly for the process to be masked behind the usual Anglican civilities, showed the intensity of the passions which flow close beneath the surface in contemporary Western Anglicanism. To see just how far, within a supposedly 'pluralist' dispensation, the marginalization of counter-revolutionaries can go, we need to look at the Episcopal Church of the USA. Its problems are by no means dissimilar to those of the Church of England and other white Anglo-Saxon provinces within Anglicanism; to suppose that the tragedy of ECUSA could never happen anywhere else is to take complacency to the point of folly.

PART THREE

FIVE

The Final Crisis of the Episcopal Church

'They have taken our Church away from us – that's what it amounts to. How are we going to get it back?' The Church in question is the American Episcopal Church (ECUSA); the speaker was an intelligent woman in a church hall in Anchorage, Alaska. It was not the first time I had been asked to answer this question, or something like it. I had heard it in places as contrasting as America has to offer: in Dallas and in Washington DC; in Detroit and in Houston; in Philadelphia and Denver; in Westwood, New Jersey, and Portland, Oregon. Now, yet again, it brought back to my mind a scene which haunted me then and which haunts me still.

In a large room in an off-campus location, twenty or thirty seminarians and their wives sat round me in a semicircle, discussing the crisis of their Church. I had been fulfilling a speaking engagement nearby; the students asked me to have breakfast with them on my way to the airport. I changed my flight as a precaution, advisedly as it transpired since the meeting lasted several hours. The seminarians were preparing for ordination to the priesthood at a well-known seminary on the East Coast which I do not name for the same reason that the meeting did not take place on campus; my presence there was kept strictly secret. These were students set apart, ignored and pilloried by many of their fellow-students, under considerable pressure from teaching staff and from their own dioceses.

One major reason for this treatment was their refusal to attend celebrations of the Eucharist presided over by women priests. More recently, they had declined to attend also the experimental 'inclusive language' liturgies for the Eucharist and for Morning and Evening prayer then being officially conducted in most Episcopal seminaries.

One diocese had asked for a list of non-attenders; the faculty refused to supply this, less because of any libertarian principles than on the grounds that nobody had to attend anything anyway. Lists of course are in any case unnecessary. A bishop only has to ask an individual seminarian the $64,000 question: Do you or do you not recognize the women priests in my diocese? If not, the seminarian is himself increasingly unlikely to be ordained, despite the 'statement of conscience' made in 1987 by the American House of Bishops promising that there would be no victimization of those who in conscience could not accept women's ordination.

The Roots of Crisis

How is it possible that in a seminary of the Anglican communion, one belonging, that is, to a tradition which values intellectual liberty, such a scene could occur: a secret gathering of young men and women, fearful of the consequences of meeting to discuss the condition of their Church? How is it possible that Anglicans should be pressured and isolated in this way? How has all this come about? Though Anglicans in England tend to suppose that undesirable American developments cannot happen to them (presumably through some imagined cultural superiority that renders them immune), the increasing influence of American culture in Britain, together with the recent history of the Church of England, ought to suggest caution.

As Garry Bennett suggests in the preface, 'The problems of modern Anglicanism are highlighted by the case of the Episcopal Church in the United States'. In America things tend to be seen in vivid colours and sharp contrasts; but the problems, as we shall see, are not dissimilar, even though Americans are less inhibited in their words and actions than the English with their famous 'reserve'. When British reserve snaps, however, the results can be just as wild and unregulated as anything imaginable on the other side of the Atlantic, as the *Crockford's* affair amply demonstrated.

The Episcopal Church has now been in decline for over 20 years. In 1968 ECUSA had 3,588,435 members. By 1989, this had dropped to 2,420,000. This decline has taken place against a steady increase in churchgoing in the American population as a whole, an increase which has been going on steadily since the 1950s. During the same period, the classification of ECUSA by the Library of Congress in Washington has changed: it has now been demoted from the status of a 'denomination' to that of a 'sect'.

It takes little imagination to be able to link the decline in membership of ECUSA since the late 1960s with the beliefs and policies of its ruling caste since that time. These policies, however, were followed, not with any intention of producing a kind of spiritual élite, a Church 'leaner and fitter' to proclaim the gospel; their intention was to make the Church more relevant to society's perceived needs so that more and more Americans would find those needs answered within the Episcopal Church. The Church was seen in the 1950s by Episcopalian liberals as in need of renewal; it was out of touch, stagnant, conventional. Nevertheless, from the 1930s, until the 'new insights' of the 1950s and 1960s began to percolate through to the parishes, the story of the Episcopal Church had been one of continuous growth. The steady rise in the membership figures begins to flatten out in the early 1960s, and from 1968 onwards goes into a sharp reverse. This sudden downturn in the graph can be clearly related to a radicalization in ECUSA's public profile. Under the 'liberal' presiding bishop John Hines, between 1967 and 1970, the Episcopal Church distributed some nine million dollars in what they described as 'reparations' to 'empower the powerless'; among the recipients of such funds were the Black Panthers at home, and guerrilla groups abroad.

Until the late 1960s, though, few American Anglicans had the remotest inkling of what lay ahead. Partly, their self-confidence was a reflection of the position enjoyed by Episcopalians in American society, even of the new importance of America in world affairs. As Bennett puts it in the preface, 'to become an Episcopalian has traditionally been a sign of upward mobility in American society. In the 1950s English visitors were impressed by the vigour of the Episcopal Church which seemed to reflect its nation's new confidence as a world power'.

But there was something else going on, and had been for decades past, which Bennett does not acknowledge. It was a period, too, of steady and sometimes striking missionary activity. In some dioceses, quite large numbers of missions were started, which in due course became vital and established parishes: one notable example was the diocese of Dallas, which grew in this way to the point at which it split into two dioceses, those of Dallas and Fort Worth. Anyone who, like this writer, has had any part in the life of an orthodox Episcopalian parish of this kind has witnessed something rarely present in even the most successful parishes in England, something one is tempted to evoke New Testament times to describe: a Christian community to which its members are entirely committed, containing a high proportion of adult converts, in which a faith is practised which combines in its members a decent level of instruction and intellectual engagement with a lack of embarrassing pietism.

Whatever the reasons, Episcopalian congregations, as the preface says, were full and finances were healthy. There were, Bennett went on, weaknesses: bishops were often 'pastoral activists' rather than theologians; the Episcopal Church sometimes gave the impression of shallowness, with much of its preaching devoted to the propagation of 'American values'. Within a short time, Bennett goes on, 'the Episcopal Church acquired a strong party for liberal causes, among them a movement for the ordination of women'. It was an issue that conservatives handled inadequately, being theologically ill-prepared, and given the strenth of current opinion on what were seen as 'civil rights' issues. There was a vociferous campaign. In 1974, three retired bishops irregularly ordained six women. Two years later this action was endorsed when, by the slenderest of majorities, women's ordination was accepted by the General Convention. 'If six votes had been cast differently,' comments Bennett, 'it would have failed.'

The Liberals Move In

'The consequences for American Anglicanism,' he continued, 'were momentous, and have not been sufficiently understood in the communion at large.' Many Episcopalians would fervently agree. The perception even within America that opposition to women's ordination, and other liberal causes, has largely died away has been due to several reasons. Partly, to the political adroitness with which over the last two decades liberals have captured the House of Bishops, giving a misleading impression of near unanimity in the Church as a whole; partly, to the ruthlessness with which they have used their newly acquired power; partly, to the brilliant public relations skills of the Episcopalian establishment during this period. Thus, as Bennett points out, by 1987 it was possible for Episcopalian bishops to claim that the ordination of women question was no longer causing serious difficulty. Only twelve dioceses did not ordain women; numbers in the breakaway churches were small. 'Unfortunately', Bennett continued,

they did not tell of the methods by which this effect had been achieved or the change in the character of their church which it involved. It is clear that a major casualty has been the comprehensiveness of the Episcopal Church. In 1977 the House of Bishops issued a 'Statement of Conscience' which affirmed the wide tolerance of Anglicanism and promised that none should be coerced or penalized for conscientious objection to the General Convention's decision. It is, however, apparent that this statement was given a minimal interpretation. Many bishops, including even some who had at first been cautious, exerted great pressure on dissenting clergy to conform, while some liberal bishops acted in ways which were not only in total breach of the spirit of the statement but seemed to be aimed at driving conservatives out of the church. Except in a few dioceses dissenting clergy were denied diocesan office and vetoed for the episcopate. Within a short time the commanding heights of the church were occupied by the liberal party. And the result is obvious to those who have spent some time in the United States, though it may not be readily appreciated by senior English Bishops on carefully arranged short visits. The liberal ascendancy has transformed the younger clergy of the Episcopal Church into a national force for radical secular causes.

The number of ordinands, Bennett goes on, from the Catholic and Evangelical traditions has diminished. Episcopal seminaries have ceased to teach theology in the Anglican tradition. Prayer and spiritual formation in most of these establishments are ignored. Last, but by no means least, 'the sexual mores of both staff and students appear to have broken with the standards usually associated with the Christian ministry'.

It is worth lingering over this last charge, for the question of sexual morality is, in fact, a key issue for the Episcopal Church. Nowhere can we observe with greater clarity two key features of the modern Anglican disarray; on the one hand, the disaffection of large parts of the laity as a result of current trends and, on the other, the process of theological liberalization from which these trends derive. Dogmatic theology is often ignored by the laity; but moral theology, particularly when it has to do with sexual activity, has immediate practical consequences, certainly, it seems, in the USA. Sex and religion in America would make a fascinating and lengthy study; the chapter on the Episcopal Church would be substantial.

Anecdotes abound. I cite one among many examples gleaned from despairing clergy, anxious over the effects of current teaching. I have heard the same story from several sources in the same diocese and I am satisfied that it is substantially accurate. A married couple went to see their priest for counselling. The husband had been reluctant and did not like what he heard. He stormed out, but decided to calm down and return to the counselling session. On entering the room, he saw his wife and the priest together on the floor, *in flagrante delicto*. The husband acted swiftly. Placing his right foot on the clerical posterior, he pinned the guilty couple to the floor. With his left hand, he reached for the telephone and summoned nearby witnesses; he then quickly telephoned the bishop. 'Bishop,' he roared, 'I have my foot on the adulterous ass of one of your priests.' He then informed the Vestry (the Parochial Church Council).

After due consideration, the Vestry asked the bishop for the priest's deposition, not because of his behaviour *but because he refused to admit that he had been wrong*. The bishop was furious, *but not with the priest*. The Council was, he said, unchristian and unloving. They should accept both the priest and his loving relationship with the adulterous wife.

The story has a sequel. The bishop subsequently sent the priest to look after a parish in the diocese which was going through a long interregnum between clergy, until such time as a new parish priest could be elected by the Vestry, the appropriate selection procedure in America. The adulterous priest moved into the rectory with the unfaithful wife, representing her to the people as his own wife. The parishioners discovered she was nothing of the kind, and went to see the bishop to demand an explanation and the removal of the offending clergyman. The bishop refused, and demanded they elect him as their rector. The Vestry refused. The bishop replied that he would accept nobody else. There was stalemate. The parish, formerly thriving, declined rapidly and fell into debt. The day after I heard this story, I heard about the bishop of the next diocese who had resigned quietly so as to be able to live far away with his mistress.

Behind such incidents, and there are many, there lies the long saga of the surrender by the leadership of the Episcopal Church to the powerfully insistent ethos of twentieth century American culture. Modern American liberal theology, including moral theology, might be summed up in a single phrase: if you can't beat them, join them. The 1960s was the decade of the great collapse; the assumptions of the present leadership of the Church, on both sides of the Atlantic, were formed then; few seem able to move on from the ethos of those times, or to see how hollow its supposed new understanding often was.

It was above all the age in which the young were supposed to have new insight; the young were going to remake the world their elders had wrecked with war and hatred and repression. Bogus sub-Freudianism, with an admixture of bogus sub-Marxism of an undemanding kind, floated in the atmosphere like a kind of all-purpose ideological ectoplasm. Love and freedom would soothe away all conflicts, dissolve all principles, remove the necessity for all hard moral decisions. A classic example of the 1960s breakdown (he would say breakthrough) is described by Paul J. Moore junior, later to be a controversial 'liberal' Bishop of New York, in his book *Take a Bishop Like Me*:

In the sixties, our children, one by one, established close relationships with lovers. . . . Were we being sensible in [our] acceptance of 'living in sin', or were we being weak? I rather think we were being pragmatic. It was quite clear that our children were not going to break off these liaisons no matter what we said. . . . Our fallback position was that when they visited us, they would stay in separate rooms. Even that fell apart late one night in the Adirondacks where we were vacationing. Our family camp there has separate cabins . . . when I arrived, exhausted, about midnight, [my wife] told me that my son and his girlfriend were together in another cabin. . . . They were to be with us for a month. Perhaps we were too tired to fight it. Perhaps we knew that sooner or later this last rampart of respectability would crumble. Perhaps beneath it all we really did not object. We decided to let them stay together.

The law, Bishop Moore goes on to say, 'is an instrument of love, the servant of love. When the law goes against this higher command-ment, it can be broken.' 'All you need is love, love,' sang the Beatles; 'love is all you need.' Or, in the words of a slogan daubed on many of the walls of Paris during the student revolution of 1968, 'It is forbidden to forbid.'

Sex Rears its Ugly Head

The effects in more recent times of this collapse of leadership in the field of sexual ethics may be conveniently studied in the history of a proposed religious education curriculum, prepared for use in parishes and schools and published by the Episcopal Church Centre. In 1982, the General Convention of ECUSA passed a resolution that educational ways should be developed 'by which the Church can assist its people in their formative years (children through adults) to develop moral and spiritual perspectives in matters re-lating to sexuality and family life'. To this end, a body sonorously entitled the Task Force on Human Sexuality and Family Life was appointed. In due course, the Task Force presented the fruits of its labours: these were accepted by the Episcopal Church Centre, field-tested, cosponsored by the National Association of Episcopal Schools, and published in September 1987 under the title *Sexuality: A Divine Gift*, with a commendation by the presiding bishop.

The aim of the document is made clear from the outset; it is to design a sexual morality based on the supposed demands of con-temporary society rather than on those of Christian tradition and biblical teaching. The document takes it for granted that if we 'ignore the sociological data and . . . follow the so-called traditional standards of . . . strict heterosexual monogamy', the consequence will be that 'noncommunication and enmity result', and that the Church will be divided. Ethical principles were to be derived from 'sociological data'. At no point is it specified what this data actually consists of, but the intention is clear enough. What already *is* would now determine what ought to be. Thus moral theology would become a matter of helping individuals adapt to the status quo with the minimum of conflict.

The theological presuppositions underlying this teaching material for children and young adults are clearly spelled out in the document. Firstly, it is based on the presupposition that revelation is continuous, an 'on-going process'. As one critic, Dr Stephen B. Smith commented, 'Questions quickly surface such as who is to discern this revelation and how will we know it when we see it? Is the group that produced *Sexuality: A Divine Gift* offering a component of that revelation as part of the process?'

Perhaps so, Dr Smith continued. Certainly we need some kind of revelation, as he goes on to comment wryly, if we are going to affirm, as the document does, that 'sexual intercourse is ... a Christian sacrament'. A sacrament, according to traditional Anglican teaching, is an 'outward and visible sign of an inward and spiritual grace'. Thus, according to *Sexuality: A Divine Gift*, 'our sexual encounters can be moments when our physical and emotional connections ... can open our eyes to ... the promise of our loving relationship with Almighty God'. Marriage, however, is not mentioned: sex is clearly conceived as being sacramental without it. Indeed, the language of this passage suggests more than one sexual partner, perhaps many; 'encounters' and 'physical and emotional connections' does not suggest a context of fidelity within Christian marriage.

The recommended educational resources accompanying the course make it clear that this is the case. One of these is another 'curriculum', *About Your Sexuality* by Deryck Calderwood, produced by the Unitarian Universalist Church. This has the aim, *inter alia*, of providing 'accurate information to young people about heterosexual, bisexual, and homosexual lovemaking'. Several 'approaches' are suggested at the 'initiation' stage, 'designed to promote interaction among the group members'. These include discussing songs about intercourse to discover what feelings they arouse, listening to songs about 'gay' and lesbian lovemaking, and performing such exercises as the following:

If available, play 'I'm in love with a wonderful guy' from *South Pacific*, or 'The man I love' from Gershwin's *Lady be Good* and ask the group if they could imagine a man singing these ballads. Even without these specific songs, you can engage in the same activity, using everything from 'golden oldies' like 'Night and Day' (Cole Porter), 'Goodnight Sweetheart' (Rudy Vallee) ... to the latest hit songs that imply a man or a woman or leave the object of affection anonymous. If any of your group is a guitar player/singer, you might arrange to have a few appropriate songs sung, and if possible, have the whole group join in the second time around.

Two filmstrips showing heterosexual and both male and female homosexual lovemaking, together with two cassette recordings, accompany this material. The descriptive material about the cassettes, for the use of group leaders, includes the following, selected at random:

SUSAN: A woman explains that she began her sexual experience on the heterosexual end of the continuum and moved toward relating to both sexes where she feels most comfortable. (3 minutes)
RICK: A man explains how he began his sexual experiences on the homosexual end of the scale, originally believing he was gay. He describes the attraction each sex now holds for him. (3 minutes)
SHARON: Shares her lesbian lovemaking experiences and how they enabled her to feel like a complete woman for the first time. . .

The filmstrip includes visual depictions of heterosexual intercourse (including oral-anal contact), lesbian lovemaking, and male homosexual intercourse. It also features a man masturbating and tasting his semen. The Episcopalian 'Task Force' recommended this material warmly: it 'does a nice job', they say, 'of showing representative young people'. They do, however, counsel caution:

These materials are excellent with older teenage and adult audiences. Because they are sometimes explicit, they are best used by an educator with some experience, and parental consent is strongly recommended.

On the publication of *Sexuality: A Divine Gift*, a lively controversy ensued, widely reported in the secular press; the Episcopal Church in general arouses less interest in the American press than the Church of England in the British press. Protests from the faithful flooded in. A campaign against the curriculum was mounted and given great impetus by a young deacon, Kendall Harmon, who with the support of his bishop prepared a swingeing and weighty critique entitled *A Deeply Disturbing Document*, copies of which, with accompanying documentation, he proceeded to distribute in considerable quantity all over the Anglican communion. When the General Convention voted on a motion thanking the task force for its work, it did not pass; but there was no explicit condemnation of the 'curriculum'. There are no plans for it to be reprinted officially. But any diocese which wishes to may use it.

Revolution Not Reform

Two things became clear during the course of the controversy. Firstly that, though several bishops had opposed the curriculum strongly, support from the leadership of the Church was considerable. The presiding bishop himself had commended it; it was officially published by the Church itself. Secondly, that there was a groundswell of opposition from the laity at large to changes which were clearly perceived as a dissolution of traditional Christian teaching. This is not to say that there was no lay support for the document; as Dr Bennett pointed out, there has been a liberalization of ECUSA as a whole, and not just of the leadership: 'The Episcopal Church', he asserted, 'has a rapidly changing membership with conservatives withdrawing and liberals from other denominations, notably from the Roman Catholic Church, joining in'. There was considerable support for the document from activist lay delegates at the General Convention. But there are many Episcopalians who oppose current trends who are now, possibly too late, beginning to find a voice. Certainly, it is clear that in general the membership of ECUSA still tends on most issues to be more conservative than its leadership, and sometimes much more conservative.

Episcopalians, however, are not (as once they used to be) a homogeneous group within American society. There has been a polarization of attitudes and opinions. Within the Episcopal Church, there are now two worlds. Women's ordination is seen as a key symbolic issue defining the line of separation, and has possibly done more than any other single issue to open out the divide. But it is not the only issue to have split the Church. There are several others of crucial importance: the right, not everywhere allowed, to use the old Book of Common Prayer; sexual ethics (as we have seen); the authority of the biblical revelation and of two thousand years of Christian tradition. Whether logically or illogically many Episcopalians group these issues together. If you are against women in the episcopate the likelihood is that you will be in favour of the right to use the 1928 American Prayer Book, against homosexual 'marriages' in Church, and in favour of upholding biblical authority in matters of doctrine and morals. If you are for women priests and bishops you are more likely to believe in social activism and a generally radical political stance than if you do not.

These divisions did not arise overnight. By the late 1980s, the Episcopal Church had been undergoing a process of fundamental change for nearly thirty years, a process consciously planned and executed issue by issue, and achieved by dedicated activists determined on seizing the structures of power within ECUSA. The first stage of their revolution is now complete; the second is under way. The metamorphosis of ECUSA has now entered a new stage. The real issue will increasingly be whether or not the Church is to undergo a revolution in faith and moral teaching so profound that questions seriously have to be asked – as C. S. Lewis predicted in his essay 'Priestesses in the Church?' (1948) – about whether or not 'a new religion is being embarked on'.

The radicals who have all but achieved this revolution are now so confident of victory that they hardly bother to hide what they are about. The best-known of these is the Rt Revd John Shelby Spong, Bishop of Newark, New Jersey, of whom it would be tempting to say that he is the David Jenkins of North America, were it not for the fact that he is taken very seriously indeed within his own Church. He is admirably frank about his intentions. Like C. S. Lewis, he sees the feminist reconstruction of Christian tradition as effecting a fundamental change. 'The liberals', he says,

tend to see the women's movement . . . primarily in terms of justice and human rights. That is too shallow a judgement in my view. The conservatives, on the other hand, see the women's movement as a fundamental break with history and tradition. . . . *They recognize . . . that much of what we Christians think of as crucial to the life of the Church will not survive the revolution. . . . They are correct.*

One clear and unmistakable sign of the revolution was the election in 1988 of Anglicanism's first woman bishop in Boston, Massachusetts. The character and opinions of the successful candidate are important here. For, though the official line of the liberal hierarchies on both sides of the Atlantic is that women's ordination is neither divisive nor revolutionary, this election seems to indicate otherwise. It is firmly believed by many Anglican bishops in England, including the Archbishop of Canterbury, that women in the priesthood are being accepted in the USA as part of a gradual reform of the ministry, that this development is working peacefully, and that it has no necessary connection with extreme political and theological radicalism. Their carefully arranged American tours insulate them from contact with the very large minority (at least 40 per cent, 60 per cent on women bishops) of Episcopalians who differ from the official liberal line, and who are shockingly underrepresented within the governing structures of the Episcopal Church.

The Harris Effect

What American traditionalists had feared was the election of a woman bishop who would seem to confirm the hierarchy's claim: one of the quieter and more apparently moderate women clergy who could be used to demonstrate by her mildness that nothing has really changed, that no one is threatened. This is not what has taken place. Barbara Harris, above all else, represents the spirit of hard, dedicated, intolerant liberalism which has become more and more powerful within the Episcopal Church, and which has caused such an exodus from the Church during the 1970s and 1980s. For some years now Ms Harris has written a weekly column (entitled *A Luta Continua*, Portuguese for 'the struggle continues'), whose dominant tone is that of a strident social activism. Perusal of this column does not make reassuring reading.

She does not see herself as a focus of unity. In 1987, for instance, she assailed the Primate of her Church, Bishop Edmond Browning, for being insufficiently radical over gay liberation. Bishop Browning's aim of 'building bridges' within the Church she thinks inessential. 'The role of prophet calls for far greater risk of alienating or disaffecting some in the community'. Although, according to Susan Levine of the *Philadelphia Inquirer*, at her post-election press conference 'there was little of the stridency or activism for which she long has been known', those who know her think there is little likelihood that she will mellow in the radical atmosphere of the House of Bishops (though there will be, for a time, a tactical withdrawal from public activism).

She knows who her enemies are. More than one of her columns has been dedicated to attacking the American Prayer Book Society, the surely unexceptionable aim of which is to achieve a state of affairs in which congregations and clergy who want to use the old Prayer Book have the right to do so. In America they have no automatic right to this, and some bishops forbid it: in this 'Anglican' Church, several priests have been deposed by their bishops for the crime of using the liturgy they grew up with. Nor does she believe in the right of bishops *not* to ordain women, or of dioceses not to license them, despite the House of Bishop's declaration of a 'conscience clause'. The 'conscience clause', she says, simply allows those who dissent to stay in the Church, nothing more.

The Harris package, of radical feminism (including God the Mother), left-wing political activism, the sexual revolution, and theological and liturgical modernism (to be enforced if necessary) increasingly represents the prevailing philosophy of the ruling élite of the Episcopal Church. It is a package which now forms the basis for much, if not most, theological education within ECUSA. The radical complexion of ECUSA as an institution seems set for the foreseeable future. Those opposed to current tendencies, it seems safe to say, will be increasingly marginalized. Some sign of this was given at the 1988 General Convention in Detroit. For eighteen months before the convention took place, a working party appointed by the Primate of ECUSA, Presiding Bishop Edmond S. Browning, had been meeting regularly to try to work out some compromise formula whereby those who could not in conscience accept women bishops, or the ministrations of any bishop who consented to her ordination, could nevertheless remain within ECUSA. One obvious problem was the provision of acceptable episcopal ministrations at confirmations (Anglicans still insist that only a bishop may confirm). The working party, after great expense of time and money, arrived at a formula which satisfied both sides; that the presiding bishop of ECUSA was empowered to appoint an 'episcopal visitor' to care for dissident parishes within a 'hostile' diocese. After debates in both houses of the General Convention, in which little evidence was shown of charity or pastoral intention towards those who argued in favour of this solution, it was thrown out in favour of a provision so watered down as to be meaningless. Such visitors would now be appointed only with the consent of the diocesan bishop concerned. But since in most cases it was precisely the unacceptability of the diocesan that was in question, such provisions could, to say the very least, not be relied upon. The convention passed a high-sounding resolution, which included the words 'this Church is confident that the Bishops of the Episcopal Church will deal pastorally with those bishops, priests, deacons or lay persons who may not be able to accept women as bishops'. The simple fact was that, because of their actions in the past, traditionalists within ECUSA had no such confidence in most bishops of the Episcopal Church. Their mistrust was to prove well-founded. Within days of the election of Barbara Harris, bishops who had indicated their intention of consenting to her election were already making it plain that there would be no 'episcopal visitors' in their dioceses.

The Dissidents' Dilemma

Since 1976, as assurances of toleration rang more and more hollow with the passing of the years, life has become increasingly difficult for those who could not accept what had happened. For those who have refused to leave the Episcopal Church over the ordination of women, it has been a matter of retreating into safe areas: that is, into parishes where historic mainstream Christianity is still taught and practised. And, as Garry Bennett puts it in the preface,

Perhaps the most difficult position has been that of the traditionalist clergy. Many felt a great loyalty to Anglicanism as they had understood it: they had no desire to join a schismatic church nor did they wish to become Roman Catholics. . . . Most have endeavoured to keep their heads down and make their parishes enclaves of an older kind of Anglicanism.

But this was always bound to be a temporary expedient. And with the election and consecration of Barbara Clementine Harris as Suffragan Bishop of Massachusetts, the real crisis of the Episcopal Church was upon it. For those who truly believed that women can be neither priests nor bishops, an almost impossible situation now presented itself. Most obviously for those in the dioceses most closely concerned. But there were problems for those whose own bishop was male: if a bishop is no bishop, then the priests she 'ordains' are not priests. Those who wish to remain within a Church with women bishops they do not recognize must ascertain the pedigree of everyone claiming to be a priest before they receive his ministrations. The situation becomes absurd. It is at this point, of course, that those opposed to women in the priesthood are most likely to be accused of pedantry and obscurantism, even of attempting to stifle the Holy Spirit (those in the movement to ordain women are for the most part wholly convinced of their monopoly of the guidance of the Holy Spirit in this matter).

One answer to such accusations, from the American experience, is that if the objections to women priests were a matter of simple prejudice, it would by now have become clear, from people's experience of some thousand women priests ordained since 1974 in America, that there are no more substantial objections to women priests than there are to women doctors or women pilots. This is far from having happened. In a survey conducted by the Episcopalian journal *The Living Church* in 1986, ten years after the vote to allow women priests, slightly more than 50 per cent of those expressing an opinion were in favour of women's ordination, just under 40 per cent opposed, around 10 per cent neutral. Nearly 50 per cent, that is, were not convinced. These figures are based on a poll with a low sample; but they are confirmed by the almost identical findings of a Gallup poll carried out in the diocese of Atlanta the previous year, which found a similar degree of opposition to women priests after nearly a decade's experience of them. The opposition would, of course, be even higher if the million or more Episcopalians who have left over the last two decades had remained. Certainly the very least that may be asserted is that there is no sign whatever that a consensus in favour of women's ordination is likely soon to emerge among the laity, and that this issue has split the Episcopal Church very seriously indeed. Opposition to women bishops is even more substantial. A Gallup poll conducted in 1988 by the American Prayer Book Society found that well over 50 per cent of Episcopalians are opposed to women in the episcopate.

The extent of the opposition in America is not acknowledged by the English Movement for the Ordination of Women to whom it is a great embarrassment. The *Church Times* – which has consistently supported MOW – gives a grossly slanted picture of the American Church, and it is probably the case that in England many bishops who support MOW genuinely imagine that in the USA little opposition remains. The House of Bishops of ECUSA, elected by electoral college, does not – as we have seen – represent lay opinion accurately, and is overwhelmingly in favour. Liberal Churchmen have shown themselves over the last fifteen years to be skilled political manoeuvrers. Getting their candidates on to the right committees, and particularly on to the important but low-key diocesan standing committees (which decide on what names shall appear on the slate of candidates for election to episcopal office), has been their particular skill. 'The American House of Bishops', said one observer to me, 'is the product of endless meetings behind closed doors in smoke-filled rooms. The Episcopal church is the last refuge of Tammany Hall politics.'

Lex Orandi, Lex Credendi

Outside America, attention has been focused more on the ordination of women in the Episcopal Church than on any other single cause, for obvious reasons. With so many women priests actually functioning, ECUSA has become a kind of test bed. Much less well understood has been another Episcopalian controversy, that arising from a process of liturgical reform which seemed – at the time – to come to its logical conclusion with the adoption of a volume confusingly known as the *Book of Common Prayer* in 1979. In contrast with the English equivalent, this is not an *Alternative Service Book*; it officially *replaces* the existing prayer book and becomes the norm. In some dioceses, use of the old *Book of Common Prayer (1928)* is actually forbidden. And since in Anglican tradition worship and doctrine are bound up together on the principle *lex orandi, lex credendi*, the 1979 book became, also, the norm for doctrine, if any such thing as norms can be said any longer to exist in the Episcopal Church. The consequences of this have been little short of revolutionary, though it is a revolution that is still largely unseen. But once a generation of Episcopalians have been taught from this book, a major doctrinal shift (already, as we have seen, being encompassed in other ways) will have been consolidated.

One example (though one involving a fundamental change in belief) will suffice to show what is involved here. The sacrament of

Baptism, all Christians agree, is the basic sacrament of the Christian life. Through Baptism we become Christians. And the effect of Baptism is that by God's power the falling away of humanity from God's grace which Christians believe has in some way occurred, so that the human race goes its own way and not God's way, is reversed. Mankind's 'original sin' is overcome, through the death and resurrection of Christ. In Baptism, we die with Christ and rise again with Him. There is, in the words of the Prayer Book, 'a death unto sin, and a new birth unto righteousness'. 'Except a man be born again of water and the spirit', said Jesus, 'he can not enter into the Kingdom of God' (John 3:5). This is known as the doctrine of baptismal regeneration, and it is fundamental to mainstream Christianity, both Catholic and Protestant, and certainly Anglican. It has been simply removed from the baptism service of the 1979 prayer book. Regeneration, to which there are four references in the old prayer book, has been replaced by the undefined term 'initiation'. There is no controversy about what is intended. Since the Anglican tradition is that doctrine is embodied in the Church's authorized prayer book, one bishop is reported as having said, Episcopalians need no longer believe in the doctrine of original sin.

Despite such occasional moments of frankness, Episcopalian liberals have tended to claim that no revolution, doctrinal or otherwise, is intended in its liturgical practice, simply an evolutionary process of renewal by which no one except extreme reactionaries need be alienated. This has become more difficult to argue since the publication in 1987 of a slim black paperbound book unassumingly entitled *Liturgical Texts for Evaluation*. It was published by ECUSA's official Standing Liturgical Commission, for experimental testing in seminaries and selected parishes. The original intention was that it should be discussed by the 1988 General Convention and that some version of it should then be authorized for general use. Like *Sexuality: A Divine Gift*, however, it aroused strong and widespread opposition from traditionalists. Some courageous seminarians refused to attend services employing these rites. One seminary, the Trinity Episcopal School for Ministry, (TESM), refused to cooperate in the experiment and published its objections in a substantial document. (TESM is the establishment of which Bennett wrote in the preface, discussing the decline in standards in Episcopalian seminaries generally, 'It is significant that

Evangelicals have for the first time felt it necessary to establish a separate seminary for their own ordinands.') The book was withdrawn from discussion at the pre-Lambeth General Convention in 1988. It, or some version of it, will undoubtedly surface again at some point in the future, and it is undoubtedly worth study as an indication of the Episcopalian Establishment's long-term aims.

The aims of these liturgies were set out in an accompanying paper and in a 'leader's manual'. These made their underlying intention quite clear: to go as far as possible towards phasing out the New Testament perception of God as 'Father' and of Jesus as being his Son, and to installing a liturgy based as nearly on radical feminist norms, as can be achieved without the laity becoming too conscious of the shift that has taken place. The real revolution is not to occur yet. 'The time may come', as the 'leader's manual' put it, 'when, by using the images of this rite in prayer, another generation may well reform and renew the perceptions and images of God sufficiently to actually call God "Mother" without hurting and alienating many faithful people.'

In the meantime, God the Father and God the Son are heavily 'de-emphasized'. This is particularly the case in often repeated texts, like the 'Gloria Patri', traditionally said or sung after the recitation of psalms and canticles in Morning and Evening prayer. Thus, 'Glory be to the Father, and to the Son and to the Holy Spirit' becomes 'Honour and Glory to God, and to God's eternal Word, and to God's Holy Spirit'. It is not only masculine terms which are targeted but any language which emphasizes God's power and majesty; these are unacceptable in an egalitarian age. The word 'Almighty' is excluded, because 'the concern to minimize hierarchical, domineering pictures of God makes frequent use of this title seem out of place in liturgies focusing on God's tender and intimate concern for all people in community'. Such notions cannot be entirely excluded, of course, from such historic texts as *Sanctus* and *Benedictus*: here, the processing is confined to the filleting of masculine language. But the 'Black Mass Book', as its opponents called it, did not confine itself to the censoring of historic texts. There were two new eucharistic liturgies, entitled 'Image of God' and 'The Nurturing God'. Space does not permit a detailed analysis; suffice it to say that they were both, by any traditional standards, clearly heretical, and were withdrawn even before the Convention:

this does not necessarily mean, of course, that they (or something similar) will not reappear at some later date. 'The Nurturing God' in particular, despite spurious claims to be based on biblical imagery, was very close indeed in spirit to the neo-pagan Mother God liturgies of radical Christian and 'post-Christian' feminism (examined in detail by this author in his book *What Will Happen To God?*).

Unsheathing the Mailed Fist

The 'Black Mass Book' brings me back to that room full of young men and women who refuse to participate in such performances and who reject the whole revolution of which they form part – a revolution initiated by women's ordination but now well into its second phase, with the full backing of those who hold power within the Episcopal Church. Some of these young people have already paid the price for their defiance, and it was very clear from their words and demeanour that they knew what to expect. It was a grim but by no means uninspiring meeting. By the end of it some were in tears; but there was in all those present a courage and resolve I found deeply impressive. One ordinand who had just completed his training, clearly a young man of exemplary learning and piety, asked my advice in some agony of spirit as to whether or not he should proceed to ordination in such a Church. For what it was worth, I said I thought he should, that in times like these the people would need faithful priests more than ever. I could have saved my breath. I learned three weeks later that his bishop had subsequently refused to ordain him. His story is not uncommon.

It is one of the great features of the revolution in the Episcopal Church (one which has clear implications for Anglicanism as a whole and clear parallels in other parts of the communion, notably England), that as any idea of clear and objectively held doctrine has crumbled so intolerance has grown. As 'inclusiveness' has increased, so has the feeling of exclusion among those who have not accepted the 'liberal' revolution. Despite calls at the Lambeth Conference for 'mutual respect'; despite a statement of intent by the presiding bishop that during his term of office there would be 'no outcasts'; despite such claims as that in *The Episcopalian*, in the aftermath of

Barbara Harris's election, that 'we go forward together – always with concern for those who hear a different beat from the drum', there has been a heavy price to pay for such 'concern': acquiescence and silence. As the Bishop of Quincy, the Rt Revd Edward Mc-Burney, put it in the same issue of *The Episcopalian*,

Whatever Lambeth may have said, within our own Episcopal Church dialogue is muted, respect is minimal, and harsh invitations to depart are issued.

What bridges can there be to the other side? . . .

The chief reason for our failure in relationships is remarkable spiritual arrogance. We, the minority, have been assured that the Holy Spirit is doing a new thing and we are to 'get with it'. Or, 'Be open to the Spirit, and then you will agree with us. . . .'

We, on our side of the divide, have experienced an outpouring of triumphalism from those who carried the day, by the narrowest of margins, at Minneapolis [in 1976, in the vote on women's ordination]. Triumphalism, spiritual arrogance, and ridicule will clear the field of any possibility of dialogue or any hope of unity.

The Great Exodus

With or without 'harsh invitations to depart', there has been a rapid decline in the membership of the Episcopal Church since the late sixties. At least part of the explanation for this must surely be the feeling of many former Episcopalians that they had become strangers in their own church. There have, of course, been other analyses: it is hardly a matter that can be ignored, and few are likely to accept that their policies have had such a result. The Episcopal Church's falling membership was, according to the writer Bob Libby, an observer at the 1988 General Convention in Detroit, a major topic of discussion for the delegates. The questions on everyone's lips, as he wrote later in the weekly *Episcopalian*, were these:

Why is the Episcopal Church losing members? Why are we not growing?

Nearly everybody at General Convention, from the Presiding Bishop to the Prayer Book Society, raised these questions. Bishop Browning suggested it is due to lack of 'clarity of mission' while the Prayer Book

Society editorialized, 'We have departed from our Anglican heritage'. David B. Collins, president of the House of Deputies, attributed the decline to 'lack of intensity of faith'.

Listening to conversation in the exhibit hall or in the elevator one could hear everything from 'we are not inclusive enough' to 'we are so inclusive that anything goes'.

The traditionalist explanation – that the character of their Church has changed; that mainstream Christianity has been all but officially abandoned; and that their Church has become, in Bennett's words 'a national force for radical secular causes' – seems to this writer the correct analysis, as well as the most obvious one. But, as we have seen, there is no shortage of alternatives. According to the Revd Wayne Schwab, 'executive for evangelism' at the Episcopal Church Centre, the real explanation is demographical. 'Main-line middle-class church families', he is reported as saying, 'have a birth-rate that is one-half that of evangelical fundamentalist denominations'. It seems a curious explanation for the loss of nearly a third of a Church's members during a period of general growth in both churchgoing and in the population at large; the claim seems to imply a considerable fall in the Episcopalian birth-rate. But this is not, so far as I know, an explanation yet offered by the Episcopal Church Centre.

Other explanations are harder to assess, simply because hard evidence, in the nature of things, is difficult to come by. Presiding Bishop Edmond Browning, whose early public statements left Garry Bennett with 'no doubt that the primacy of the American Church has come to a deeply committed liberal', addressed the question in his opening sermon at the Detroit convention with a series of further questions: always a liberal instinct at moments of perplexity. But these particular questions implied a clear answer: that without the liberal revolution of the 1960s and 1970s the health of the Episcopal Church would have been even shakier than it was in the 1980s:

What if the Episcopal Church did not allow for open discussion and discernment, if our structures did not allow and encourage each and every one of us to bring together revelation and our human experience of that revelation? Would we be a better Church – a Church more prepared for mission? . . .

What if the Episcopal Church had not voted to ordain women to the priesthood and the episcopate? Would we be a better Church – a Church more prepared for mission?

What if the Episcopal Church had not taken a strong position on South Africa? Had not voted disinvestment, sanctions and the breaking of diplomatic relations? Would we be a better Church – a Church more prepared for mission?

What if the Episcopal Church had not taken a courageous action and declared that homosexual persons are children of God? What if the standing Commission on Human Affairs and Health had found other matters to discuss than human sexuality? Would we be a better Church – a Church more prepared for mission?

And so on. The individual questions invite varying responses of an obvious enough kind, including the observations, which I offer in passing, that 'open discussion and discernment' is a luxury less and less available – especially in seminaries – to those who dissent from the official line, that no traditionalist known to me has ever had any doubt whatsoever that 'homosexual persons are children of God', and that to 'declare' any such thing is not courageous action but deeply patronizing attitudinizing.

The real question, however, is this. If the Episcopal Church had persisted with the policy of growth and mission, based liturgically and doctrinally on the 1928 Book of Common Prayer – a policy which was continuously and strikingly effective from the 1930s until the early 1960s, until it was overturned by the revolution of the 1960s and 1970s, *then*, to put the Presiding Bishop's question once more, would the Episcopal Church 'be a better Church – a Church more prepared for mission?'

The Presiding Bishop would very firmly say 'no'; far more Episcopalians than he would be prepared to admit would say 'yes', and with equal emphasis. Who is right? If an organization decides on radical changes in its operations, and half way through the implementation of the changes a loss of effectiveness becomes apparent, those who were opposed to the changes will claim to be vindicated, those who had pressed for them will say that the decline would have been worse without them, and that to reverse the decline the revolution must be completed. Who is right? Neither side can prove their case, unless there is a similar organization that has resisted change which can serve as an experimental 'control'.

Anglicans in the Desert

Such an experimental comparison is arguably available, for groups of Episcopalians have, in fact, broken away from ECUSA or – as they would put it – have remained faithful. They are, they claim, 'continuing' Anglicans, while the revolutionary Church based at their expensive offices at 815, Second Avenue, New York, has ceased to be the Episcopal Church and become something else. This exercise is not, at first sight, promising to the traditionalist cause. The numbers of continuing Anglicans, particularly at first, were very small. Not only that: soon after its inauguration, the new Church broke up in apparent disarray into several feuding groups. 'The schismatic Church', one hostile commentator put it to me, 'was simply showing its schismatic nature by going into a whole new series of schisms'.

The reasons for this break-up of the breakaway Church are many and complex, and may have as much to do with the personalities and history within the Episcopal Church of its first generation of bishops as with any other single cause; they were all men of strong character who had fought for years from within ECUSA to preserve what they saw as the historic faith, sometimes having created in their parishes what might be seen as 'no-go' areas, in which their personal style and authority had been paramount. Once they had episcopal authority, and the chance to mould the Church according to their vision of it on a wider field of action than that of their parishes, friction between them was inevitable. One 'continuing' bishop, indeed, said to me that 'until my generation of bishops has died or retired, the continuing Church movement will not reach its full potential'.

Whether the leaders of the 'continuing' Church were right to leave is not for me to say here. The same bishop also said to me that 'we are not the answer: we are a sign of the tragedy'. If he had not left, he said, his people would have left without him, to join the great limbo of the unchurched who form the majority of the million and more of former Episcopalians who have voted with their feet. The question is this: small numbers and fragmentation apart, what has happened to these first continuing churchmen since? Have they grown fewer? Are they disappearing altogether? If so, are they disappearing at the same rate as ECUSA, or faster? Or are they actually growing? These are not questions often asked by the leaders of the Anglican Communion, to whom their very existence is an anathema. A member of the Church of England is, whether he likes it or not, officially in communion with Bishop Jenkins of Durham and Bishop Spong of Newark, New Jersey, who many would say are apostates. They may share the same mainstream Christian faith as a 'continuing' bishop, but they must not receive communion from him.

Traditionalists who have remained within ECUSA have in the past been as hostile to the 'continuing' Churches as the liberal establishment, sometimes even more so. They tend to believe that if the continuing Anglicans had remained within the fold to continue the fight, then the opposition to the liberal revolution might have been more effective. Continuing Churchmen, for their part, feel that if the traditionalist Episcopalians who remained inside (to engage in what they themselves believed from the first to be a futile struggle) had all joined them, the continuing Church would by now be a real and viable alternative, that it might by now have reached 'critical mass'.

However this may be, the continuing Church movement is small in numbers and it is fragmented. The question remains, however, is it growing or disappearing? The answer is beyond dispute; the movement, though still small, is growing steadily. According to one source, there are now some 15,000 to 20,000 continuing Anglicans. In the nature of things, figures are difficult to come by but at the present rate of growth, and the present rate of decline of ECUSA, it is possible to surmise that they will be more numerous than members of the Episcopal Church at some point during the next century.

What, however, is the character of this continuing movement? Is it simply a resting place for the weary and the reactionary, for former Episcopalians who wish to live in the past? These are questions it is difficult to answer except from within. What follows is based on my own experience of one part of the movement, the Diocese of Christ the King, whose bishop, the Rt Revd Robert Morse, invited me on a three week speaking tour early in 1988.

I began by attending the tenth anniversary celebrations in San Francisco of the founding of the diocese and of Bishop Morse's own consecration. I then spoke to parishes and other groups in

Southern California, Alabama, South Carolina, Washington DC, Connecticut and New York. I slept in a different bed almost every night for three weeks. What I saw was outside my experience in the Church of England or the Episcopal Church – a missionary church on the move, outward-looking and positive in its mood and attitudes. Ten years before, the diocese had begun with a bishop and six priests. Now it had two bishops and over fifty parishes. Most of these had begun by meeting in houses, garages, rented halls, churches lent by other denominations; everywhere I went I spoke and preached to substantial congregations who had just finished building their own churches or were in the process of building, or were drawing up plans to build soon.

Wherever I went, for the first time, I found myself among Anglicans who were truly united by a common faith with their bishop and all the clergy and laity of the diocese. It may be objected that this is not surprising given the circumstances. It was a heady experience, nevertheless, to be among men and women of the American Anglican tradition who were looking forward to the future and who were entirely free of the necessarily embattled defensiveness of those so close to them in faith but who were still struggling within ECUSA with the growing apostasy of that institution. This is in no way to impugn ECUSA traditionalists, whose mind-set was, before the 1989 ECM Synod in Fort Worth, in many ways identical with (but one stage more desperate than) traditionalists within the Church of England. But to be within a diocese (however scattered) in which a confident and mature acceptance of the faith once for all delivered was so notably present, not among an embattled minority but as a basic assumption of membership, is not an experience I shall easily forget. To say that its members were one in faith is by no means to say that there was, as liberals tend to say of the orthodox, a tendency to closed minds or easy answers. But there was an absolute unity over essentials; the expression *consensus fidelium* continually sprang to my mind. One memory remains strong. At the tenth anniversary eucharist in St Peter's Cathedral, I looked from the sanctuary at the clergy of the diocese, occupying the front rows of pews in the nave. As they sang the hymn, 'Onward Christian Soldiers', I noticed that several were in tears, as they sang the familiar words:

We are not divided,
All one body we,
One in hope and doctrine
One in charity . . .

Nearly all of them were former Episcopalians, though a new generation was beginning of young priests who had known nothing else.
Most of them had known, all too bitterly, the experience of a
divided Church, with little hope or charity to go round. They had
paid a heavy price, many of them, to be standing where they stood
now. They had withstood persecution and ridicule; some of them
had lost pension rights, all of them had suffered serious financial
loss. These were not easy or sentimental tears; their joy was hard
won.

I had been warned to expect crankiness and eccentricity; I found
little, simply a straightforward Anglicanism, liturgically simple and
unfussy, doctrinally mainstream Christian. I was told that I would
find extreme right-wing attitudes. Certainly, the political ethos was
conservative. But in one city I visited in Alabama, when a group of
Nigerian Anglicans had tried to attend the local Episcopal Church
with all its 'liberal' ecclesiastical positions in place, they had not been
made to feel welcome. It was at the hard-line traditionalist 'continuing' parish that they found what they were entitled to expect – total
acceptance as human beings, as well as the orthodox Christian
teaching they had known in their own country.

The Last Stand of the Faithful Remnant

Whatever may be said about the ecclesiological legitimacy of the
'continuing' Church movement (a subject on which the last word
has certainly not been spoken), the very least that must be asserted
is that it has given an example of courage and steadfastness uncommon in Western mainline Christendom in our times. It is clear,
however, that for most traditionalist Episcopalians it is simply not
an alternative they are prepared to consider. They are entitled to
their choice; they too have withstood persecution and ridicule and
they too have kept the same faith. What divided traditionalist
Episcopalians and continuing Anglicans before the great historic

watershed of the Fort Worth Synod in June 1989 was their different assessments of the historical situation of the Episcopal Church itself. 'Continuing' churchmen firmly believe that from the moment the Episcopal Church decided to ordain women it had become irreversibly compromised and that any struggle to save it was futile. ECUSA traditionalists have stayed to fight over women priests and other issues, believing that the present secular captivity of the Episcopal Church could eventually be ended. Now that a woman had been consecrated bishop, it became clear to all that current tendencies were locked, apparently irreversibly, into the institutional structures of the Episcopal Church.

What then is the future for orthodox Christian witness within ECUSA itself? In the wake of the election of Barbara Harris, most Episcopalians finally accepted – if they had not done so before – that the institutional Church centred on the General Convention and ruled from the Episcopal Church Centre at 815 Second Avenue, New York, was now definitively in 'liberal' hands. But in the midst of the confusion and decline the whole liberal revolution had brought about, a curious phenomenon had already begun to be noted: that numbers were not falling away in all parishes, and in all dioceses, at the same rate. The liberal diocese of New York, for example, was declining fast, but the orthodox diocese of Fort Worth was growing steadily. Liberal parishes and dioceses were often in financial difficulties while orthodox enclaves were flourishing. There were signs too that the opposition of traditionalist Episcopalians, hitherto low-key and ineffective, was at last gaining in resolution. The tactic that seemed to be emerging in the wake of the Harris election was not to attempt to recapture the 'General Convention' Church; that was now impossible. The aim now was to hold the orthodox together and either to allow the rest of ECUSA simply to wither away or to leave ECUSA in a body; at the time of writing it is impossible to say which of these courses will prevail.

Holding traditionalists together, it was clear, was an urgent priority after the election of Barbara Harris. Many now believed that this was the end of the road; in one parish where I stayed a few days after the Massachusetts election, one which happened to own and control its own church buildings and to be financially independent of its diocese, I found that the rector had just written to the local Roman Catholic archbishop to inaugurate negotiations about the possibility of establishing the entire parish, lock, stock and barrel, under an 'Anglican rite' Roman Catholic jurisdiction (a path a handful of parishes had already taken). Events persuaded him otherwise; but his was not the only parish in which it was a close run thing. One parish, in Atlanta, Georgia, left early in 1989 to join the Roman Catholic Church.

The urgency of the situation was one element that precipitated a group of bishops who were members of the Evangelical and Catholic Mission, a traditionalist fellowship founded in 1976 after the Minneapolis decision, to issue a pastoral letter to all its members. Its tone was both dramatic and sombre. It opened with a strongly worded preamble, calling on traditionalists to 'forgo precipitate and individualistic reactions' to the election, while awaiting 'the enactment of a comprehensive reaction to the crisis'. The bishops called a Synod, to 'consider how we shall be the Church within the Episcopal Church and to adopt a detailed and unified plan for active witness in the face of the institution's present disintegration'. The preamble minces no words:

The final crisis of the Episcopal Church is now upon us. We, as bishops in the Church of God who exercise our ministry within the Episcopal Church, are deeply aware of the anguish of many of the institution's members over the progressive disintegration of its faithful witness to the gospel over the last two decades. . . . we are convinced that there is a crucial distinction to be made between the God-given order of the Church and the humanly invented institutions in the Church. . . . Considered as an institution, the Episcopal Church is in rebellion against this order. The venerable Anglican principle of comprehending nonessentials within clearly defined doctrinal and moral limits has been replaced in the practice of this institution by a vague and sentimental notion of 'inclusivism' which sets at naught the classical Christian standards of belief and behaviour. It is ever more evident that the tenderness with which this notion is set forth is but a thin velvet glove sheathing the mailed fist of intolerance.

Has the Episcopal Church gone past the point of no return? Certainly, as an institution, it is hard to see how, in its present form, it can be reclaimed. And it is the institutional shell – the boards and conventions and synods and bureaucracies – that people tend to identify with the Church itself. When the institution is doing its work faithfully, this does little harm. When it is not, disillusion, even disaster, are inevitable. By the late 1980s such a disaster seemed to have overtaken the Episcopal Church, at least for a generation. As Smith Hempstone, a nationally syndicated columnist, put it in the wake of the Harris election,

the point is that the Episcopal Church has ceased to be a vehicle through which ordinary men and women worship God and seek to do His will. Instead, it has become a platform for the promotion of fractious radical causes, receptive to every ephemeral wind . . . at the end of the day one wonders if one is not trying to preserve that which has ceased to exist.

Certainly, the Church of the General Convention and of 815 Second Avenue prompts such questions. The Episcopal Church as we have known it, the Church in which a quiet but deep Anglican spirituality, with its roots planted firmly in the rich soil of the Christian centuries but clearly able to function confidently amid the confusions and insanities of modern Western culture, that Church has gone forever. But the Church is always dying and being reborn, its message kept alive by a faithful remnant who nurture the divine spark through dark and dangerous times until, of itself, it ignites once more. It would be a brave man who would predict the future of the Anglican tradition in America. But the remnant of true and faithful believers – inside and outside the institutional confines of the Episcopal Church – is numerous and it is brave. Surely such faith and such courage will not be without their reward.

SIX

The Anglican Communion: Impairment or Disintegration?

At the beginning of the third week of the 1988 Lambeth Conference, the assembled bishops debated and voted on two resolutions concerning the consecration of women to the episcopate. The first was a complex composite motion, the interpretation of which was later to cause some considerable confusion:

This conference resolves

(1) that each province respect the decision and attitudes of other provinces whether in favour of or against the ordination and consecration of a woman to the espicopate, maintaining the highest possible degree of communion with provinces who differ.

(2) that bishops exercise courtesy and maintain communications with bishops who may differ, and with any woman bishop ensuring an open dialogue in the church, to whatever extent communion is impaired

(3) that the Archbishop of Canterbury, in consultation with the primates, appoint a commission:

(a) to provide for an examination of the relationships between the provinces of the Anglican Communion and ensure that the process of reception includes continuing consultation with other churches as well;

(b) to monitor and encourage the process of consultation within the communion and offer further pastoral guidelines.

(4) that in any diocese where reconciliation on these issues is necessary the diocesan bishop should seek continuing dialogue with and make pastoral provision for those clergy and congregations whose opinions differ from those of the bishop in order to maintain the unity of the diocese.

(5) that the conference recognizes the serious hurt which would result from the questioning by some of the validity of the episcopal acts of a woman bishop and likewise the hurt experienced by those whose con-

science would be offended by the ordination of a woman to the episcopate. The church needs to exercise sensitivity patience and pastoral care towards all concerned.

A phrase indicating that support for the motion did not necessarily indicate recognition of women in the episcopate was inserted during the course of the debate, so that those who could not accept women bishops could still vote affirmatively; and before the resolution ever saw the light of day it had been negotiated, by a working group which included both conservatives and radicals, to the form in which it was debated. In the end, a resolution whose original draft was worded so as to convey recognition of women in the episcopate had become a motion phrased to convey, willy-nilly, recognition of the confusion and division into which this issue had plunged the Anglican Communion in general, and the provinces determined to proceed in particular.

Another motion, uncomplicatedly requesting all bishops to refrain from proceeding to consecrate women, was supported by 40 per cent of the bishops voting. If the grossly overrepresented North Americans had not voted on either side, this motion would certainly have been carried.

Some idea of exactly how overrepresented the dwindling American Church was, and of how underrepresented other more thriving parts of the Anglican communion, can be grasped from the fact, strange but true, that the province of Southern Africa alone has more communicant members than the whole of the Episcopal Church of the USA, but that, nevertheless, it had only twelve episcopal votes in comparison with the 120 of ECUSA: 2.5% of the world's Anglicans were represented by 25% of its bishops. Another way of explaining the true message of the vote was to say that four provinces (by no means the largest) supported the consecration of women without further delay, and the other twenty-four did not.

Confusion and Dismay

Despite all this, the perception of the outside world was that there had been an overwhelming vote in favour of women bishops. The BBC television news interpreted the result of the ballot on the composite resolution as a decisive endorsement of women bishops, by

423 votes to 28, with 16 abstaining. In fact, as we have seen, it was nothing of the sort. But the second vote, urging restraint, was generally ignored. The BBC version, having winged along the airwaves, filled Anglican traditionalists around the waiting globe with despair and foreboding. Telephone lines from East to West began to vibrate with imprecations directed at the chaplains and secretaries of absent bishops who were thought to have sold out. Back in Canterbury the news of this reaction filtered in slowly, causing some consternation. There was talk of anti-traditionalist plots at the BBC (BBC religious broadcasting in London, as the *Crockford's* preface indicates, has a reputation among conservatives for liberal bias). But the BBC news desk certainly meant to tell the truth; they simply got it wrong.

This unwitting misrepresentation was still, however, culpable, given the explicit nature of an 'explanatory note' appended to the resolution, which makes it all the clearer that what the sprawling composite resolution had become by the time it was voted on was a kind of corporate recognition of the ecclesiological chaos into which the Communion had now fallen:

It is recognized that deep differences of opinion and the continued impairment of communion have resulted from the ordination of women to the priesthood. It is recognized that the ordination of a woman to the episcopate would result in a further impairment to communion. While impaired communion is not the same as a breaking of communion, such a development would require a reexamination of the relationship between the provinces of our communion.

The conference recognizes that the decision by a province to consecrate a woman as a bishop would touch fundamental concerns about the threefold ministry and would need ultimately to be affirmed by the whole church or (using the word in the technical sense) to be 'received'. Such a step should not be taken without an acknowledgement of the need to offer such a development for a full and open process (including the possibility of rejection) by the whole Communion and by the Universal Church. It would need to be accompanied by a high degree of pastoral care and support both for the women so ordained and for others affected by the decision. There would also need to be a strengthening of channels of communication between the provinces in order to aid theological reflection and to stimulate mutual sensitivity and care.

The language of this explanatory note, like that of article four of the resolution itself, reflected a growing realization of the human consequences of proceeding to such a step without real consensus. Such a public recognition, in an official document overwhelmingly accepted by the conference, was part of the price paid by the progressives for conservative agreement to recognize the inevitability of provincial autonomy. Their own preference would undoubtedly have been to continue their insistence on the illusory version of events they have propagated ever since women's ordination in America: that this development was widely accepted and working well; that opposition was confined to the comparatively small numbers who had left to join the continuing Churches; and that the claimed general acceptance of women's ordination among those remaining in ECUSA was demonstrated by the overwhelming support for women-priests within the House of Bishops.

The American bishops were obliged to accept the wording of the main motion. But when they returned home, they gave it a very different interpretation from that of the explanatory note. Like the BBC TV news, but with very much less excuse, many of them represented the overwhelming vote in its favour as Lambeth's endorsement of women in the episcopate.

It takes little imagination to see that the 'pastoral' section of the composite motion, together with that motion's pious sentiments regarding consultation (embodied in its proposal for a commission 'to monitor and encourage the process of consultation within the communion and offer further pastoral guidelines') will prove largely cosmetic in effect, however sincerely intended by some of the bishops who voted for it. Quite simply, it will be (indeed, already has been) ignored by the *nomenklatura* of the American Church wherever its recommendations are not to its liking. Underlying the whole motion, and infinitely more important than any of its other clauses, are the implications of its first article: 'that each province respect the decision and attitudes of other provinces whether in favour or against the ordination and consecration of a woman to the episcopate'.

Effectively, this means that the conference recognized that, even if it were to become clear that the overwhelming mind of the Communion was for caution, those determined to proceed would ignore them and proceed regardless, and this despite the admitted knowledge of the damage their action would cause. The same recognition of national independence was also embedded in the second motion, though the whole point of that motion was to warn of its dangers:

this conference affirms the office of bishop as an instrument of unity both within a diocese and in the interrelation of dioceses and while recognising the constitutional autonomy of each Anglican province urges that for the avoidance of further impairment of communion both within and between churches, provinces refrain from consecrating a woman as bishop.

The bishops who voted for this motion, though a large minority at Lambeth, nevertheless represented the overwhelming majority of Anglicans throughout the world. Despite this fact, and despite all the misgivings enshrined in both motions, within six months of the conference ECUSA had elected, confirmed, consecrated and installed a woman-bishop. In many dioceses in America, parishes which in the wake of the election of Barbara Harris had asked for special pastoral arrangements, of the kind envisaged by both the General Convention and the Lambeth Conference, were from the outset denied them. And almost the first action of the Commission set up by the conference was to request bishops from provinces which had not decided to ordain women to stay away from her consecration, in the knowledge of how such an action would cause divisions to surface.

Unreality

All this took place amid repeated assertions that nothing had really happened, that unity had been preserved by the Lambeth Conference, that the communion was intact after all. The fact was, however, that it was nothing of the kind. The conference and its aftermath revealed nothing so much as the capacity of many senior Anglicans for living in a state of heightened unreality. After the Harris consecration, the *Church Times* outdid itself. 'It seems probable', declared the Church of England's in-house journal, 'that the Anglican Communion will survive in more or less its present shape until the time comes for a reunion with the Roman Catholic Church, or another Christian family, after an agreement which accepts that a proportion of Anglican priests and bishops are women.'

The possibility that such a time will never come is rarely considered in such circles: and yet, it is not merely possible but almost certain that the Roman Catholic Church will never accept such an agreement, if only because it would rule out its own reunion with the Orthodox Churches for all time. (If one thing *is* certain it is that the Orthodox will not ordain women.) Within weeks of the Lambeth Conference, Catholic ecumenists like the Jesuit Father Edward Yarnold, who has dedicated many years to the quest for unity with the Anglican Churches, were saying that the way forward for unity now had to be sought province by province rather than with the Anglican Communion as a whole. The Conference had insisted on provincial autonomy; now, its ecumenical partners were beginning to take it at its word.

If, in the words of the *Church Times*, 'The Anglican Communion will survive in more or less its present shape', the question has to be asked what that shape is. One English diocesan (not the Bishop of London) was saying, within days of Lambeth, 'We are no longer a communion, we are an association of Churches.' The Anglican Communion might have preserved its visible structures and communications more or less intact for the time being: but it had been at the cost of redefining its own nature in a quite substantial way. It had very little leeway for such a redefinition; it was not as though the bonds had been loosened because they were already excessively tight or constricting. As Bennett wrote in the preface a year before the conference,

Though it is usual to speak of the Anglican 'provinces' this is to give the false impression that there is a single Church of which the provinces are sub-divisions. The real fact is that there is a loose association of independent national churches with some weak consultative bodies which attempt to ensure agreement in faith and order and advise on common action. Seasoned observers at meetings of the Anglican Consultative Council know that the level of theological and ecclesiological discussion is not high and their most notable characteristic is the way in which the representatives of the churches come with opinions already formed.

The problem already, even before Lambeth 1988, was to hold together coherently so loose an entity. Now the bonds were slipping; by the end of the year, some provinces were already floating freely. Some were floating towards ever more overt radicalism; it was not only the gender of Barbara Harris that was significant about her election but the way in which she represented the general direction of Episcopalian liberalism. One province was floating towards conversations with Rome about the possibility of 'going over' lock, stock and barrel. Several American dioceses called a Synod to discuss an independent existence within ECUSA, possibly leading to eventual secession from it. All these developments were widely predicted at the time of the Lambeth Conference, not only by 'irresponsible' or 'ill-informed' commentators, but by many of the Lambeth Fathers themselves.

Conference Euphoria

Most bishops, however, left Lambeth in an optimistic mood, firmly believing that the unity of worldwide Anglicanism had been preserved. Even those who did not like all that had happened seem to have enjoyed their weeks on campus. It is here, partly, that we have to look for an explanation of how it was that some normally realistic men seem to have come to believe that by passing a resolution to empower a commission, and by calling for consultations, unity had been preserved; that the wording of motions and the counting of votes somehow had the power to change things. There is a psychological phenomenon known as 'conference euphoria', one characteristic of which is precisely the belief that the conference itself represents the reality of things, that it only remains to take that reality to the grass roots. One striking example of this was the English Liberal Party conference at the end of which the party leader, David Steel, told cheering delegates to return to their constituencies 'and prepare for government', shortly thereafter undergoing an electoral rout.

The mood at Lambeth was described the following year, in a signed preface to the *Church of England Year Book*, by Derek Pattinson. 'There was an increasing sense of confidence and cohesion among the bishops as the days went by', he wrote. 'They accepted that there might be some impairment of communion if the ministries of some could not be accepted by all – but there was felt to be a depth of spiritual unity.' He went on to quote Archbishop Runcie's summing up on the last day:

Common life – that is what we have experienced here, a common life which lies at the heart of communion. There has been much talk about being 'in' or 'out' of communion, about 'full' communion and 'impaired' communion. But the communion we have known together is something other, something far, far deeper. . . . Our communion is real, but it is not for our own enjoyment but for a purpose. . . . Humility, generosity and adventurous Christianity – these are the things I hope you will take from this conference back to your dioceses, where I pray you will dare to do great things for God.

As the Archbishop finished, Pattinson recorded, 'the Primates rose up and gathered round him. It seemed as if they were going to take him on their shoulders: it was *that* kind of moment. It had been *his* Conference in a special sense. . . .'

Those who to the best of their ability objectively reported the ecclesial chaos which had now been officially accepted into the structures of worldwide Anglicanism were, predictably enough, accused of distortion. Only those who accepted the Conference at its own valuation were thought to be dispassionate. Michael Marshall, formerly Bishop of Woolwich, now a successful Episcopalian publisher in America, attacked this writer's *Daily Telegraph* coverage in an instant 'book of the Conference', published within weeks of its end:

. . . for those who are looking for a streamlined catholicism, the 1988 Lambeth Conference only evoked further frustration. Dr William Oddie, with predictable rancour, asked rhetorically when it was all over: 'Should the bishops agree to go their separate ways?' . . . And then, as a prophet of gloom and doom, he continued, 'The Anglican Communion is in for a rough passage; it is battening down the hatches and attempting to install damage limitation equipment'. No, that is not what Bishop Browning had meant by 'structures of grace'. Certainly not for anyone attending the Conference, and least of all for those waving farewell at Canterbury West, did it feel as though they were leaving to 'batten down the hatches'. 'Anglican bishops believe in independence far more strongly than in unity', William Oddie proclaimed somewhat questionably. 'And quite simply, you cannot have them both.' Can't you?

There are, of course, worse things than to be a 'prophet of doom and gloom', if that is what simply speaking the truth entails. It was the false prophets, according to Jeremiah (one of the true prophets, the gloomiest of them all), who were to be heard 'saying Peace, peace when there is no peace' (6:14); this was a procedure which the prophet Ezekiel likened to whitewashing a collapsing wall (13:10–12). Nobody expected a 'streamlined catholicism' from the Lambeth Conference; what had been hoped for by some was the slowing down of the movement into the incoherence they now feared. They certainly did not expect the application of quite such large quantities of whitewash to cover the cracks. Even among the bishops, 'conference euphoria' notwithstanding, there were not lacking those who were far from seeing the results of the vote on women bishops in the same rosy light as Bishop Marshall. More than one of them, afterwards in the cold light of day, told me that they regretted voting for it; and they certainly (as it turned out, realistically) had no very exalted hopes for what was to become the Eames Commission, even while they were 'waving farewell at Canterbury West'. 'Damage limitation', it became clear enough, was a perfectly realistic description of the Commission's function and expectations. Of course, the conference had not ended in anything so tasteless as open and formally ratified schism; that is not the Anglican way. Whether it intended to or not, what the Conference *had* ratified, nevertheless, was an ecclesiology whose ultimate consequence could only be the weakening if not the eventual dissolution of the Communion itself – at least, *as* a communion rather than a loose association of Churches.

This result was predictable, and widely predicted, for obvious reasons. Quite simply, it was difficult to see how, without an unaccustomed unity of will and purpose, the assembled bishops could bring under control and then reverse an underlying historical trend already so well established. Already, before the bishops assembled, they knew that their discussions would be confined within the boundaries they and their predecessors had delineated ten years previously at the 1978 Lambeth Conference over the question of the admission of women to the priesthood. The formal acceptance of provincial autonomy over that issue made the outcome of the 1988 Conference a foregone conclusion; it only remained to be seen how successfully the appearances could be saved. Worldwide Anglicanism was no longer held together by a common liturgy or a common doctrine; its ministry, no longer interchangeable, was to become even more than it had been a source of disunity. Gareth

Bennett's verdict, in the preface, on the 1978 Lambeth Conference might well have been issued, with only minor adjustments, as a commentary on the Lambeth Conference which met ten years later:

They burked the ecclesiological issue and fixed their minds on the legal right of each province to act according to its own canons; they contented themselves with lofty exhortations that each side in the dispute over women-priests should respect the convictions of the other. Yet in one respect they had made a decision, and one which was to affect the very nature of Anglicanism. They had consecrated the notion of an ever-increasing Anglican diversity and the obligation of all provinces to 'accept', at least in the sense of co-operating with, anything decided by a particular province. It now remains to be seen whether there will emerge any determinable parameters to Anglican diversity.

Ecclesial Chaos

The recognition by the 1988 Conference of the principle of provincial autonomy was inevitable, perhaps. But one thing had become clear to the Lambeth Fathers by the time they met; provincial autonomy notwithstanding, here was an issue which had unavoidable implications for worldwide Anglicanism, and which demanded to be seen in an inter-provincial context. For, as Bennett puts it in the preface, 'not only would women-bishops make the episcopate itself a cause of disunity but those whom they ordained, men as well as women, would be unacceptable to many'. The interchangeability of ministries – on which full communion between churches is built – already impaired by women priests, would be made even more problematical by the necessity for those who do not recognize women as bishops of verifying the source of a priest's orders before recognizing him as being a priest at all.

The problems for the communion at large, indeed, were and remain similar to those of an individual Episcopalian, looking for a Church where he may receive the Eucharist on a Sunday morning in the United States. If he accepts the priesthood and episcopate of women there is no problem. If he does not, he has the problem of finding a male priest; and now that a woman has actually been consecrated must ensure that that male priest is ordained by a male bishop. For him right order in the Church has broken down, and he must live from hand to mouth.

Over a year before the Conference met, Garry Bennett had, as we have seen, accurately indicated the ecclesiological consequence of provincial autonomy over an issue such as women in the episcopate (an institution, it is worth reiterating, one of the main purposes of which is the maintenance of ecclesial unity). These consequences he saw as inevitable, particularly in the context of the breakdown of classical Anglican Divinity under the onslaughts of the liberal relativist theology of radicals like the Bishop of Newark, New Jersey. 'Those of us,' he wrote in the preface,

who are regular readers of the writings of Bishop John S. Spong of Newark will be aware of the type of mind which sets no store by tradition, and has scant regard for the ecumenical process. Bishop Spong's interpretation of Anglican Comprehensiveness is that everyone should do what seems right to him in conscience and that everyone else should accept it. It is not hard to describe his views as ecclesiologically simplistic and basically sectarian and a recipe for the destruction of Anglicanism as a meaningful communion. On the other hand there will be those like the Bishop of London who would regard the consecration of a woman-bishop without a wider ecumenical consent as so serious a breach of Catholic order that it would dissolve the terms of communion.

Both Bishop Spong and Bishop Leonard, nevertheless, were in the end both supporters of the composite resolution which (whatever the intentions of those who drafted it) recognized in effect that this 'basically simplistic' ecclesiology was now inevitable – had indeed for some years been in place. But the resolution did not itself install provincial autonomy; nor even had the resolution of the 1978 Lambeth Conference, despite Garry Bennett's view in the preface that the assembled bishops had then made a decision on the matter – had in fact 'consecrated the notion of an ever-increasing Anglican diversity and the obligation of all provinces to "accept", at least in the sense of co-operating with, anything decided by a particular province'. The decision had already been taken unilaterally two years previously in 1976 by the American Episcopal Church. It was then, by *force majeure*, imposed on the rest of a Communion only too willing to put off the evil hour in which it would have to face up to the consequences of what had been done. Ten years later, the reality of what provincial autonomy could actually mean in a climate of theological 'pluralism' had to be confronted. It meant the 'impairment' or actual breaking of communion between dioceses and provinces; for many of the faithful it now meant facing the possibility of being out of communion with their own bishop. In a word, it meant schism.

What had brought the Anglican communion to this point? The answer is obvious enough in all conscience. If a world-wide association of this kind is to have any real coherence, all its members have to agree that when divisive issues arise, there has to be some restraint on all sides until a general consensus emerges. This necessarily involves a voluntary surrender of absolute freedom of action by individual members. Provincial autonomy and ecclesial unity are ultimately irreconcilable during a period in which theological consensus has been destroyed. And the trouble now was that certain members of the Anglican communion – most notably the Episcopal Church of the USA – had made it clear that it intended to do exactly as it pleased at all times whatever anyone else said.

It is important to note here that freedom for some is not necessarily extended willingly to others. It is another illustration of how what appears to be a process of liberalization can take on a momentum of its own and become transformed into an engine of intolerance and strict conformism. 'Anglican Provinces', as Gareth Bennett commented in the preface, 'increasingly lacking a common mind, tend to look inwards for the formation of opinion and to the concerns generated within their own societies.' This leads to the formulation of local demands which are then pressed on others:

Having full canonical power to make changes they develop a strong disposition to put into effect what a local majority wishes and then expect the rest of the communion to follow suit. The issue of the ordination of women to the priesthood provides a cogent illustration of this point. When it was first proposed to the ACC meeting at Limuru in 1971 it was in terms of allowing the small diocese of Hong Kong in special circumstances to be allowed a dispensation from the usual practice. But a plea for tolerance easily passes into a demand that others should conform, and as certain provinces from the prosperous first world began to ordain women it was not long before the Church of England in particular came under attack because it did not receive the ministrations of these women priests.

In 1983 this culminated in an imperious speech from Archbishop 'Ted' Scott of Canada before the General Synod of the Church of England in which he soundly berated it for not accepting a decision in which it had not been consulted and to which it had not given its consent.

The Fruits of Autonomy

Thus, provincial autonomy is not necessarily a means whereby tension between different parts of the communion is avoided; it may indeed itself bring about such tensions. As the 1988 Lambeth Conference drew ever nearer, it was clear to many that provincial autonomy had led not only to tension but to crisis.

In a way, the conference had its theological justification for provincial autonomy and its consequences already in place. The idea of theological 'pluralism', expounded in such Conference documents as *For the Sake of the Kingdom*, can be seen, in a sense, as an attempted rationale for provincial autonomy, a rationale, that is, for a reality of Anglican life which had been imposed willy-nilly by particular events in the past and the expectation of further connected events in the future. The problems posed by these events had loomed over the preparations for Lambeth 1988, including the theological preparations, for several years.

The idea of theological 'pluralism' in this context, more than the traditional Anglican notion of 'comprehensiveness', can be perceived as having a specifically cultural dimension. Its effect is to give a positive gloss to what has often been seen as a weakness in the way the English model was exported: not as a universally understood faith but as the particular religion of a particular people which was then adapted in a variety of different ways so that it fitted other particular people. The cultural transcendence of the Christian gospel, an essential element in the Christian revolution as the first-century Church broke loose from its Jewish moorings, had thus in a sense been partly reversed. Unlike the Catholic model for an international world Church – which begins from a universal human faith which has to be incarnated in particular human circumstances – the Anglican model is based, not on the Church understood as universal but on the culturally based autonomous national church, the international dimension of which derives from its links, now increasingly tenuous, with others similarly based. At Lambeth 1988, this model now found its justification in the theology of 'pluralism'. 'To affirm pluralism', wrote the seventeen joint authors of *For the Sake of the Kingdom*,

> . . . is to affirm not one but two things. On the one hand it means to assert that there is good in the existence and continuing integrity of a variety of traditions and ways of life; on the other hand, it means to assert that there is good in their interplay and dialogue. For Christians, moreover, such affirmation of pluralism has a special meaning. It embodies a recognition that every human culture has God's Kingdom as its horizon in creation and redemption. At the same time, it acknowledges that, in the dialogue between traditions, people's understanding of the meaning of God's Kingdom, and of the Christ who bears it, may be enhanced.

This document was itself a masterpiece of what I have called elsewhere 'the theology of negotiation and ambiguity'. Most obviously, we can see this in the way that every time a view is expressed, it becomes qualified by another view. Thus, if the document appears at any point to be veering towards one or other variety of relativism, it protects itself against 'misinterpretation' by stating a corrective view (which may then be qualified in its turn). The whole document ends with a ringing statement reaffirming the centrality of Christ, for those who insist on the objectivity of revelation; but it does so in the setting of a simultaneous reiteration of the subjectivist view which underpins the entire document. The rhetorical tone of this passage is high; the word 'inspirational' comes to mind. This serves to hide the fact that what is being said is far from being either clear or coherent:

> It is not pluralism but the risen Christ as the bearer of God's reign, who is the ground of Christian repentance as well as of Christian faith, because he is the one in whom the unity of humankind is established and promised. Pluralism is to be affirmed not as it divides people, and not as a recipe for indifferentism, but as the context in which the heirs of God's Kingdom may engage with one another more richly and variously than hitherto and may thus be enabled the better to know and follow Christ – the Second Adam, the new humanity, and into whom all are called to 'grow up'.

The tactical value of such writing is that it gives a justification and a respectability to the current state of a 'communion' which is in the throes of facing the reality that it has no commonly accepted norms whereby doctrine may be understood and stated, whereby moral theology may be conducted, whereby even a generally recognized ordained ministry may be maintained. Chaos is miraculously transformed into 'pluralism'; what is clearly destructive becomes part of a creative process leading to the emergence of a new and higher state in which 'the heirs of God's Kingdom may engage with one another more richly and variously than hitherto'. Thus there is no crisis to be faced, there are no problems of authority within the Anglican communion; where we are turns out to be where we wanted to be all along. And once again, those who believe that there is a crisis to be faced are marginalized. It is the way the establishment mind always works: the first iron law is the maintenance and justification of the institution you have in the form in which you have it. If it is going badly wrong, you find a new rationale according to which it is ticking over perfectly. Crisis is never traced back to its roots: it is simply redefined.

Pluralism and Coercion

In modern times, it seems to be a major function of the Lambeth Conference to perform this kind of redefinition of a crisis already in full swing. In 1978, the Lambeth Fathers met in the aftermath of a decision unilaterally taken two years previously by the General Convention of ECUSA (by a small majority), to ordain women to the priesthood. As Gareth Bennett comments in the preface:

if six votes had been cast differently it would have failed. But by 1978 over 90 women had been ordained as priests. The Episcopal Church thus acted unilaterally with less than a two-thirds majority in its House of Bishops and a bare majority in its House of Deputies.

Ten years later, according to two different surveys of opinion, around 40 per cent of those left in ECUSA were still opposed to women in the priesthood, and around 10 per cent still unconvinced one way or another. Of those theoretically in favour, only a tiny proportion were prepared to accept a woman priest when it came to electing a rector for their own parish. Nearly all those women priests actually employed (most were not) were in diocesan administration or in special jobs created for them or in mission parishes where they could be appointed directly by the bishop without the consent of the laity. Nevertheless, this lack of enthusiasm at the grass roots had in no way deterred the overwhelming majority of the American House of Bishops – who remained as indifferent to the necessity for consensus within ECUSA as beyond it – from their determination to proceed to the revolutionary and irreversible stage of consecrating a woman bishop, whatever the consequences.

The Anglican Communion is often compared (by both its admirers and its detractors) with the British Commonwealth. It is the American influence within Anglicanism that makes this comparison inappropriate. The American bishops at Lambeth were not only twice as rich and twice as numerous as the English bishops, even though they represented a much smaller church; they were also, though for tactical reasons quieter than many had expected, twice as politically self-assertive.

Although considerably to the political left of most Americans, the American House of Bishops continues to represent a strain of cultural imperialism which in American foreign policy it would undoubtedly deplore, many ECUSA bishops having taken up the liberation theology package with some enthusiasm. Their determination to push their own line, deaf to all others, caused a certain resentment at Lambeth. 'Over-represented, over-paid, and over here' one Commonwealth bishop was overheard to say, *sotto voce*, as the bishops assembled.

Most bishops of ECUSA are entirely convinced of their world leadership role, and they are not given to undue delicacy in their exercise of it. The 1978 Lambeth Conference may have decided that over the women-priests issue, each province must respect the decisions of the others; this in no way deterred many American bishops from the most aggressive kind of proselytizing. Over forty of them refused to celebrate the Eucharist in England in the Lambeth summer of 1988, in 'solidarity' with their sisters who were unable to exercise a priestly ministry in England (though it has to be said that in the event this gesture went virtually unnoticed).

American pressures do not stop at this kind of demonstration. More than one African bishop told the author before the conference started about the way some American bishops use financial inducements more or less subtly to pressure African bishops, for the most part running desperately impoverished dioceses, in favour of their policies – in particular, of course, in favour of the ordination of women to the priesthood. The process can be quite subtle. 'What happens is something like this', the former bishop of an African diocese told me:

A diocese in America has a great fund-raising drive for mission in Africa. A quite substantial sum is raised for an African diocese with which the ECUSA diocese is 'twinned'. This is how the money is spent. First, the American bishop has a trip to Africa, where he establishes warm relationships with the diocese. That's easy, they are very friendly people, it's not hard to like them. Funds are made available for some large diocesan project. Places are found and paid for for seminary training in America. An invitation to America follows for the bishop and his wife, they stay in swanky hotels, it's all very exciting. Then it comes: there's one more thing we would love to share with you, one of our greatest treasures: the priesthood of women. It's all very subtle. Nobody says, ordain women or these funds will dry up. But you have the idea in the back of your mind. And one day there are going to be American-trained bishops. It's a long term operation. And you become all the time more dependent on American money, we are so poor.

This fact of Anglican economic life had its effect on the arrangements of the Conference itself: the second motion on women in the episcopate, urging restraint, was voted on by secret ballot because the proposers feared that the large African vote would be lost if the names voting against women bishops were revealed; not an unfounded fear as one African bishop confirmed. 'The third world bishops are afraid to oppose the Americans publicly,' he said to me; 'we have no doubt that they would not hesitate to use economic sanctions against us if we did. The ordination of women is not an issue for us. If voting the wrong way here loses us desperately needed funds for a school or a hospital or a new church, we are going to toe the line.'

An Uncertain Future

Nor does this new brand of American imperialism confine itself to the Third World. Illegal celebrations of the Eucharist in England by women ordained in America take place more often than is generally supposed, and such forays are encouraged and probably in some cases financed by ECUSA bishops. The ugly American may be unfashionable today in the USA, but he is alive and well and flourishing in the House of Bishops of the American Episcopal Church.

Today, once more, Anglicanism is faced by a crisis caused by the refusal of the American Church (or at least of its ruling caste) to accept that membership of the Anglican Communion involves any restraint whatsoever on its own actions. And this time the issue involved is divisive in a way which will not admit of being swept under the carpet. A priest operates within a given diocese. A bishop moves on the world stage. He is the sacramental centre of unity with his own diocese; but just as important, it is his unity with other bishops that joins his diocese to theirs.

The crisis over women bishops, however, serious though it is, does no more than bring to a head an already long-standing problem. How, when there is no source of cohesion, institutional or theological, other than the bonds of affection (bonds which become dangerously strained in the heat of controversy), is the entity known as the Anglican Communion to have any real function or meaning? How is it to stay together as anything but a secular club for the bigwigs? Dr Habgood, in criticizing Dr Bennett's answer to this problem, puts forward his belief that the best way forward is by strengthening the theological coherence of the Communion. This undoubtedly comes near the heart of the problem. Dr Habgood's hopes that the international Doctrine Commission might perform such a function do not seem yet to have materialized, however. What is needed is more than a rationale for the status quo. What is needed is a real common rediscovery of the fundamentals of the Christian religion. Gareth Bennett's solution here is a purely functional one, and I strongly suspect he had little faith in it. Certainly it might have worked if more fundamental problems of faith and order had been solved first. The likelihood that they ever would be seemed remote before the 1988 Lambeth Conference; by the time the conference was over that possibility had become non-existent. Bennett's blueprint for Anglican unity remains as a poignant memorial of something that once seemed real and salvageable:

It ... becomes clear that if there is to be a central body with a clear responsibility for Anglican coherence it will have to be a reconstituted Consultative Council; it will have to meet more frequently, have an adequate secretariat and the assistance of theologians and other experts. It seems probable that there will have to be some self-denying ordinance by which the provinces agree that certain matters shall not be decided locally but only after a common mind has been established amongst the churches. Finding a constitution for a new kind of Council will not be easy but it is probably not too much to say that the future of Anglicanism in the world Christian community depends on its being achieved.

SEVEN

Dr Bennett and Dr Runcie

Two images remain vividly in the mind.

After dinner, on a lawn at New College, a young cleric has been tackled and floored by a bunch of undergraduates of the type sometimes called 'rugger buggers'. A small knot of dons watches; one of them is the head of another college. The undergraduates force out the priest's arms, so that he is in the position of the crucified Christ on the cross. They pin down his arms and legs with croquet hoops so that he cannot move. The dons are laughing. The young cleric is Gareth Bennett; he is a fellow and chaplain of the college. It is the early 1960s.

Years later, in a dark panelled room, fellows of New College are having lunch. The college doctor is there. A group at one end of a long table is listening intently. There has been a very nasty attempted suicide; a young man has tried to gas himself in his car, but the petrol ran out before he was dead. He will live on, but with brain damage. All the same, says the doctor, it's the best way, if you're going to do it; when a doctor discovers he has something like cancer, that's what he will do: drive to a layby on the ringroad and gas himself in his car. But it has to be done properly, with a full tank of petrol. He proceeds to explain, in minute detail, how it is done properly. Sitting on the edge of the small group is a priest in his forties, Dr Gareth Bennett. He sits there, silent, with a look of icy disapproval on his face.

Garry Bennett was never really happy at New College. His early years were hard. 'He was sensitive to the barbed comments of self-conscious non-Christians', remembers Dr Geoffrey Rowell, once his assistant chaplain, 'and to what he perceived as the superciliousness of some of the wealthier members of the college.' He had won his way to his fellowship on intellectual merit, and over the years his early promise was more than fulfilled. But he remained an outsider. As a middle-class scholarship boy at Cambridge, he had been sensitive to the social gap between himself and many of his contemporaries. Now, for all his starred first, his Cambridge doctorate and his New College fellowship, he was still an ex-scholarship boy in an aristocratic college full of Wykehamists. That was not all; anti-clericalism (of a kind now on the retreat in Oxford) was still fashionable. 'There were times', he wrote later, 'when I felt very solitary and as though there really were no loyal churchmen.' Devoted pastoral work over the years built up the Christian community around the chapel and the chaplain. But he was never a round peg in a round hole at New College. He was a sensitive man without the extrovert social skills on which the clergy sometimes survive in such circumstances. He was never allowed to forget his humble origins; and to add to his difficulties, he was a Christian traditionalist, disliked by 'the progressive element'. In this respect, his position was not wholly unreminiscent of the way C. S. Lewis describes the position of Canon Jewell as a fellow of the fictitious Bracton College, in *That Hideous Strength*. Bracton is generally thought to be based on Lewis's experiences in Magdalen; but the phenomenon was the same. The penalty of not being a progressive was to be excluded from 'the inner ring'.

The Making of an Outsider

In a way, he had always been an outsider. As a child, he was a lonely boy. His only companion was his cousin who lived nearby. There is a dreadful poignancy about his adult memory of an over-protected childhood. 'I was never allowed out with other children,' he wrote, years later, in an unpublished autobiographical fragment (quoted by Geoffrey Rowell), 'and I used to sit at the window watching other boys (probably older than I) walking by in gangs or groups. I recall, even now, envying them their freedom and independence.'

Memories differ. Some remember an apparently cold and distant cleric, whose sermons were remote and scholarly and whose religion, at the time from which their memories stem, did not seem particularly warm and vital. Others have very different memories. One New College graduate remembered, after his death, Dr Bennett's pastoral care at a difficult moment. He had been walking near the Bodleian one evening, obviously deeply depressed. Bennett spotted him, asked him to his rooms, gave him port, kept him there until the depression had been talked through. It was clear that he had been worried about the possibility of suicide. He is one of many New College men to have memories of Garry's kindness. Rowell quotes another of them, Jeremy Harvey, who remembers his kindness to him and other undergraduates. 'He would take me out for Sunday lunch at Burford', he wrote later, 'and I often ended up talking with a group in his rooms. Garry showed me friendship, gave me his acceptance, was himself, and knew how not to intrude. . . . I have often thought about him – and the college – often since his death. He gave us so much.'

I once asked him what was the greatest satisfaction of the life he led as an Oxford don (he had been speaking of its frustrations). He replied that it was to see a really unpromising undergraduate do well after all. 'You see him at the beginning of his first year,' he said; 'you wonder how he could ever have got in, do you know? He is spotty, ill-favoured, timid, apparently unintelligent as well. Then you gradually manage to bring him out, include him in things; you take him on reading parties, take him seriously. And you see him change. By his third year, he has become a confident young man. He might even get a good second.' Those who thought him cold and forbidding had never seen him talking to a young person uncertain about his or her future, uncertain about anything. For them he had a great tenderness and warmth, often unimaginable to others more self-assured.

He felt increasingly warm towards one particular part of his Oxford life; his association with Pusey House, to which he left his estate. He was a governor and played a vital part in rescuing it from financial and institutional disaster in the late 1970s and early 1980s. His relations with the then principal, Canon Cheslyn Jones, who was not without responsibility for Pusey's near catastrophe, reached breaking point with the principal's enforced resignation, and the results added not a little to Garry's often undeserved reputation as a political manipulator in the Oxford manner. A story was assiduously spread all over Oxford about how badly Cheslyn Jones had been treated, and how ruthlessly Garry had behaved. This is not the place to go into the details of the affair which I observed at close quarters; but common justice requires it to be said that the governors of Pusey House had no alternative, and that Garry was among those who made sure that Canon Jones was given generous financial support until retirement age. This, however, did not form part of the story that circulated around Oxford.

As we have seen, Garry's faith was deeper than it often appeared to the casual observer. He could seem detached and donnish about his religion. The first time I heard him preach at Pusey, Canon Jones predicted that the sermon would be a dry little affair, containing an historical anecdote about New College; and so it proved. But over the five years I was on the staff at Pusey, there was a change, a kind of flowering. Underneath, his faith had never been as dry and formal as it sometimes seemed. But in the last six or seven years of his life, it deepened to the point at which it broke through more clearly for others. His sermons became more simple and more powerful. It was almost as though he had undergone a new conversion. He preached more and more about the love of God, about the power of the Holy Spirit to change lives, about the Church as a sacrament of God's presence in the world. The deepening of his faith did not come without a struggle, and this too was sometimes evident; it gave an added dimension to his teaching. In a Lenten address he gave in the year of his death, he spoke of what is a familiar dilemma for Christians, and as he did so gave a glimpse, I think, of his own painful pilgrimage towards holiness of life:

Perhaps I am not very good at prayer but my own experience is that the thought of trusting myself into God's hands actually produces in me some struggle, confusion and resistance. There are only occasional moments when I break through to some surrender to the will of God, and stop thinking of myself. The trouble is that one is having to come to terms with the kind of sacrificial love which was in Christ. 'Thy will be done' is not to be repeated parrot-fashion like some Christian mantra; it is a prayer to be made one's own amid the hard experience of life with its constant temptation to faithless self-concern.

Ambition and Faith

Like all deepening of faith, it was a breakthrough to a greater simplicity of vision. For him this was centred on the self-revelation of God in Christ as it had been recorded in the gospel, and conveyed through the centuries by the mainstream Christian tradition. His defence of that tradition was no mere obscurantist stand against change. And he became more and more concerned that the ruling caste of the Church of which he was a member did not seem to have the same instinct that all the Church's activities should be centred on that gospel. Hence his intervention in the November Synod debate the same year, three weeks before his death, which I have described in chapter two. The Lenten sermon I have just quoted moves from the problems of personal faith to a vision of the Church:

I think that this . . . sermon of mine has become a plea for a church which has the Gospel as its chief and only treasure. It is for a humble community of those who know that they have been given a great gift which was quite undeserved. They are not placed in the world to condemn it, moralize to it, or advise it but to love and serve it: to be alongside those who are in trouble, despised or neglected. In other words, their vocation and their joy is to show the mercy which has been shown to them.

The Christian religion does not necessarily make life any easier; and often it makes it more difficult. It was certainly no help, towards the end, in reconciling Garry Bennett to his life in Oxford. He became increasingly frustrated by his teaching work. He was endlessly painstaking in the one-to-one tutorial supervision which is the backbone of the Oxford system, and in his diary would record his own self-assessment of how well or badly he had met the needs of his pupils. But he was heartily sick of it; he wanted to move on a larger stage, to be less confined by drudgery and repetitive tasks after so many years of them. He needed a change. It is difficult not to see a certain fellow feeling in his description (in *The Tory Crisis in Church and State*) of Atterbury's life as a student of Christ Church. Atterbury, he wrote, 'was incurably ambitious and (as for Oxford dons of every age) the great world of London made his own round of tutorials and college business seem trivial and frustrating'. He goes on to quote a letter from Atterbury to his father:

I am perfectly wearied with this nauseous circle of small affairs, that can neither divert nor instruct me. I was made, I am sure, for another scene and another sort of conversation, though it has been my hard luck to be pinned down to this. I have thought and thought again . . . and for some years: now I have never been able to think otherwise, than that I am losing time every minute I stay here.

To the outsider, his life in New College seemed enviable; but, like Atterbury, he longed for release. Like Atterbury too he was ambitious, though unlike him, perhaps, not utterly 'incurably' so. Ambition in a churchman is generally seen as an undesirable quality, and Garry's enemies certainly made the most of his during the furore over the publication of the preface. His ambition sprang from a complex mixture of genuine idealism and personal motivations, as we shall see. But it also has to be seen as deriving from the whole ecclesiastical culture of which he was part. Personal ambition, quite simply, has been and remains one of the perennially corrupting elements of institutional Anglicanism. To say this, of course, is not to say that there is any part of the Church which is, or has been historically, wholly free of this corruption. But the lofty Anglican assumption that worldly ambition and the lust for power are the besetting sins only of others is simply untrue. The English version of these seemingly ineradicable tendencies has, of course, been most vividly portrayed by Anthony Trollope; but they are still alive and flourishing vigorously in today's Synodical Church of England. I remember sitting next to a bishop at dinner in Pusey House, listening to him saying of an American who had just been described as a successful parish priest in an English parish, 'Ah yes, but of course they never get beyond a certain point.' I had supposed that he was talking about pastoral effectiveness, and was about to deny it when the conversation made it clear that he meant something else; that, being American, he would never scale the career heights of those who became archdeacons, cathedral deans, and bishops. Garry Bennett may not have described the workings of the Crown Appointments Commission correctly; but that a power game involving the lives and careers of men (and the welfare of their families) goes on all the time and at all levels, in a way it should not in the Church of God, is beyond dispute. Peter Cornwell (a mainstream Anglican who filled exactly Garry Bennett's description of the kind of priest who could do well from his connection with Dr Runcie) gives a brief but fascinating glimpse of the power game in action in his account of how he came to resign as vicar of the University Church in Oxford, to become a Roman Catholic. He was already beginning to have his doubts about the Church of England when he was offered a new post:

As I had served about eight years at St Mary's and the job offered was interesting, I gave it serious consideration. However, in advising me to accept, a senior bishop made the mistake of going on to outline the scenario of my future Anglican career as he saw it. It was an eerie feeling, to see myself so blatantly a pawn in a game of ecclesiastical chess, and though the prospect of what might lie ahead had a distinct appeal to the ambitious side of me, I came away from that interview depressed and feeling boxed in.

Garry Bennett, certainly, was ambitious for high office in the Church of England. This was for a number of reasons, some more creditable than others. He wanted to be where decisions were made, so as to be able to do something about the state of the Church. He wanted to get away from his life in Oxford, to start afresh. Underlying it all, doubtless, there was a deep insecurity, that driving force of so many ambitious men. He wanted at last to be a real insider as of right, to count, to be important. It is the oldest story in the world, and in the Church of England not the least common.

His ambition, without doubt, was a powerful restraining force on his growing compulsion to crusade for the spiritual renewal of the Church of England. It is not to overdramatize the case to say that he was a man divided against himself. The caution, the ambition, the 'constant temptation to faithless self-concern' about which he talked in his 1987 Lenten address pulled him in one direction; and his growing love for the real Church of England that lay beneath the structures of power, not the corrupt human institution but the 'church which has the Gospel as its chief and only treasure' pulled him ever more irresistibly in the opposite direction.

A Man Divided

How was he to harmonize these inclinations? In the end, of course, they cannot be harmonized. To try to do so remained the great temptation for him, as it had been for many others during the Church's long history. If he had not been brought to his personal shipwreck when he was, his journey – if it had continued steadily and faithfully in the direction he had chosen – would have been one of increasing rejection of personal ambition. There would have been a repetition of another old, old story, the story of God's grace acting in human lives, of a dying to self, and of a commitment to the reality of the Church rather than its institutional shadow. The invitation to write the *Crockford's* preface, to speak out anonymously without suffering the marginalization he had seen others endure, and which he still feared so terribly for himself, was irresistible at the stage of his pilgrimage at which he had arrived. And so, greatly daring, he took the risk of discovery to say what he was called to say.

His decision brought him to the point at which he felt impelled to criticize not only his Church but certain of its leaders whose personal style and spirituality he saw as representing, though certainly not as causing, the condition of modern Anglicanism. He had no particular difficulty in criticizing Dr Habgood, whose reputation as a thinker he thought grotesquely inflated. But the criticism he felt he had to make of Dr Runcie undoubtedly deepened profoundly his own inner conflict. The relationship of Gareth Bennett and Robert Runcie was a complex one, difficult not only to describe but to understand in normal terms. But before anything else is said, it has to be recorded that Garry Bennett, the author of the anonymous 'attack' on the Archbishop of Canterbury which precipitated the greatest crisis of his primacy, was a real friend who had known him for over thirty years, with whom he was in regular contact, who had written many of his speeches and addresses, and who had feelings of great warmth towards him. It is too easy to say that if this was so, he was a treacherous friend; it is more just to say that Bennett became increasingly torn by what he clearly saw as an imperative duty laid upon him. The real subject of the preface – and more and more the overriding object of Bennett's passionate concern – was the condition of the Church of England itself. And Robert Runcie had become, in his mind, a kind of living symbol of the problem.

Archbishop Runcie was a symbol: and he was also a contributory cause. The underlying problem itself was, in many ways, most poignantly dramatized in the increasingly bitter struggle over the ordination of women to the priesthood. Dr Runcie had been originally opposed to this step, not least because of his ecumencial contacts with the Orthodox.

It had been Robert Runcie's commitment to Anglican–Orthodox unity which had given him the acceptability to the Anglican Catholic constituency without which – as a 'dark horse' candidate – he might never have been appointed Archbishop in the first place. Over the key issue of women in the priesthood, he was felt by conservatives to be 'safe'. But under pressure, he changed his mind: many traditionalist Anglicans now felt, not only that Archbishop Runcie did not understand them, but that he had betrayed them. Quite simply, he was not to be trusted – or so it seemed to them.

At one point during his last year, Garry's own feelings over this question brought him seriously to consider whether the battle for the Church of England was now finally lost. He was not the only one. It seemed to many at the time (myself included) that the liberal establishment had decided that the departure of those who did not accept the current dispensation was an inevitable part of their overall plan for the future of the Church.

In the last week of February 1987, the General Synod considered a report from the House of Bishops, outlining the contents of legislation to ordain women. The report was greeted with horror by traditionalist Anglicans. It had previously been proposed that, even after women's ordination, the views of conservatives would continue to be represented in episcopal appointments; now, the argument was that 'it would be anomalous to appoint a bishop who was actively opposed to the mind of the province'. The message was clear: as I wrote in the *Daily Telegraph* on the report's publication, 'Once the thing is done',

. . . the ordination of women is to be rendered irreversible. Even if the American Episcopal Church, where the opposition can be treated very roughly indeed, there has been no such move as this. Dissident bishops are still being elected, and it is still possible to talk of an ultimate reversal.

It will not be so, apparently, in England, despite the report's reassuring words about the need to respect the right of dissidents to campaign for their views. Any such campaign will have to take place in conditions which would render it no more than a cosmetic exercise, designed to give the appearance of pluralism in an increasingly monochrome liberal protestant denomination.

The dissidents – or so it seemed so many – were being told, quite simply, to take themselves off. In the silky words of the report, 'those who could not remain in communion with the See of Canterbury would need to find other ways of continuing their existence within the universal Church and would be entitled to explore such ways'.

Within days of its publication, the Bishop of London threw a spanner in the works by taking the report at its word. The report had acknowledged that the dissidents would consider themselves as representing the traditional faith and practice of the Church of England, 'and would therefore believe themselves entitled to a share in its resources'.

Bishop Leonard announced that he was considering negotiations with other parts of the Universal Church (this meant the Roman Catholics and the Orthodox) so that dissident Anglicans could leave the Church of England in a body, presumably taking with them their 'share in its resources', remaining together to preserve an Anglican identity in some kind of 'Uniate' relationship with their new partners.

The stir created by Bishop Leonard's intervention brought home to many, for the first time, that the traditionalists really meant business and that there was a serious risk of disintegration if the plan to ordain women succeeded. Though an Anglo-Catholic, Bishop Leonard was no pan-Romanist: he was a Church of England traditionalist to the core. If such as he could think of leaving the Established Church then things had indeed to come a desperate pass.

Bishop Leonard's *démarche* was mercilessly ridiculed by Archbishop Runcie in the Synod debate on the report. His speech was a characteristic example of the way in which he could sway the Synod by the use of charm and wit; in this case, in order to mobilize Synod members against those who were felt to be rocking the boat. Afterwards, Garry recorded that 'one could feel the atmosphere change to one of real hostility to the Catholic cause'. The report was accepted by the Synod as the basis for legislation.

Afterwards, Garry noted in his diary that on the train back to Oxford he felt 'quite panic-stricken'; it seemed to him that it was 'all up with the Church of England' and that he was 'already in a lost minority in a church which has turned itself into a liberal protestant sect'.

Like many at that time, he now seriously faced the possibility that he would have to leave the Church of England and become a Roman Catholic. He underwent, in his own words 'a bad attack of Roman fever'. But, even in the midst of his attack, caution held him back. 'What', he asked himself, 'is a lay Anglican historian in the Roman Church?' He decided to 'let it all settle' in his mind, and then decide his future. The following day, after the Sung Eucharist at Pusey House, he brought the matter up in conversation with Fr Walter Hooper, then still an Anglican priest, now a Roman Catholic layman. Fr Hooper himself recorded this conversation immediately afterwards in his own diary. 'Why pretend,' said Garry; 'the cause is lost.'

. . . and he admitted to being puzzled about what to do or rather how to go about it because he straightway proposed that we go to Rome together and without delay. According to what he has heard Runcie has asked the American Episcopalians to hold off creating a bishopess until the Lambeth Conference where he will throw his entire weight into the C of E creating priestesses 'so we would be just another protestant sect'. He hoped that there was still the possibility of our all going over to Rome at the same time. . . [Probably a reference to the Bishop of London's current initiative.]

By the evening, Garry's mood already seems to have been calmer, his 'Roman fever' less pronounced. In his own diary entry about his meeting with Fr Hooper, he significantly makes no mention of this confession of Romeward inclinations. But he does record a conversation with Fr Philip Ursell, who called about 10.30 that evening. Garry, said Ursell, had been behaving rather strangely: was he thinking of going over to Rome? Garry replied that he 'had no plans to do so', but that he did not rule it out.

Two things need to be said about this weekend of 'Roman fever'. Firstly, that it reflects the situation in the Church of England at that time, when the flood tide of liberal triumphalism was at high water mark. It seemed to Garry in the immediate aftermath of the debate on the Bishops' report – and to many others – that the Church of England had turned itself into a 'liberal protestant sect' (he was to tax Dr Runcie personally with his own share of the responsibility for this transformation). It was, in the prevailing atmosphere, natural for a document like the Bishops' report to be generally accepted as representing the likely eventual outcome for the Church of England. That this outcome is no longer seen as inevitable has, ironically, a great deal to do with the *Crockford's* tragedy itself.

It is important to understand, secondly, that Garry, though in the widest sense a Catholic in his vision of the Church, was not the kind of Anglican one thinks of as being inclined to Roman ways, and his Roman fever was in many ways out of character. Certainly, from this point on, there is no record of any such thoughts. As Dr Geoffrey Rowell has written, after a perusal of the diaries, 'thoughts of a move to Rome (if they were seriously there) were overcome. He believed that he should stay in the Church of England and fight for its Catholic identity and that concern lay behind the *Crockford's* preface.'

The fight to save the Church of England from becoming a 'liberal protestant sect', to which Garry now turned with great seriousness, was his overriding concern as over the next few months he composed the preface. And it became clear to him – as the controversy over the Bishops' report indicates – that the question of the condition of the Church and its future direction could not be seriously addressed without talking about the individuals whose style and policies had brought it to its present pass. In the words of the preface, a survey of the state of the Church such as he now proposed to undertake would inevitably 'point to matters which are not for our comfort and it must deal with personalities'. And, equally inevitably, the most important of those personalities was Dr Runcie himself.

But, however passionately Garry Bennett felt that Robert Runcie's personality and style had come to symbolize the problems of modern Anglicanism, Dr Runcie was still his friend. They met on the last Sunday of his life at Pusey House; Bennett received his last communion at the Archbishop's hands. Dr Runcie, to his eternal credit, remained his friend though he had read the preface some weeks before and was certain in his own mind of its authorship. The two men met on their usual terms without any discernible embarrassment. If the rest of the hierarchy had maintained the same level of charity and civilized control as Dr Runcie, Gareth Bennett might well be alive today.

It is an almost Cornelian tragedy: the conflict of love and duty. For Bennett's affection was real. The laudatory preamble of the now famous 'attack' on Dr Runcie was largely discounted at the time and has generally been seen as a tactical device, designed less to soften the blow than to establish a spurious impression of fairness by balancing the criticisms with faint praise. But the praise is not faint; and there is no question whatsoever that it was sincerely meant. It reads, in retrospect, almost like a personal message:

One may well feel great sympathy for the man whose office gives him responsibility for guiding the affairs both of the Anglican Communion and the Church of England. Robert Runcie has been Archbishop of Canterbury since 1980 and has already established himself as a notable holder of the primacy. He has intelligence, personal warmth and a formidable capacity for hard work. He listens well and has built up a range of personal contacts among clergy and laity far wider than that of any of his predecessors. His speeches and addresses are thoughtful, witty and persuasive. In the General Synod he has an ability to influence the course of debate which can be decisive for the success or failure of a motion. In spite of the lack of an adequate staff at Lambeth he has survived the work-load remarkably well with only occasional periods of exhaustion. In what must be the latter part of his primacy he has travelled extensively and has established himself as the friend and confidant of most of the leaders of world-Anglicanism.

The two men had met in the mid-1950s at Cambridge. Bennett was by this time a young don at King's, London, who had been accepted for training for the priesthood; this was to take the form of three long vacation terms at Westcott House where Robert Runcie was then Vice-Principal. Bennett's academic standing led to a certain frigidity from the Principal of Westcott, the Revd Ken Carey, who kept trying to cut him down to size. 'He kept on about his own Third in History at Oxford,' Bennett recalled later, 'as if to reprove me for having got a First; he wholly refused to laugh at my jokes; and kept on asking me if I made my confession. Since he refused to allow me to tell him jokes, I refused to tell him my sins.' In this uncongenial milieu, the Vice-Principal was a godsend. Bennett's memory of him at this time, from the autobiographical fragment, quoted in his memoir by Geoffrey Rowell, should be put together with the passage from the preface just quoted; together, they convey, with unmistakable warmth, one side of Gareth Bennett's feelings about Robert Runcie:

He was the one member of the staff who actually seemed to think it was a good thing that I was an academic and we had a number of humorous conversations. . . . He thought that all priests should have a secular side to them, and that a false or intense piety was an enemy to real religion. He took a kind of benevolent oversight of me which was more than I deserved. He was always cheering me up by asking my advice on this or that theological problem. I became quite devoted to him, and my diary is full of references to his kindness. He had intelligence, wit and style. But I can scarcely have realized that I was laying the foundation of a friendship with a future Archbishop of Canterbury.

Grasping the Nettle

Gareth Bennett's feelings for Dr Runcie were real; but the criticism had to be made, so at any rate he clearly believed. It was here that the 'fortunate circumstance' of the *Crockford's* tradition came to his aid. It was not just that anonymity would shield him, so he genuinely thought, from the consequences of his criticisms of the liberal establishment as a whole; there was a way in which it allowed him the freedom to write impersonally, to distance himself from his own feelings, to write, almost, as if he were someone else. He entered into a tradition, in which criticizing archbishops of Canterbury was almost expected: the last three archbishops – Fisher, Ramsey and Coggan – had all run the *Crockford's* gauntlet. The formula was well established: a combination of real appreciation with the elegant rapier thrust of clerical cold steel. The most famous skewering had been of Lord Fisher, then scarcely cold in his grave. 'The achievements of his archiepiscopate', editorialized the preface writer in the 1973–4 *Directory*,

are still clouded by what can only be called his misuse of his retirement.

Few figures prominent in public life can have made themselves such an embarrassment to their successors . . . [during his primacy] many wise Churchmen felt that great opportunities were missed. . . . Along with his lovableness and his endearing if infuriating ways, Lord Fisher remained throughout the highly efficient headmaster (we are informed that on one occasion he compared the other bishops to housemasters, though some of them felt at times that they were treated as fourth-form boys). . . .

The tone is a long way short of idolatry; the appreciation of Lord Fisher too is by no means as extended or as warm as the appreciation of Archbishop Runcie in Garry Bennett's preface. But there is no denying that when the tone changes, the 1987 *Crockford's* preface pulls no punches. Garry Bennett's was certainly the most trenchant criticism of an archbishop to date, and, to appreciate its full force, we need here to quote the passage in full:

His influence is probably now at its height. It would therefore be good to be assured that he actually knew what he was doing and had a clear basis for his policies other than taking the line of least resistance on each issue. He has a major disadvantage in not having been trained as a theologian, and though he makes extensive use of academics as advisers and speechwriters, his own position is often unclear. He has the disadvantage of the intelligent pragmatist: the desire to put off all questions until someone else makes a decision. One recalls a lapidary phrase of Mr Frank Field that the archbishop is usually to be found nailing his colours to the fence. All this makes Dr Runcie peculiarly vulnerable to pressure-groups. In a rare synodical moment of self-revelation he once described himself as 'an unconvinced Anglo-Catholic', though it is the latter part of that description which should not be taken too seriously. His effective background is the elitist liberalism of Westcott House in the immediate post-war years and this he shares with Dr John Habgood, the Archbishop of York. In particular it gives him a distaste for those who are so unstylish as to inhabit the clerical ghettoes of Evangelicalism and Anglo-Catholicism, and he certainly tends to under-estimate their influence in the spiritual life and mission of the Church. His clear preference is for men of liberal disposition with a moderately Catholic style which is not taken to the point of having firm principles. If in addition they have a good appearance and are articulate over the media he is prepared to overlook a certain theological deficiency. Dr Runcie and his closest associates are men who have nothing to prevent them following what they think is the wish of the majority of the moment.

This is, without doubt, severe criticism; but that in itself is no grounds for the kind of extreme hostility it attracted. The questions that have to be answered before any other are surely these. What does this analysis actually amount to, and *is it true*? For if it *is* true, it needs no other justification. It is simply not adequate to say that it is tasteless or that it amounts to washing the Church's dirty linen in public. Criticism behind closed doors is criticism which has been rendered ineffective; confining criticism in this way is how establishments always protect themselves. For the point about Garry Bennett's criticism of Archbishop Runcie, as we shall see, is how closely it follows the general lines of his more fundamental criticisms of the direction of modern 'liberal' Anglicanism. When Archbishop Coggan was criticized in the 1977–9 preface, in some ways far more offensively, no 'backlash of support' was organized in his defence; the difference was that on that occasion it was not a liberal who was being criticized by a conservative, but a conservative who was being criticized by a liberal (the omnipresent hammer of the conservatives, David L. Edwards). The criticisms then were not about uncertainty of belief, but about the opposite; Dr Coggan believed too much, too firmly:

Dr Coggan rides out as a man with his mind made up, as a latter-day Don Quixote, and there has not been the sense that there was in his predecessor's time of the Primate as the more edifying type of Canterbury pilgrim . . . it has been possible to think his key statements both splendidly clear and counter-productively simple; both attractively personal and alarmingly naive.

At the heart of Garry Bennett's criticism of Dr Runcie (and with him of the liberal ascendancy he represents) is the allegation that there is no firm core of theological belief or principle by which he is prepared to stand. 'It would . . . be good to be assured', says Bennett, 'that he . . . had a clear basis for his policies other than taking the line of least resistance on each issue.' His speechwriters, Bennett continues, make up for his lack of theological training; but Dr Runcie's 'own position is often unclear'. He has described himself as an 'unconvinced Anglo-Catholic'; but we should pay more attention to the word 'unconvinced' than to the word 'Anglo-Catholic' (one of the marks of an Anglo-Catholic – as of an Evangelical – being that he *believes*). Dr Runcie's 'clear preference is for men of liberal disposition with a moderately Catholic style *which is not taken to the point of having firm principles*'. (My italics.) And so on. It is a portrait which derives from personal acquaintance, and Dr Runcie was well aware of his friend's opinion. The accusation, for instance, that Dr Runcie paid undue attention to 'good appearance' and being 'articulate over the media' is not unreminiscent of a conversation between the two men during the week of the February Synod discussed earlier. Dr Runcie had said that what the Church needed to put over its case were men who were 'articulate and presentable'; Dr Bennett had replied that what the Church needed were men of principle. And it was here, Bennett felt, that the Archbishop was weakest. 'Dr Runcie and his entourage', he concludes, 'are men who have nothing to prevent them following what they think is the wish of the majority of the moment.' They are, that is, able to respond to the pressures of the moment because they are uninhibited by any firm belief about the nature of the faith.

The Colours on the Fence

This was very damaging criticism, all the more so for exploding, if true, a widely floated rumour, believed by many, that though the Archbishop felt it his duty to keep those of different beliefs together – and therefore tended not to take sides – his personal preferences were conservative rather than liberal in tone. But nobody really knew. It has always been difficult to pin down what the Archbishop really believes. It did not, for instance, go unnoticed that in the week of the publication of the *Crockford's* preface he had preached a sermon of impeccable traditionalist orthodoxy at Pusey House (an Advent sermon about Hell and judgement) on the Sunday and the following night had preached a farewell sermon at St Paul's for the ultra-liberal Dean, Alan Webster, a sermon which was an impassioned defence of the 1960s radicalism Dean Webster epitomized. The impression that Dr Runcie is a kind of ecclesiastical chameleon has been almost eerily compounded by his use of different speechwriters to suit the different ecclesiastical preferences of his audiences. The feeling that 'his own position is often unclear' was very far indeed from being confined to Dr Bennett.

Dr Runcie, on hearing of Dr Bennett's death, told both Philip Ursell and Geoffrey Rowell that he had not taken offence; that Bennett had said nothing in the preface he had not already said to him at different times. The following month, he spoke in a lecture of 'Dr Bennett's supposed attack on me'. But he was nettled by the charge of 'intelligent pragmatism', and the suggestion that he has no position of his own. A study of Dr Runcie's published sermons and speeches does indeed yield the impression that some of them are closer to the core of his beliefs than others; some are both personal and highly revealing. One lecture in particular has attracted a good deal of attention, particularly from Evangelicals, and since it appears to have been either written by Dr Runcie himself, or at least to have been based closely on his own experience and reflections, and since it deals with matters very close to themes we have been considering in this book, we can see it as valuable evidence for our inquiry: the Sir Francis Younghusband Memorial lecture, delivered at Lambeth Palace in 1986 as part of the fiftieth anniversary year of the World Congress of Faiths.

The underlying theme of the lecture seems, at first sight, one which ought to be congenial to Christians of all persuasions.

Through nurturing a spirit of friendship and reconciliation [says Dr Runcie in the preamble to his remarks] true dialogue can help us to overcome religious divisiveness and create new conditions for greater fellowship and deeper communion. It can help us to recognize that other faiths than our own are genuine mansions of the Spirit with many rooms to be discovered, rather than solitary fortresses to be attacked.

Certainly, Christians of the most impeccable orthodoxy are now more inclined to accept than they were that God may well speak through other religious traditions. The meeting in 1987 of leaders of world religions at Assisi, in the presence of Pope John Paul II, was an example of an openness to the religious experience of others that would have been impossible only thirty years ago, and few would say that it did not represent a real step forward from the entrenched positions of the past.

Few of the religious leaders present on that occasion, however, would have been any less certain of, or insistently defensive about, the fundamentals of their own tradition than they were before. It is here that Dr Runcie's lecture gives some cause for concern. It was given shortly after a visit to India, which seems to have left him by no means sure of the solidity or the universality of the religious tradition of which he was a leader:

India can be a stunning experience – not in some Hollywood sense – but rather as an experience which leaves one dazed and uncertain of one's own bearings. Before there were the certainties of an encapsulated western Christianity. After, there are new ways of thinking about God, Christ and the world. A number of vivid and haunting images remain and continue to pose disturbing questions.

There was a conversation with a Parsee in Bombay.... Here was someone for whom the utter holiness of God was indeed as fire... And I wondered whether contemporary Christianity hadn't something to re-discover about the awesome 'otherness' of a God we have at time neutered and domesticated.

It is, of course, precisely the man-centred liberal theology of our own times which has performed this act of spiritual neutering. One is left with the impression, perhaps, that Dr Runcie is seeking here to fill the deficiencies thus created by advancing into inter-faith dia-logue rather than undergoing the rigours of a rediscovery and renewal of his understanding of his own tradition. His lecture continues by praising Islamic architecture for its 'reminder to the Christian of the source and goal of the human search for the perfect beyond this mutable world, for the changeless behind the transitory state of human life'. But again, this is not an insight for which the Christian imperatively *needs* to go outside his own religion, unless his own version of Christianity has become *centred* on 'the transitory state of human life' – on human society and politics – rather than on what lies beyond 'this mutable world'.

The Universality of Christ

It can, nevertheless, hardly be a source of complaint that an arch-bishop should be open, whether in his own or another's religion, to intimations of the divine presence. The question one has to ask however is this: how firmly does the Archbishop believe that in Christ, God definitively revealed Himself, so that however open they may be to God's activity in other religions, Christians, *whether they feel comfortable about it or not*, are bound to the belief that it is only in Christ that the fullness of God's self-revelation is to be known? It is a question that had to be faced in the Younghusband lecture; and the answer appears to be that Dr Runcie believes that the Christian fundamentals are definitive for Christians, but that they do not have the kind of absolute and universal significance, belief in which throughout Christian history has animated missionaries and evangelists to sacrifice everything so that souls may be converted to Christ. It seems, at first, that he is in fact not saying this at all:

For Christians, the person of Jesus Christ, his life and suffering, his death and resurrection, will always remain the primary source of knowledge and truth about God . . . . *For the Christian*, this is firm and fundamental – it is not negotiable. [My italics.]

It becomes clear on closer examination, however, that this is a view of the faith not wholly dissimilar to that expressed by Dr Habgood in *Changing Britain*: Christianity is for Christians; it does not necessarily 'have validity' for those who are not already believers. But it has been one of the fundamentals of the Christian faith that the death and resurrection of Christ were not simply 'a primary source of knowledge and truth about God', as though He had laid on a demonstration to convey information about Himself. The resurrection of Christ, Christians have always believed, was not simply a demonstration of love and power. *It actually changed everything.* Because God had been made flesh, had lived among us as a man, had risen from death and passed into the heavens, taking our humanity into the very Godhead, everything was now different, whether we knew it or not. The whole creation had shifted on its axis; and this was knowledge the Church was bound to share with others, a faith it was solemnly enjoined by its master to take to all nations and all peoples. And however powerfully God had acted in other ways and through other religions (a new perception Dr Runcie is right to value) God's incarnation as man and His victory over death were 'non-negotiable', not simply as a resource 'for Christians' but for the Christian understanding of how God works to make himself known to all humanity. Christianity is in its essence a universal faith, and its message is definitively for all men.

It becomes clear, as the Sir Francis Younghusband lecture

proceeds, that such absolute claims of universal validity are ones that Dr Runcie firmly rejects, and that he has adopted an unambiguously relativist view of the Christian revelation. The doctrine of the incarnation itself is, for Dr Runcie, no longer fundamental and definitive; on the contrary, it is an embarrassment in an age of dialogue between world religions. Dr Runcie's position is spelled out with a clarity which makes misunderstanding impossible.

One of the greatest challenges of interfaith dialogue which Christianity must face is the question of the universality of Christ and his mission: the question as to the meaning and significance of the incarnation within the context of religious pluralism . . . what is at stake is our understanding of the finality and significance of Christ's life and work. . . . *For Christians* the coming of Christ is the ultimate sign of the fullness of God's grace. But in an age of radical historical consciousness an understanding of the incarnation as the central Christian event must also be linked to an understanding of the historical circumstances in which this belief first took root and developed. . . . If we want to find viable and helpful answers in a situation of great need, we will have to abandon any narrowly conceived Christian apologetic, based on a sense of superiority and an exclusive claim to truth. [My italics.]

An idea of exactly how this new understanding actually works out 'on the ground' is now given by the Archbishop himself. In Calcutta, he visited Mother Teresa's Home for the Dying. He had not realized that her hospice was built on temple property dedicated 'appropriately enough' to the Goddess Kali.

Here [reflected Dr Runcie] was the love of Christ given and received by men and women of all faiths and none alongside the goddess who symbolizes a mixture of destruction and fertility. In the hospice there was at work a saintly woman dedicated to the mystery of dying and rising. That juxtaposition speaks powerfully of the universal power and significance of the love of Christ.

One is led to wonder how much the Archbishop had really discovered about the cult of Kali, a fiery-tongued ogress garlanded with coils of writhing snakes and human skulls. The city of Calcutta is named after her; once, infants were sacrificed in her honour in secret temples near the city; in her honour, too, the notorious Thuggee practised ritual murder on unfortunate travellers. Later, her adherents practised animal sacrifice, drenching themselves in their victims' blood. If there were any reflections to be made on the 'juxtaposition' of the two religions in Mother Teresa's hospice, it ought surely to have been to the effect that here, at least, the love of Christ had driven out this horrible religion of blood, skulls, snakes and death; that if ever there was an illustration that God does not reveal himself equally in all religions, here it was; and that evangelism and the work of conversion to Christ had become a dangerously neglected priority.

Conversion of the unbeliever and the kind of interfaith dialogue envisaged by Dr Runcie are, of course, incompatible, though the Archbishop himself does not explicitly say so. The kind of theological company he is in here was illustrated vividly by the radical Bishop John S. Spong after a visit to Hong Kong in 1988. He had, he tells us, been prepared for dialogue with Buddhists in Hong Kong by an earlier dialogue with Hindus in south India in 1984. Like Archbishop Runcie, Bishop Spong challenges the uniqueness and universality of Christ's mission. 'We had', he wrote in his diocesan magazine *The Voice*, 'raised disturbing questions that scream out for answers':

Can we any longer claim a unique universal ultimacy for our Christ? Can we with integrity continue to support and engage in a missionary enterprise designed to convert? What is the meaning of that enterprise we call evangelism that seems to assume the narrow and traditional claims for Christianity that we have made throughout the ages? . . . I will not make any further attempt to convert the Buddhist, the Jew, the Hindu, or the Moslem. I am content to learn from them and to walk with them side by side toward the God who lives, I believe, beyond the images that blind and bind us all.

The Enigma of Dr Runcie

Bishop Spong, of course, likes to play the rôle of the wild radical bent on the swift dismantling of the Christian tradition as it has been received from the past. Dr Runcie is more oblique, even enigmatic in his public postures; the Younghusband lecture is unusually revealing of just how radical his views are. Dr Runcie differs profoundly from Bishop Spong in his personal style and in his perception of what it is wise to say openly and consistently. Nevertheless it has to be said that on this clear evidence there some theologically very little to choose between them.

The elusiveness of the Archbishop's views is a matter of clear and conscious policy. He allows such revealing occasions as the Young-husband lecture (which he probably did not expect to gain the attention that it has) to take place on rare occasions and in front of carefully selected audiences. Occasions on which too much might be said are avoided, even to the extent of withdrawing from projects already agreed on. Ludovic Kennedy tells us in his memoirs that he had persuaded the Archbishop to take part in a television programme on the subject 'what is a Christian?' The two men discussed the venture at length over lunch and Dr Runcie, Kennedy later told journalist colleagues, seemed keen on it. The following day a long handwritten letter was delivered at Kennedy's office. The programme was off, for fear of what 'the Evangelicals' might make of the Archbishop's opinions on certain questions. 'The Evangelicals', Mr Kennedy informed his readers, were not a pop group but 'a band of fundamentalists'. This may be Dr Runcie's view; but in fact 'the Evangelicals' are distinguished by their views (which are wholly within mainstream Anglican tradition) on the authority of scripture and on the importance of personal conversion; Anglican Evangelicals are not mindless fundamentalists and they have given the Church many distinguished biblical scholars. Their churches tend to be full, and they are now training more clergy than anyone else in the Church of England. More than others, they have been concerned by the liberal drift of Anglicanism since the 1960s, and Dr Runcie himself has probably attracted more criticism from this quarter than any other.

If the Younghusband lecture establishes clearly how far Dr Runcie has moved from the classical Anglicanism whose decline Dr Bennett so poignantly records in the preface, it exemplifies, too, the pastoral instinct which has animated liberalism at its best. I have argued that theological liberalism has within itself a real tendency towards intolerance; that its assumptions are, in the pejorative sense of the word, just as 'dogmatic' as those of traditional mainstream Christianity; that we can observe repeated examples in recent years of liberal illiberality, of what one observer has called 'the stern unbending face of liberalism', the most striking instance being the 'backlash of support' after the publication of the *Crockford's* preface.

This illiberality, however, is probably as often as not unintentional. The leaders of the Church of England are not monsters; they are, most of them, men of pastoral instinct who have too lightly abandoned their theological moorings and are now often anxious and uncertain as the Church's drift takes it further and further into dangerous crosscurrents beyond their control. Nobody exemplifies this combination of personal warmth and decency with what one might call softcore theological drift more clearly than Dr Runcie himself. If we need an explanation of the confused and divided feelings he evoked in Garry Bennett surely here it is. Decades before, Robert Runcie had befriended him in Cambridge, and had been a friend and pastor to him ever since. But Dr Runcie had also come to embody for Dr Bennett what he more and more came profoundly to believe were tendencies in modern Anglicanism utterly destructive of the Church, a Church which, as his faith deepened, he came to love more than individuals, more than his own hopes for advancement.

The Shipwreck of Gareth Bennett

He had seen in the American Episcopal Church a terrible object lesson of what might happen here, if the views of men like Bishop Spong, as we have seen so close to those of Dr Runcie, were to prevail. He wrote what he wrote, not from personal spite but out of a concern for the Church of England which came to be more compelling than ambition, than mere affection, than personal comfort. And so he sowed the wind, hoping that the whirlwind would be containable. He imagined that he could both speak and protect his own position. His whole life had been one ruled by caution and control; in writing the preface he sailed into deep and dangerous waters he did not know. His concern for the Church had overruled his longing to count for something in the Church; but the longing had never really left him and when the storm broke he knew he would be exposed, that he would now count for less than nothing.

Was his crime so very heinous? Being on the margin was something he had always suffered from very deeply. He had suffered from it as a child who had not been allowed to play with other boys. He had suffered from it as a scholarship boy looked down on by wealthy undergraduates. He had suffered from it as a young chaplain in an anti-clericalist and aristocratic college. He had suffered from it as a conservative don at loggerheads with 'the progressive element in college'. By no means least of all, he had endured it as a traditionalist in a Church dominated by 1960s liberalism. He wanted at last to come in from the cold, he was tired of being lonely and disliked and powerless.

To such a one, the violence of the 'backlash of support' was bound to be wholly devastating. It is facile to say that he ought to have foreseen it; nobody could have foreseen it, it was utterly unprecedented. It was directed, not at his arguments, but at him personally. He was accused of being a 'disappointed cleric', taking revenge on Dr Runcie for failing to promote him. Certainly, he was disappointed; and with good reason. But that he should be accused of using his opportunity to make the preface an instrument of personal vengeance made him realize how deep were the antagonisms he had aroused, how utterly he would now be cast out. 'There is a sourness and vindictiveness about the anonymous attack on the Archbishop of Canterbury,' wrote Dr Habgood, 'which makes it clear that it is not quite the impartial review of church affairs which it purports to be.' Dr Habgood, himself so resentful of those who quoted him 'out of context', now ignored most of the essay over which Garry had taken such pains to 'get it right'.

For Dr Habgood to accuse the press of bringing to bear the intolerable pressures and the fear of personal exposure which brought Garry Bennett so quickly to the point of personal disintegration was like aiming a bomb and then blaming the manufacturers for the resulting devastation. Why should Garry Bennett fear the press? What was the press to him? It was the Church of England he cared about, and it was in the Church of England that he now knew he would be an outcast. He would be exposed by the press perhaps, but only because the press was being used as the instrument of his disgrace. It was not a notoriety of a few weeks he feared; it was the rest of his life as a pariah.

In the end the question to be asked, the question that will not go away is this: what kind of Church is it in which it is possible to be so afraid of the consequences of speaking one's mind? It will not do to say that Garry Bennett should have been braver, that he should have cared less about the rejection and the contempt of the Church's ruling caste: that was the way he was made. But that a part of the Church of God should defend the authority of its rulers by making dissidents into lepers, by killing hope, by refusing so adamantly the love and care which it is its whole purpose to spread among men – that is the deep shame of the Church of England. And it failed in Gareth Bennett's case, not simply during the retaliation of the days before his death but in the pastoral failure which, over the years, had left a man of his stature so isolated, without a fitting part in the ministry and councils of the Church to which he had devoted his life.

How shall we remember Garry Bennett? He was not a martyr in any generally accepted sense; a martyr is one who, knowing what he is doing, and having done everything he reasonably can short of betrayal to avoid his martyrdom, accepts death at the hands of others for the sake of the truth. But neither was his death without honour. He cared for the truth and he spoke it, not fearlessly, but in spite of his fear: in the end, this, too, is courage. Because of his death, what he said came to be read and pondered throughout the world, wherever Anglicans have come to be distressed by the confusion and secularism of their leaders. The preface has become the *samizdat* of the Anglican counter-revolution. If he had cared less for truth and for the future of his Church he would be alive today. If this is not martyrdom, it is not far from it.

Index